a novel
SINGER OF AN EMPTY Day

a novel
SINGER OF AN EMPTY

FLORA ANN SCEARCE

TATE PUBLISHING & *Enterprises*

Singer of an Empty Day
Copyright © 2009 by Flora Ann Scearce. All rights reserved.

No part of this publication may be reproduced, stored in a retrieval system or transmitted in any way by any means, electronic, mechanical, photocopy, recording or otherwise without the prior permission of the author except as provided by USA copyright law.

This novel is a work of fiction. However, several names, descriptions, entities, and incidents included in the story are based on the lives of real people.

The opinions expressed by the author are not necessarily those of Tate Publishing, LLC.

Published by Tate Publishing & Enterprises, LLC
127 E. Trade Center Terrace | Mustang, Oklahoma 73064 USA
1.888.361.9473 | www.tatepublishing.com

Tate Publishing is committed to excellence in the publishing industry. The company reflects the philosophy established by the founders, based on Psalm 68:11,
"The Lord gave the word and great was the company of those who published it."

Book design copyright © 2009 by Tate Publishing, LLC. All rights reserved.
Cover design by Kandi Evans
Interior design by Stefanie Rooney

Published in the United States of America
ISBN:978-1-60799-081-9
1. Fiction, Biographical 2. Fiction, Family Life
09.04.01

The future is for the young,
The past—forever gone,
But he who hath his memories
Will never walk alone.

S.W.S.

Selena "Sippy" Wright age 9

Rachel and Jim Wright - circa 1902
Selena "Sippy" Wright - about 2yrs. old

This book is dedicated to the children, grandchildren, and great-grandchildren of Selena "Sippy" Wright Davenport Sanders, my mother.

F.A.S.

PREFACE

I must have contemplated the writing of *Singer of an Empty Day* a year or more before undertaking it. The work would be a long and lonely journey to the past—tearing at my heart strings, followed only by the emptiness of letting go. It would take three years.

My mother, Selena Sanders (who was "Sippy"), died in 1989, leaving a wealth of written material—her own life stories, reminiscences, and songs. "Sippy" embodies her early years, pointing toward all that followed, always with her unfaltering faith in the future. In life, Selena Sanders more than surpassed her childhood dreams.

This work could not have been completed without the encouragement of my husband, Herman. Many times he came from work to find me at my keyboard and, uncomplaining, started supper. My children, Jan, Rebecca, and Phil, have been very supportive, along with their spouses. They wrote prologues (at my request) that I shall treasure and that I've incorporated into my own:

> Life's experiences are enjoyed best from the perspective of hindsight...I (Sippy) could not see

beyond the peaks surrounding Utah Mountain, let alone into an adulthood so completely different from my childhood... God blesses us all with imperfect knowledge. Had I known the fate awaiting my family on Utah Mountain, could I have born the burden of fear? Could knowledge of my mother's dying struggle have brought any more than despair? No preparation can steel us for the saddest of life's turns, yet they come, and we survive because there is nothing else we can do.

–Phil Scearce, Murfreesboro, Tennessee

So this is happiness, she thought. The house, the family, the money. It was what she had worked for—ached for—all those hard years. Years of starvation ... She drifted back to reality. It was almost dark. She switched on a light and looked out the window of her two-story house. How very strange! Maybe it was convolutions on old glass... but staring at her in the window was the face of Sippy, from many years ago.

–Jan Scearce, Carolina Beach, North Carolina.

I am grateful for all who aided and encouraged me in the endeavor. Tom Jordan, former Minister of Youth and Music, Temple Baptist Church, New Bern, North Carolina, did the arrangements of folk songs—those I could remember from my mother's renditions. It was a tough job! Thanks, Tom. The "Writing for

Publication" class at Craven Community College, Maxine Harker, instructor, were my best critics as well as my most verbal boosters. Who was "that feller what bigged Nellie Sue?" they kept asking.

Flora Ann Scearce

PROLOGUE

Soon Jay will be home for lunch. We'll talk about our children, grown up now, our grandchildren, and how good life is. He'll admire the flower arrangement I spent all morning creating for the two o'clock garden club meeting. "It's beautiful, darling," he'll say. But, to him, whatever I do is fine.

"You have a natural talent," a fellow club member will say, more to the truth. And I'll remember my mother. In memory she runs with me through fields of anemones and black-eyed Susans. We stop to pick Painted Trillium and purple violets in spruce-fir forests. On the mossy banks of Jonathan's Creek amid the ferns, she stoops to marvel at a pink lady-slipper, and I wonder, *Was she, too, a flower "born to blush unseen" in a wilderness of poverty?*

Beyond my front porch a little girl is playing in a neighbor's yard. Gusty winds blow her skirt while she clutches a rag doll tightly. A thin child with stick legs and curly no-color hair, she catches me staring at her from the window of my two-story home ...

So let me sing of names remembered
Because they, living not, can ne'er be dead,
Or long time take their memory quite away
From us poor singers of an empty day.

-William Morris
"An Apology" from The Earthly Paradise

CHAPTER 1

November 1907

Mournful as a locomotive winding its way through the rugged passes of North Carolina's Great Smoky Mountains, the blustery winds seemed foreboding. They whistled around the gabled roof of our log cabin home in Haywood County. Yet inside, where my mother prepared the evening meal, all was cozy.

Using her homemade grater, a can with nail holes punched in one end, she grated enough corn for bread. Then from the open fireplace, she shoveled red-hot coals onto the smoke-blackened clay hearth and, with pothooks, lifted an iron Dutch oven and set it on the coals. Sweat gleamed on her brow, and wisps of dark hair clung to her neck. She wiped them away with the back of her hand.

Pulling several split logs from a pile nearby, she

added them to the fire then glanced at the mantel clock. It was time for Papa to come home. Hastily she patted out two egg-shaped corn dodgers, knuckling them into the hot grease of the oven. She put the lid on and spread red coals over its lipped top.

"Sippy-gal," she said to me while turning slices of salt pork in a skillet. "I cain't leave these vittles a-cookin'. Grab that water bucket and fetch a bucketful from the spring afore yer papa gits here." She stirred a pot of boiling cabbage. "Hurry now. He'll be a-wantin' a cool drink soon's he gits in."

"Yes'm." I wrapped Liddy, my rag doll, in her cotton-sack cloak to take with me. Mama'd made Liddy for my birthday. We'd both giggled as she sewed on black button eyes. At twenty-three, Mama was at times like a little girl herself. "Let's call 'er 'Button-eye,'" she'd said, laying the long-legged doll in my lap.

"I don't like 'Button-eye;' her name's 'Liddy,'" I replied.

"Don't take that doll with you." Mama mopped her face with an apron-tail. "It's high time a seven-year-old learned to do housework 'stead of lollygaggin' around with a doll. When I was seven, I knowed all sorts of work, did all sorts, fer that matter. Didn't hurt me none."

"Yes'm." I laid Liddy gently on a bed and went to the corner cupboard. Stoneware dishes were stacked on open shelves and below sat milk crocks, a butter churn, and wooden pails. I grabbed a pail and headed out the door.

"Come on, Blue," I called to our dog, who waited patiently for my summons. Ragged heads of burdock and fennel weed bobbed crazily in the wind, and russet leaves spun around my legs as I wandered down the path swinging the bucket. Ole Blue followed at my heels.

"Sippy! Sippy-gal!" Mama shouted from the door. "Quit playing, and git that water right now, you hear me?"

"Yes'm." I plunged the gourd dipper deep into the spring and filled the small pail to the brim. Water sloshed out with each step as I wobbled back up the hill.

"Just look a-there! Just look a-there!" Mama slapped at my dress-tail. "Wet as a drownded rat, you are. Now git in and git them clothes off. You're a-fixin' to cough all night."

"Can I wear my new dress?"

Mama sighed. "'Spose so." A blazing log in the fireplace cast flickering lights across the room where two bedsteads rested against a far wall. Worn and faded garments hung from nail hooks like shadowy ghosts. The rest of our clothing was folded neatly on a low bench under heavy piles of quilts. Mama pulled a red calico dress from the bottom of the stack. She'd finished making it in time for my birthday, November 10. "Keep it nice, now," she said. "You can wear it again Christmas. Then we'll put it away fer school."

Marietta, whom we called "Met," slept in her cradle pulled close to the fire. Met was two and getting big for the cradle, but when Mama was busy, it was the best place for a nap. I rocked it back and forth, watching her suck her thumb, a rag doll nestled to her cheek.

"Quit rockin' that cradle, Sip. Can't you see the baby's done asleep?" Mama poured water from the bucket into a small basin, mixed in a splash of witch hazel, and bathed her face. "Um-mm," she said. "That fire's such a hot 'un. Smoke blows out awful, it's so windy." She eased into a chair at the homemade dining table, hub of our activity. Taking combs from her long black hair, she twisted it into a neat coil at the nape of her neck, then applied a dab of sweet oil to her brows and lashes—something she did when Papa was due home.

Papa was gathering firewood at the edge of the forest. There could never be too much. We used it for cooking, heating, building huts and fences. According to Papa, this was the very best working weather—cool, crisp, and dry.

The pendulum clock ticked at its place on the fireboard between an oil lamp and our small coffee mill. Mama rested her hands on her abdomen.

"My back's hurtin' something awful," she told me. A pensive look deepened her dark eyes. "Listen to that wind. 'Minds me of the day you was born. Lordy, that was a bitin' cold day! Seven years ago, it was."

"Mama, tell me about bein' borned."

"Shucks, gal. You ask such pesterin' things. 'Sides, I've told you a dozen times. You were born right here on Utah Mountain, November the tenth, nineteen hundred. It was writ down in your grandma's Holy Bible the very day." She was sixteen, she said, and Papa eighteen on the day I was born on a rocky flat called "Rattlesnake Den." Her mother, Nancy Burzilla Robards Robinson, was midwife, and I was named Selena "Burzilla" Wright for her. "Sippy," my baby sister, Marietta, said when she tried to say "sister," and it stuck.

"When I was borned, why'd you and Papa git me 'stead of somebody else gittin' me?"

Her face softened. She got up, holding her back with both hands, and peeked at each cooking pot. "I done told you, honey. We found you under a fodder stack in old man Kingsley's cornfield."

"How come you found me way down there?"

She stirred the cabbage pot with a long wooden spoon. "Fact is, your papa and me was clearin' that field for old man Kingsley when we found you. You was so little bitty and so purty, we just couldn't leave you, so we brung you home. Now git on and set that table."

"I'm glad you didn't let old man Kingsley find me; he's so ugly. Did you find Met under a fodder stack, too?"

"Shh! Shh! I hear your papa a-comin'." She began ladling food from steaming pots. "He'll shore like these vittles. Um-mm, um-mm! I sweetened this stewed pumpkin with 'lasses and nutmeg. Smells so good." She piled wedges of steamed cabbage into a bowl and placed fried salt pork with milk gravy and fried onion rings on a small platter. The aromas filled the cabin, and I could hardly wait for my plate to be served.

"Whoo-ee!" Papa hurried in, slamming the door. "That wind's a-blowin' somethin' awful. And they's fire on the mountain. I saw smoke a-risin' over toward Rattlesnake Den."

Mama groaned. "Oh, Lordy, don't tell me that. I'm so scared of fire. I remember how pore old Huldy looked a-layin' in her coffin-box burnt to a crisp."

"Rachel, fer Gawd's sake, hush sich talk at suppertime. I'll be pukin' up these vittles afore I git 'em down." He washed his hands carefully in the tin basin on the shelf near the door, took a peek at himself in the mirror above, and sat down at the table. Papa was not vain, but he knew women found him attractive. Long-legged and brawny, his freckles and red hair contrasted with intense blue eyes. "'Sides that," he added, "if you'll just recollect, it was old Huldy herself what started that fire and burnt herself up—a-pourin' kerosene on hot coals. She orter knowed better."

Mama heaped his plate with hot food. "You know what a cold winter that was. Pore old Huldy was just tryin' to git warm."

Papa grunted. "Well, she shore did."

"Mama, I don't want no fried onions, nor cabbages—just meat and gravy," I said.

Papa gave me a stern look. His rule for the table was that children "should be seen and not heard." "You'll eat whatever your maw puts on your plate. And don't talk when grown folks is a-talkin'."

"Yessir." I nibbled at the cabbage Mama placed on my plate.

Papa looked at Mama. "Hain't been no calls fer lumber, but tomorrow I'm a-goin' to eat my dinner at the grist mill and talk to old man Kingsley. Maybe he'll see fit to pay me fer what I've got cut."

Jacob Kingsley owned the land we lived on. He'd turned most of it into a range for beef cattle, and Papa had to build split-rail fences to keep cows out of his planted fields. Still, Papa was only a tenant, and part of his meager harvest went to Mr. Kingsley. The one hog Papa could afford to raise had been slaughtered, the hams going to Kingsley for farm tools. The shoulders were swapped for salt, sugar, and coffee. The rest, salted down, hung in our lean-to.

"Honey, we don't owe that old feller a red cent. Finished payin' him off with that last cured ham." Papa piled his plate high with a second helping of fried onions. "Leaves only sides and middlin's to last till next year, but I figured we can do that."

"Shore we can. We got enough to eat, thank the Good Lord. But we're plumb out of coffee. This here's bran coffee." Mama had made her strong "hard times" brew by roasting cornmeal bran in a skillet until brown, adding water and molasses, and straining it through a sieve. She refilled Papa's cup and passed him a pitcher of milk.

"Well and good. Your bran coffee's better than no coffee. But I'll see if I cain't git us a pound of Arbuckle's when I git paid fer my four days' work at the sawmill." Met had woke up and was crying to be taken. "Fer pity's sake, honey, git that baby afore she squalls her eyeballs out."

Mama took Met into her lap and fed her with morsels she'd mashed or chewed to tenderness. These were alternated with sips of milk and coffee. Met wanted to hold the cup, but Mama didn't trust her.

"Reckon I'll take me another look at the ridge afore dark," Papa said, pushing his chair from the table. "Come on out; see fer yourself." I followed them, afraid of what we'd find.

Papa squinted, shielding his eyes with his hand. "Lookee yonder at that ridge. Hain't that fire a-crossin' Rocky Branch?"

Mama grabbed his arm. "Hit shore is. If this wind keeps up, I'll be a-feared to go to bed. All that dry brush makes wildfire."

"No need to be scared, honey." His voice was calm. "I done cleared that tract over there. Hit'll burn plumb out afore it's nigh our house." He kicked a small stone toward the menacing black puffs high above the stacks of corntops and fodder on the hillside. "Damn fox hunters."

Fall was the season for forest fires, and we always kept close watch for telltale wisps and acrid odors of smoke. But fall was also the season for hunters, and wild game was free for the taking. When sportsmen came from the city to hunt foxes, the mountains echoed with blasts of bugles and baying of hounds. Listening to the fox chase was exciting for us children but worried older folks. Some fires were caused by lightning, but Papa knew, likely as not, careless hunters had simply failed to douse their campfires.

We started back inside. "Better fetch some more kindlin'," Mama said.

Papa and I went to the lean-to where salted-down hog sides and middlings hung from the ceiling. Loops of golden pumpkin, strings of beans, and bunches of white onions Mama was drying for late winter and early spring eating dangled from walls and across joists. On the earthen floor rested crocks of pickled vegetables, fermenting apple-peel vinegar, and preserved fruit.

Papa liked checking the contents of his full storehouse. He picked up a jar of peaches, blew dust off the lid, and placed it back with the others. "I think me and you can rest easy, gal," he said. "I think we'll git by with what we got laid up." Stacked neatly next to the split-log bench holding Mama's washtubs and batches of her lye soap were piles of kindling wood. Papa and I gathered sticks of it.

As soon as the sun sank red and hazy behind western peaks, the wind picked up. It howled like a hungry wolf. Mama was clearing the supper table. "I'm powerful uneasy, Jim. Go, see how fer away the fire looks now. I cain't rest with it on my mind."

"Ain't nothin' out there but smoke a-risin', but I'll take another gander afore goin' to bed."

"When I cain't sleep, I just give plumb out." Mama clasped her abdomen. "It won't like this a-carryin' the others. I won't so give-out with them."

Papa pulled her to him, wrapping her in his long arms. "Maybe this'n's a boy, then." He grinned as he placed a hand on her bulging apron. "It just takes more fer a boy."

"Sh-hh!" Mama took away his hand and motioned toward me, staring at them wide-eyed. "When you git back in, you need to help me git a dose of boneset down Sippy here. Else she'll keep us awake all night a-coughin'." The words "boneset" and "pennyroyal" were among the most dreaded I knew. Teas from them and wild cherry bark were used for treating colds, grippe, and other symptoms.

"No, no," I pleaded, but it was no use. There was no escaping Mama's prescriptions from her "medicine chest" of herbs and roots. Only one thing was worse—hot onion poultices applied to my chest. They burned while I had to lie still. Mama glared at me and placed her kettle of water on hot coals.

Papa came in shaking his head. "There's fresh smoke a-risin' toward Chestnut Ridge. I figure we're safe, though. Ain't no trees nigh our house, and Spring Branch's 'twixt us and them woods. All the same, I tied Ole Blue to the doorstep. As scaredy as that rascal is, she'll yelp her danged head off if fire gits close."

Mama agreed. "She's a barkin' dog if I ever knowed one. She'll bark at her own shadder." She picked up the steaming cup of herb tea, and I started kicking and whimpering. "Come on and drink it like a purty little gal."

I pushed it away, my lips tightly closed.

"Help me hold 'er, Jim." They both held me hand and foot to get the bitter tea down.

"Git on to bed now!" Mama snapped, breathing hard from the struggle. "See how much good all that bawlin' did?"

The harsh dose set my teeth on edge. I spit and spit till I had no spit left. No matter how many times I had to take it, the routine was always the same.

On cold nights, all of us slept in one bed, huddled on straw-filled mattress ticks beneath layers of homemade quilts. Met was already asleep, and I gently eased her from her warm spot and myself into it, then lay still as a mouse, making sure she did not wake up.

With the warm tea inside, I soon felt drowsy. I pictured Ole Blue standing by a pot of boiling molasses. Without warning she toppled in and commenced barking wildly, trying to get out. Her sticky paws grabbed for the sides. "Blue! Blue!" I woke up frightened and cold. Papa was snoring peacefully less than an arm's length away, but something was very wrong. Outside Ole Blue's desperate yelps were not a dream. Above her howls an eerie crackling sounded like thousands of chestnuts popping in the fireplace. Slipping to the cabin wall, I peered through the crack in the chinks. The world appeared in flames! "Mama! Mama!" I ran and jumped in the bed bedside Mama.

Papa bolted out, grabbing his pants and pulling them quickly over long underwear. He flung open the door and stood framed by a reddish glow. Dragging bedclothes, Mama carried a dazed Met out the door behind him. I followed, wrapped in a trailing blanket.

"Oh, Lordy, have mercy upon us!" Mama wailed as wind roared through burning timber like thunder.

Fiery darts leaped skyward, and blazing trees ignited the ground. A giant pine split and fell in a mighty inferno, spewing white-hot fagots onto underbrush.

"I want to go to Grandma's; take me to Grandma's!" I screamed and jumped up and down, while Met stood transfixed, holding onto Mama. Mama's head was bowed. She cradled her large belly.

Papa looked at her. "Air you all right, Rachel?"

"I'm a-prayin'," she said. "I'm a-prayin' the fire'll burn out afore mornin', afore it's nigh our house."

"You take the baby," Papa told her. "We'll git on to yer maw's and stay the night." He caught me up in his arms, and at last I felt safe. I'd ridden his back down the mountain many times but never more willingly.

"Come on, Blue, you crazy dog!" I called. "You want to git burnt up?" Ole Blue whimpered and followed on our heels.

Mama took Met astraddle her hip. We edged our way along the banks of Spring Branch, Papa searching out footholds for Mama. She followed close behind.

Grandma Robinson lived far down the mountain in a sheltered cove. It was still dark when we reached the clearing where Spring Branch emptied into Jonathan's Creek. The earth lay moist and fertile in this quiet hollow where my grandfather had built the two-room cabin and brought Grandma as a bride. We crossed the creek and found the familiar path through a field of stubble to Grandma's door. As we neared, Papa cupped his hands to his mouth: "Hullo! Hullo! Open up, Maw. Open the door!"

"'Smatter out there?" Grandma yelled, holding a lantern high and peering into the darkness. "Who air ye?"

"It's Jim and Rachel." Papa came close to her light. "We had to leave the house, Maw. Lookee yonder."

"Good God A'mighty!" There was no mistaking the ominous red haze. "Some danged fool's ornery business."

"Cain't help who done it. I gotta git Tom and git on back to look after my stuff."

Mama was gasping for breath after the mad rush. "Honey, you'ns go on to bed," Papa told her. "Don't worry none 'bout Tom and me. We'll be back afore long." Uncle Tom was up and dressed. The two took shovels and buckets and marched into the darkness back to our house.

Grandma scanned the heavens before closing the door. "'Twon't be long afore daylight," she said. She placed a huge log on the smoldering coals in the fireplace. "Rachel, you and the gals git in Tom's bed. It's still warm. I'm goin' back to bed whilst this firelog ketches up."

"I'm puttin' these young'ns to bed, then I'll just

set a spell," Mama said. "I'm too uneasy to sleep a wink. Go on, git yer rest, I'll tend yer fire."

Deep in Tom's pine-scented bedtick, I slept soundly till daylight. When I woke up in the strange bed, it all came back—the fire, racing here in the cold night. Shivering in my thin shift, I went to where Mama sat asleep in front of the smoldering fire. Met was curled on a pallet by her feet, one thin arm around Mama's ankle.

By late morning, Papa and Tom returned with good news—our cabin was still there. "Didn't I tell you, Rachel honey?" Papa said proudly. "Didn't I tell you? Now let's git on back home. Me and Tom's goin' to see Kingsley. I got some pay a-comin' from 'im. Then we're gittin some scrap lumber to build me a meat box. I need a good meat box."

From our vantage point, the smoke appeared less dense, dark tendrils trailing here and there among misty blue hills. The air was pungent with it. Light rain had fallen, and Papa surmised the fire had burned itself out. It was colder, and a stiff wind was biting as we climbed the steep ridge toward home. Falling leaves swirled and fluttered across our path like birds searching for roosting places out of the wintry blast. Mama stopped every few yards to catch her breath.

Approaching the clearing, she hollered. "Oh, Lordy, Lordy, have mercy! It's on fire!"

Smoke billowed from the top of our cabin. Papa

yelled. "I gotta git my stuff out! All my meat, all my corn's in that lean-to." He sprinted across the field, Tom right behind him.

"You cain't go in there, Jim. You won't never make it back out." Tom grabbed Papa and wrestled him to the ground.

"You dang fool, let me up. Let me up, I say!" Papa struggled against Tom's strong arms. But he knew it was too late. Flames licked the windows and streaked over the roof.

I stamped my feet, screaming at the top of my lungs. Mama buried her face in her apron, bawling her heart out, as the sweet smell of cured meat filled the air and smoke spiraled skyward, blending into the clouds.

Papa raked long fingers through his mop of red curly hair. He got up from his knees. "All my meat," he moaned. "All my corn." His voice broke. "Every damn thing I had in the world—gone."

His words seemed to prick Mama's ears. She wiped her eyes with an apron-tail. "Don't talk like that, Jim." She blew her nose softly. "You've still got us." She clasped his big freckled hand with her small brown one. They stood side by side watching the flames leap, consume, and finally smolder to ashes.

An eeriness had settled in when I heard a mewing sound. From a clump of scorched weeds walked my spotted kitten, cold and shaking. I ran to pick him up. "Lookee, Papa, Kitty-cat's still here. He ain't burnt up." I cuddled him tightly as we walked back to Grandma's.

FAMILY TREE OF SELENA "SIPPY" WRIGHT

Monteville Wright m.   Alvis Averal "Bud" Robinson m.
Kate Stuart   Nancy Burzilla Robards

John m. Roxie   Mary
   -France   -Burzilla
   -Raymond

                        Alex m. Loulie

Sallie

                        Ruanna

Harve

Anne m. Greenberry Waldrop
   -James William
    (Waldrop) Wright m.   Rachel Johanna
      -Selena "Sippy"
      -Marietta "Met"   Tom

                        George

                        Effie

CHAPTER 2
Grandma's House

My grandfather, Alvis Averal Robinson (called "Bud"), built their log home in Shingle Cove when he and my grandmother were newlyweds. Defying snakes and wild beasts, they acquired four hundred acres of rugged mountain terrain and eked a living from it. They cut timber and, with teams of oxen, dragged it down the mountainside to sell. Fields were planted on the cleared land. Their harvest grew and so did their family.

Then Bud Robinson was killed in a hunting accident, and my grandmother's dreams died with him. Her children were too young for the back-breaking work of logging, and she lacked business knowledge. With no one to advise her, first she mortgaged, then she sold outright to opportunists like Jacob Kingsley, who bought her best for a pittance. Now Kingsley owned Utah Mountain and its beautiful valley.

With nowhere else to go, Grandma remained at Shingle Cove, farming rocky land that now belonged to someone else. It was a daunting task. Years of timber cutting left flats dotted with stumps and large rocks. These were grubbed out or planted around till gullies streaked the hills, draining substance from the soil and into valleys where landlords farmed fertile fields.

Grandma had three children still at home, but only Tom, seventeen, was strong enough to farm. George, thirteen, helped. Effie, the youngest, was ten.

Her house was built in two sections, each with a fireplace. The larger cabin was a combination living room, dining room, bedroom, and kitchen. Out back, the smaller served as a spare bedroom. With three generations lumped in cramped quarters, Papa fretted and walked the floor like a bull in a holding pen, while Mama moped and cried.

"Don't cry, Mama," I kept saying.

"Oh, Sippy-gal, I don't know what we're a-goin' to do, with our home all burnt up."

I looked to Papa for an answer, but his face was pinched from lack of sleep, his blue eyes bleary. He rubbed his palms as he paced. It took Uncle Tom to break the spell.

"Fer Gawd's sake, Jim, set down! You've damn

nigh wore out the puncheons. And you, Rachel." He faced his sister squarely. "If it hadn't been fer me, that man of your'n would be a-layin' up yonder just like Old Huldy, burnt to a fare-thee-well. That lean-to of his was a-blazin' when we got there. I held onto that rascal like a derned bulldog, else he'd a-gone smack-dab into them flames, he's so hellbent on gittin' that hogmeat of his'n."

It was like Tom had splashed him with cold water. Papa heaved a big sigh and dropped to a chair. "I did sorter go crazy when I see'd everything I had to live on destroyed. I thankee fer what you done."

"Lord knows I thankee," Mama said. She went to where Papa sat. "I'd rather have this man than anything else on Gawd's green earth."

"C'mere, honey." Papa pulled her into his lap and held her close. He placed his hand on her bulging abdomen. Seeing them, Met ran to Mama and jerked at her apron-tail, trying to wrench her from Papa's arms. When Mama didn't move, Met started to cry.

"Pore hungry little gal," Papa teased. "Go-on, honey, feed 'er afore she makes herself sick a-bawlin'."

"*All* you'ns come and eat," Grandma called, surprising us with platters of hot food she and Effie were ladling to the table. "Tain't nary bit o' use sittin' and a-groanin' over what cain't be helped." Her breakfast of oatcakes with sorghum molasses and butter, fried fatback, applesauce, cold milk, and hot coffee soon had us all in better spirits.

When Tom finished his food, he pulled out a tobacco pouch. Removing a cigarette paper from a pocket, he spread a thin line of tobacco on it. I put down my fork to watch. While drawing the pouch string closed with his teeth, he proceeded to roll the cigarette with one hand then licked the paper to seal it. Rearing on his straight-backed chair, he placed the finished cigarette in his mouth and lit it. Effie clapped her hands at Tom's prowess while Grandma rose hastily from the table, trying to hide her admiration.

George wanted to try it. Grandma huffed. "Smokin' ain't fer the likes of you." She raked food scraps into her slop bucket noisily.

Papa eased from the table and patted his full stomach. "I'm a-goin' down to old man Kingsley's. A-goin' to ask him fer my four days' pay in cloth, 'stead of cash money. What we'uns need more'n anything else is clothes." He squeezed Mama's shoulder. "Honey, write down what sorter cloth you want. I'll git what I can. And don't fret none about our chickens. Tom and me'll seek 'em out tonight when they go to roost."

"I'm a-goin' with you," Tom said. "I'm a-takin' one o' my Dominecker roosters to swap the old man fer a ball of sewin' thread and a box of snuff. Maw cain't sew a lick without that lip o' her'n full of snuff."

"Fiddle-faddle! Ain't nary one of ye got no room to talk." She gave Tom a teasing shove. "Now git on with ye."

Tom raised his arms, dodging her make-believe swipes. "Yes'm, yes'm."

"Can I go, Papa?" For me, a trip to the Settlement was better than munching roasted chestnuts and listening to George's goriest haint tales.

Papa gave me a doubtful look. "I ain't a-listenin' to no squawkin' fer peppermint sticks."

"I'll be good. I'll tote a basket of eggs and not break a single one."

The way to the Settlement followed Jonathan's Creek to the gristmill dam, where the rambling stream spilled into the river. There the trail crossed a bridge and widened into a macadamized road to the Settlement and on to Waynesville, five miles away. Years before, timber was floated down the racing river from forests of Utah Mountain to factories and builders in the lowlands. Now timber of value was scarce on Utah. Lumbermen had turned to the lofty peaks of Saunook where stands of spruce, white oak, locust, and poplar remained tall and plentiful. For men like Papa and Tom, work was harder and harder to find.

Near the bridge, Papa pointed to neat hacks of wood and mounds of sawdust where a sawmill once stood. He and Tom had worked there. "If I had some of that lumber, I could build myself some furniture," Papa said.

"Yeah, and if a hoppy-toad had wings, he wouldn't bump his rump ever time he jumped," Tom replied. "Takes money to buy lumber."

"Such as I got no hopes of ever havin'." Papa sighed loudly.

Tom gave him a hard look. "Well, I'll say one thing. You got a mighty lot to be thankful fer. You got yer gals, and their maw to take care of 'em." Approaching a small chapel, we slowed as we always did. "Now take yer brother, John. His pore wife, Roxie's, a-layin' yonder in the ground. Since he lost her, he's got them two young'ns to raise by hisself." We strolled to a hard clay mound with a weather-worn wooden cross. Aunt Roxie had died after childbirth and the stillborn baby was buried in her arms. Papa and Tom took off their hats and bowed their heads.

"Pore Roxie," Papa said finally. "I wish to Gawd John coulda kept 'er."

"He done all in Gawd's name a man could do. It was Roxie's time to go and the Lord took her." Tom put his hat back on. He was just seventeen, but Tom had taken a fatherly role toward George and Effie. He and Papa shared a common lot, working together for years farming and cutting timber. They turned to go. Both were silent for a long time.

Short and stocky like most of Grandma's children, Tom walked fast to keep pace with Papa's long-legged strides. I lagged behind, cradling my basket with both arms, pausing at times to watch other children at play.

Several crossroads branched from the broad paved road and circled fields where Jacob Kingsley and other prosperous merchant farmers lived in well-kept two-story homes. Papa and Tom stopped to check our mailboxes that hung from posts by the main road. Mountaineers seldom got mail. When we did, it was usually an ad or a free publication such as *Barkers Almanac*. Papa pulled a copy of one from our box.

"Goody, goody." I jumped up and down.

Good for Man or Beast, Barkers Liniment ad claimed in bold type above a list of items for young and old. Papa flipped through to my favorite, a puzzle with hidden faces of animals and people. "How many can you find?" the caption posed. Try as I might, I could never find them all.

"Let me see it, let me see it," I begged.

"Wait till we git home." Papa's best pages featured planting guides with phases of the moon and weather predictions. Mama's were the sewing section. She traced quilt patterns from its instructions, cut scraps of fabric, and stitched them to form intricate tops. In spring, quilting frames were brought from the loft, and she, Grandma, and all females old enough to hold a needle gathered for a bee. Papa rolled the almanac up and stuck it in a hip pocket.

Tom was squinting at a dingy white envelope. "Well, I'll be dad-blamed if we hain't got us a letter. Hold onto this here chicken-rooster, Jim. I'll see if I cain't make it out:

> My Dear Brother,
>
> It is with much pleasure I set my hand to write this letter to you, to let you know that Loulie and me are both as well as common. Truly hoping this letter comes to your hand and finds you all the same. I still work at the railroad station. I make good wages. I am able to buy anything we want to eat. We eat wheat-bread any day of the week, and have beef or chicken every Sunday.
>
> Tell Ma and Rachel that me and Loulie joined a church. We bought Sunday clothes as everybody dresses up to go. I bought myself a blue serge suit, a John B. Stetson hat, and a white shirt with button-on celluloid collar. I bought Loulie a plaid wool coatsuit, beaded handbag, and a fascinator to match.
>
> It will be June before we will be able to come to see you all. Please read this letter to Ma.
>
> > From your loving brother,
> > Alexander

Tom gave a yell. "Shoo-ee! That Alex—'scuse me. I mean *Alexander*, the biggity ole booger. I'm damned if he ain't got too high-falutin' fer me."

"Hellfire!" Papa exclaimed. "If he's gittin' on that good, I'm a-goin' to Asheville and look fer me a job."

Tom settled down at Papa's quick words. "Shorely you ain't a-takin' Rachel nowhere, her feelin' porely, expectin' that young'n."

"I hain't a-takin' 'er *now*. But, I swear to Gawd, Tom, I'm a-goin' to find a way to make a livin' fer my family."

"You'ns ain't a-goin' hungry as long as we've got a mouthful of vittles. You know that, don't you?"

"Shore I do. And powerful obliged to you'ns fer it. I just hope I can do somethin' to pay you back someday. But a feller has to make a livin' fer his own family."

Tom folded the letter and began reading an ad he'd gotten. "Look what we got here. Appears they's hirin' men fer work in Tuscola. They's clearin' land over there fer a big lake." He handed it to Papa. Tuscola was a few miles from where we lived. Papa perused it carefully and stuck it in his pocket with the almanac.

The Settlement was a small village with a school, church, coffin factory/carpenter shop, and general store, the latter owned and operated by Jacob Kingsley. Approaching, Papa cast glum looks at the coffin factory. His brother, my uncle John, still owed them money for Roxie's casket. John had purchased her silk-lined box by mortgaging his mule and cow. Now he worked at the shop every chance he could, applied most of it to the debt, and considered himself lucky. Folks with no land or livestock had to buy unpainted, unlined coffins for a few dollars, or wood and nails to make their own.

We stopped at a clapboard building with a blue sign and black lettering: *J. Kingsley General Merchandise.* Next to it, a raging bull advertised Bull Durham Smoking Tobacco.

"Minds me, I need tobaccy," Tom said. He and Papa stomped clay from their boots, spat tobacco cuds into the weeds, cleared their throats, and entered the store. I spat hard into the same weeds and marched in behind them.

A tangy potpourri of ground coffee, coal dust, and tobacco smoke greeted us. Posters covered every wall—Fairbanks Gold Dust Washing Powder, Arbuckle's Coffee (green or roasted grains), Horsford's Bread Preparation, Cottolene Shortening. My eyes came to rest on a counter where sticks of peppermint candy gleamed in glass jars. Papa hadn't said not to look.

"Come right in, gentlemen! Come right in." The raspy voice from behind the sugar barrel yielded to the sight an old codger in pince-nez glasses. He tottered our way.

"Howdy-do, Mr. Kingsley," Papa and Tom each said in turn.

Mr. Kingsley opened wide the door of his iron potbellied stove, picked up two hunks of coal from a bucket, and tossed them into the flames.

Papa looked around, shuffling nervously. He took my basket of eggs and set it on the counter while Tom browsed among pitchforks and axes near the pickle barrel.

"Did you hear 'bout my bad luck?" Papa asked. He watched Mr. Kingsley take his poker to punch hot coals.

"Can't say as I did, what kind of trouble?" The old man slapped his hands together and wiped them on his apron. He got Tom's rooster and stuck it in a wooden coop.

Papa looked incredulous. "Why shorely you see'd the fire on the mountain. Burnt the cabin clean to the ground. Ever'thing I had to live on burnt up with it."

"Come to think of it, I did see that blaze, Jim. You mean you couldn't save a thing? Where's the family?"

Papa told about the night of the fire—how he took us to Grandma's, how he and Tom thought the fire was out but returned to find everything in flames.

"I just never expected the fire would git to the house, else I'd a-moved out afore it did."

"Hindsight's better than foresight. Timber will grow again is what I always say. I'm truly sorry about your loss. Of course, that cabin was mine, but you needed it more than I did." He looked at Tom, who'd worked for him off and on since the age of fourteen. "By the way, I hate to tell you boys, but I'm out of the sawmill business for good. Tell you the truth, I've taken some losses lately. You're both steady fellows, so I'm sure you'll find something. I'm willing to help as far as I can."

"I didn't come to ask fer no help," Papa shot back. "I come to ask fer my four days' pay I got comin' in cloth from yer store. My young'ns need clothes worse than anything right now. All we saved was what we had on our backs." Papa placed a hand on top of my head. I glanced up at Mr. Kingsley. "As fer a job, I just told Tom here, I'm a-goin' somewhere else and find somthin'. I'd a-gone long ago, 'cept fer Rachel. She loves Utah Mountain, always has. Alex is makin' good in Asheville. I'm a mind to go there, or maybe Tuscola—where they's building that big lake."

"Yes, sir," Tom piped up. "That brother of mine shore got hisself a fine job at the depot in Asheville."

"Your brother was just plain lucky to get that job," Mr. Kingsley said. "Asheville's a summer resort town. If the trains didn't pass through, your brother wouldn't have a job. Nothing there for Jim, not this time of year." Tom seemed taken aback by the old merchant's words. He stared out the grimy storefront window. Mr. Kingsley hunched over a lined ledger, penciling figures in while Papa leaned on the counter. "Looks like you've got three dollars and thirty-two cents coming to you. I'm prepared to give you more piece goods for that amount than you'd get in Waynesville."

"Well and good," Papa said. "Here's the list Rachel give me." Papa handed a scrap of paper across the counter. "I'll be proud to git as much as I can."

"Let's talk again about that job situation," Mr. Kingsley said as he pulled bolts of cotton flannel and calico from a shelf. "I'll tell you what my son-in-law's doing, and since you two are mountain men, you might just get in on it. Remember my son-in-law, Jim? He's about your age."

"Seems I recollect."

"Well, he's getting a crew of men together to cut timber off Mount Saunook. Big company down in the lowlands wants some fancy timber. They pay good wages. I've known big companies to furnish necessities to workers who're really in need. Go talk to my son-in-law. Name's Rance Hoaghan. Tell him what happened. Here's his address—tell him I recommended you."

Papa's face brightened. "Much obliged, Mr. Kingsley."

"I've added several yards of gingham to the flannel and calico Rachel wanted. It's some of my very best goods. Just call it a gift for your two little girls."

Papa was truly moved. "My goodness, I shore thankee, sir. My gals'll be struttin' like peacocks."

"I weighed your chicken," Mr. Kingsley said to Tom. "According to the price of roosters on foot, he's worth thirty-seven cents. I'll make it forty in trade, if you want."

"Yes, sir," Tom said. "I'll take a box of Bruton's Scotch Snuff and two balls of sewin' thread, one white, one black. Whatever's left over, give it to me in tobaccy."

The old merchant smiled down at me. His face was like a big dried apple. I ducked my head behind Papa's legs. I was tired and anxious to leave. I wanted to see Mama's eyes when she saw the beautiful piece goods. She'd hold it up to me, saying how pretty it would make up.

"And here we have a peppermint stick for little Selena," Mr. Kingsley was saying. When I caught the words, "peppermint stick," I came from behind my papa's legs to see the old man lifting the lid from the glass jar and removing a red and white candy. He held it out to me.

"Thankee." I took the striped stick from his gnarled fingers and ducked my head.

Papa and Uncle Tom picked up their bundles, wished Mr. Kingsley a pleasant day, and we were on our way.

CHAPTER 3
Winter Work

All the way home, Papa kept studying the Tuscola job Tom had gotten in the mail. "Sounds better ever' time I read it," he said.

"If you wanta seek it out, I reckon Rachel'll be fine with Maw," Tom offered. "As fer me, I got my harvestin' to do and plowin' fer early crops."

Soon Mama was busy cutting out dresses for my sister and me. Grandma made a trip to the loft and found old hand-me-downs for Mama and Papa. She shook them out good and pressed them with hot irons till the mustiness was gone and all moth holes discovered. Papa's change of clothes was a uniform from the Spanish-American War left by Grandma's brother, Zebulon Robards, when he departed for the final tenting grounds. Slightly faded with a button missing, it was a pretty good fit. The trousers were a tad short, but that could be fixed.

"Looks a sight better on Jim than it did on Zeb." Grandma smoothed away wrinkles and held buttons up for a match.

"Jim's a heap purttier'n Uncle Zeb," Mama said. Like a soldier off to fight the wars, Papa stood tall while Mama stretched to plant a kiss on his neck.

Papa noticed Mama reading Alex's letter over and over—mostly the part about "church clothes." In bed that night, he whispered, "When I git to makin' good, I'll buy you a coatsuit purttier'n any Loulie's got."

Mama shushed him. "I cain't wear no coatsuit. I cain't wear nothin' 'cept a Mother Hubbard."

Husky with emotion, Papa said, "After our little boy's borned, you can."

With everyone pitching in, Uncle Tom's crop was harvested, except for final strippings. These were left for the cows and old mule to eat when the ground became frozen and bare. Nothing was wasted.

Mama's back was getting painful, and she had trouble walking. At times she was dizzy, and despite her protests, Grandma would make her lie down. Papa talked constantly to Tom and Grandma about the timber-cutting job, but not when Mama was near. She was afraid he'd leave before the baby came.

"This'n's different," she told Papa. "I cain't hardly move my legs no more." When Papa and Tom were out working, I kept watch by her chair, though I longed to be outside with Effie and George. They were out of school and would not return until early summer after crops were planted. As soon as Papa came inside, I hurried out to forage among fallen leaves with my young aunt and uncle, searching for chestnuts and chinquapins. We strung the chinquapins like brown beads, hung them around our necks, and trudged the five miles to Waynesville depot. Waynesville was a mountain resort for the wealthy who came in summer and fall, traveling mainly by rail. They spent money on local crafts and produce, and especially liked our chinquapins on a string. So did the town children. Chestnuts sold for five cents a quart and chinquapins for five cents a string. With the money earned, we felt like millionaires till it was quickly spent—and we were paupers again.

Before snow and freezing weather forced us inside, the three of us scoured the woods for firewood. Uncle George split the logs by driving in an iron wedge and finished the job with an axe. We piled great stacks of it against the house. Afterwards we gathered straw and broomsedge, stuffing bedticks with new straw and making brooms of broomsedge—enough to last all year.

Mama and Grandma's part of winter work was

food preparation. Mama stuffed a pillow behind her back to ease the pain of sitting while she shelled corn to be ground into meal. She cut pumpkin rings, and Grandma strung them to dry above the fireplace on poles laid across rafters. Apples picked at peak of season were placed in the sun to dry, and beans were strung on twine into garlands. Mama and Grandma called these "shucky-beans" because they rattled like dry shucks. But Papa insisted on calling them "leather britches" like his grandmother always had. This is because they "turned brown as shoe leather when they got good and dry."

When the winds became bitter and our stacks of firewood dwindled, Papa and Tom went out with saws and heavy mauls, taking an oxcart to bring the logs back.

The thud of the massive hammer echoed throughout the cove, and I watched and listened as they sang to ease drudgery:

> "Oh, President McKinley
> Why didn't you run
> When you saw Czolgosz
> With that hammer-less gun?
> In Buffalo-oh-oh!
> In Buffalo-oh-oh!"

Whamming and thudding at the end of each line, the song had to wait while they shifted logs.

> "Czolgosz was a rascal,
> He shot him on the sly,
> He shot him through the heart,
> The president had to die.
> In Buffalo-oh-oh!
> In Buffalo-oh-oh!"

Another pause, shifting of logs, wiping of brows, and the song resumed, punctuated by groans and sighs.

> "Yonder comes forty-eight coaches,
> Decorated in black,
> To take him to Washington,
> And never bring him back,
> To Buffalo-oh-oh!
> To Buffalo-oh-oh!"

By nightfall, there was a feeling of security, knowing the woodshed was chock-full. We gathered around a blazing-hot fire, as if in celebration, and talked about the bad weather Grandma said "was bound to come." As usual, she was right. The first week of December we were snowed-in, the cabin wrapped snuggly in a white blanket, marked only by unbroken streams of chimney smoke.

Young Aunt Effie kept Met and me amused with old ballads passed on from her grandmother, our great-grandmother. Grandpa Robinson's mother had come from England in the early 1800s, bringing songs about lords and ladies and medieval English life. Passed down orally, they were sung in a quivery sing-song fashion, sometimes accompanied by fiddle or banjo. Effie taught me "Lord Thomas," "The Rolling Mill," "One Morning in May," "Barbara Allen," and my favorite, "The House Carpenter."

"Well met, well met, my own true love."
"Well met, well met!" said she.
"I have returned to my native land,
Just for the sake of thee.

"I could have married a king's daughter, dear,
 I am sure she'd have married me—
 Yet I've refused a crown of gold,
  All for the sake of thee."

"If you could have married a king's daughter, dear,
 I am sure I am not to blame,
 For I have married a house carpenter,
 And I think he's a fine young man."

"Will you forsake your house carpenter
  And go along with me?
 I will take you where the grass is green,
  And you can have your liberty."

"Then who would shoe my little baby's feet?
 And who would glove her little hand?
 And who would kiss her rosy little lips
  When I'm in a faroff land?"

"Her papa dear will shoe her little feet,
 He will also glove her little hand,
 And you will kiss her rosy little lips
  When you return again."

They hadn't been gone but about two weeks—
  I am sure it was not three,
When she began to weep and she began to moan:
 "It was all for the sake of thee."

"I don't want to hear you weep, my love,
 And I don't want to hear you moan,
 And I don't want to hear you sing that song
  'I wish I had never left home.'

> I wish to the Lord I had never been born,
> Or died when I was young,
> I never would have seen your pretty blue eyes,
> Nor heard your flattering tongue."
>
> They hadn't been gone but about three weeks–
> I am sure it was not four,
> When the ship began to leak,
> And the ship began to sink–
> It sank to rise no more.

The song always left me sad. I wondered why a mother would want to leave her beautiful baby to go off with a man. I was glad when Effie and George decided it was game time. Passed down in the same tradition were "Old Grandma Hump-Bump," "How Far to London-town?" and "King William Was King George's Son." Grandma kept chestnuts roasting on the open grate when we played contest games, and we used them as fines.

Also on long winter nights, Papa and Tom took turns telling funny stories about Pat and Mike, the foolish Irishmen. I didn't always understand the stories, but they made Mama laugh. When Mama laughed, I was happy; the times were so rare.

When Met finally dropped off to sleep, Effie and George began their gory "haint tales" of Rawhead and Bloody Bones. Toward the end, the action slowed, and I hung on their every word. All else to be heard was a low crackling of burning logs. Voices trailed.

Then a piercing "I've got you." Though I knew it was coming, I always screamed. Afterwards in bed I lay frightened, unable to sleep. "No more haint tales for you," Mama threatened. And I agreed—till next time.

That winter George taught me how to make deadfall triggers, trapping any bird that touched them. "Come 'ere, Sip," he hollered on a snowy morning. "Take a look at your trap." I ran to see my first catch, excited at success. Instead, there before us lay a beautiful white-throated bird, crushed flat.

"No!" I cried. "I ain't a-goin' to kill him."

"You done kilt 'im." George laughed devil-like, pointing to the bird. "You done kilt 'im deader'n a door nail! Now we're goin' to skin 'im, gut 'im, roast 'im, and eat 'im."

Scruples aside, soon I began hunting and trapping as avidly as George and Effie. Still, if I bagged a pretty one, I could not bring myself to eat it.

Sometimes we tracked rabbits through snow to their hollow-log nests, built a smoldering fire at one end, and waited at the other with a club. The prize catch was held up by the hind legs and struck hard on the back on the neck. George always dealt the blow. Effie and I had the task of preparing it for the pot. Our hunts weren't just for fun. They supplied the table with meat.

Grandma's way of cooking rabbit was to parboil

it till tender, then place it in a skillet of hot grease to brown. As it browned, she put whole black peppercorns in a cloth bag and beat them fine with a hammer, then sprinkled the pepper over the rabbit. To get the meat good and tender, she placed an iron lid on the skillet and shoveled red coals on top. Cornbread was also cooked by the "hot coals on the lid" method and, except for special times like Christmas, was the only bread we had.

Shortly before Christmas, Tom made a special trip to The Settlement to trade chickens for wheat flour. Mama wanted to help with the Christmas cooking, but her feet and legs were swollen twice their size, and she felt "dizzy as a bat" every time she got up. Grandma insisted she get to bed and stay.

Grandma carefully removed eggs from their straw packing to prepare her once-a-year treats. She made thin pumpkin pies and stacked them six or seven tiers high. She baked large cookie-thin cakes and, like a master mason, layered them spread between with her choicest dried apples, stewed, sweetened, and flavored with allspice. The tall cake was mounted on top with extra applesauce and allowed to "set" a day or two for moist blending. She called it simply "fruitcake." The spicy aroma was intoxicating to our senses, and only her tenacity kept it from being gobbled up before Christmas Day. Then and only then it would be brought to the table with a flourish and served with hot coffee, a glass of milk, or tea made from sassafras root or spicewood bark sweetened with sugar or wild honey. Though some mountain folk kept beehives, Papa had "robbed a bee-tree" for this honey and saved it for the holiday.

Met and I were looking forward to Santa Claus's visit, though we did not expect the kind of things children in town received. Maybe Santa had trouble climbing the snowy heights. Whatever his reason, this was part of life, and we did not dwell on why it was so. Christmas morning we were thrilled when we found an orange, peppermint sticks, and a small toy in our stockings.

Late on Christmas Day 1907, I learned that babies weren't really found behind fodder stacks in Mr. Kingsley's fields. Mama nearly died giving birth to a stillborn baby boy, and for the first time ever, I saw my papa cry. This was why my mama had been sick and gotten so fat. I had not known. I felt helpless and confused.

On our "gathering" walks, Mama had told me about a God who was powerful and knew everything, and that we could talk to him. I begged him to let my mama live.

CHAPTER 4
Granny, Herb Doctor

Mama was too weak to get up, even if Grandma had allowed it, when Papa left the following Monday for the timber-cutting job. The tract of land being cleared was the proposed site of Lake Junaluska. There he found lodging and came home every two weeks, bringing whatever pay was left after room and board were deducted. He was dead-tired on the trips home, lugging groceries and an occasional household item we'd need when we moved into our own place, but he was also excited to be earning real money. One of few workers who could read and write, Papa earned extra by helping set up pay records.

"Some of them 'Injuns' hain't got but one name," he told Tom. "I sign 'em up, give 'em Christian names—names they can be proud of, so's they can git paid."

"Such as?"

"Like Tom Laughingface and Luke Graywolf. I named old Tom after you."

Tom's look was somewhere between flattery and suspicion. "What kinda feller is he?"

Papa laughed. "Hardworkin'—same as you. Now that Graywolf is another case. Son-of-a-gun gits paid, you hain't a-goin' to see him fer a while. Gits all likkered up."

Grandma owned two cows, so there was plenty of milk and butter for all of us. Shortly before our planned moving day, Mama was busily churning when Grandma came and stared down at her middle daughter. Mama began to churn faster, but Grandma wasn't there to find fault. "Rachel, I hain't never fergot how you saved that red cow's life when she was a little bitty calf. She weren't a-goin' to make it without you doctorin' 'er through it all. Now I'm a-sayin' Cherry's your'n." The cow could be grazed all spring and summer without feeding expense, she explained, and by winter we'd have plenty of roughage and corn nubbins. "Now, go on, take her when you leave."

Mama's churning stopped, and she started sniffling. She hid her face in her apron-tail.

"Fiddle-faddle and fiddle-dee-dee!" Grandma pretended disgust at Mama's quick tears. "I cain't abide a growed woman bawlin'. Now git that milk churned, then you can help me get supper cooked." So saying, she sliced thick rashers of sidemeat and placed her largest skillet over hot coals.

On the first of April, we moved into our own place, a log hut slightly larger than the one that burned. It was within hollering distance of the cabin owned by my great-grandmother, whom we called Granny. Living with Granny was her son, my great uncle John, and his two sons, France and Raymond. France was ten years old. Raymond, almost seven, had been only four when their mother, Roxie, died.

Papa's job at the lake kept him away most of the time, but until food crops could be planted and harvested, that money was needed for survival. Uncle John stopped his own farming to help us get our corn in the ground. He took his plow and Buck, his mule, to the steep hills above our cabin that he, Papa, and Tom had cleared of timber in the fall. Buck clung like a fly to the rock-studded terrain as John guided and cajoled. Soon rough rows emerged among bare tree stumps.

School had not started, and we children pitched in to get seeds planted before black or yellow skies signaled bad weather ahead. With France and Raymond helping, Mama sowed furrows not far below John's plow. I'd never learned to plant corn, so my job was to keep the water pail filled. I watched from my perch atop a hollow stump.

Uncle John halted Buck and mopped his face with a bandanna. He scanned the darkening skies and cupped his hands to yell down at Mama. "Rachel! Rachel!" His voice resonated from years of practice at shouted messages. "Lookee yonder. They's a cloud blowin' in f'om the east." He pointed to an ominous mass of dark gray that loomed on his right. "You best git all them seed in today."

"Sippy, Sippy-gal," Mama called. "Come help us git this corn a-planted." I ran to where she stood in the middle of a plowed row. She handed me a bucket of seeds. "Now, you take three long steps." She measured her strides. "Then you drop three grains of corn." She dropped three onto the ruddy soil. "Do that till all this corn's a-planted. I'll come behind you with the coverin' hoe. Now git to it!"

"One, two, three," I counted, like it was a game. "One, two, three. One, two …"

"Watch out below!" Uncle John was jumping up and down, yelling at the top of his lungs, "A log's a-rollin'." A huge log, dislodged by his plow, was bounding down the hillside, heading straight for Mama and me.

I screamed and ran toward her. "Mama, Mama!"

"Gawd have mercy!" I heard Mama say as everything became black.

I woke to the sharp sting of pennyroyal beneath my nose and a wet cloth on my forehead. I was on Mama's bed. My head reeled and my knee and thigh throbbed with pain. "Mama, my leg's a-hurtin' so bad."

Mama patted my cheek. Someone else was there, breathing hard, stretching my leg out, pressing my knee. I recognized Granny. She had brought her medicine bag.

"'Tain't broke," I heard her say with authority, "just bruised. She'll be all right soon enough."

Hovering in the fuzzy light, Uncle John sighed loudly. "Praises be to Gawd. If that young'n hada got kilt, it woulda kilt me just studyin' on it bein' my doin'."

"Well now, it weren't your fault," Mama said. "You hollered—'at's all a body could do. It was a-fallin' in soft dirt what saved 'er."

"Praise Gawd fer it," John repeated.

Granny brushed them aside like fussy children. "Rachel, git me a dipper of cool water."

Mama went to a shelf near the door where the water bucket sat and moved the ruffle-trimmed cardboard box that held combs, important letters, and Papa's razor from there to the mantle so Granny would have room to work. She ladled a cup of water.

Granny put mint leaves in a cloth bag, crushed them, and placed the bag in the cup. She pressed it hard with a spoon, then held the tea to my lips. "Now drink this, Sippy. It'll settle that stomach." Next she crumbled dried plantain leaves into a shallow bowl to soak.

Mama watched Granny's every move, like a student observing a master. All mountain women learned early the medicinal value of certain plants, but Mama knew that as a practicing "herb doctor," Granny was unsurpassed. Granny's "black bag" stayed packed—with plantain, pennyroyal, boneset, Shawnee plant, and butterfly weed. There were salves she'd concocted herself of balsam, wintergreen, and alumroot, prepared with mutton tallow or ground-hog oil. At home, the ceiling of her loft "pharmacy" was strung with tea herbs for female ailments—feverfew, squaw vine, shepherd's purse, and tansy root. Whatever the malady, Granny was ready.

With the soaked plantain leaves, she formed a cooling poultice and patted it onto my leg. As the herbal scent permeated my senses, the throbbing in my leg began to ease. Mama was hovering like a shadow and Granny seemed uncomfortable. "Whyn't you git on back and git them seeds a-planted," she told Mama. "I'll take care of Sippy. And Met, too."

Despite her seventy-odd years, my great-grandmother's days were devoted to raising my cousins, France and Raymond. I knew she was spry and "tough as nails." Papa said so. But I'd never spent much time with her.

As soon as Mama was out the door, Granny

put a kettle on to brew some tea. "This here tea I'm a-makin's got 'opium' in it." It would calm me down, she explained, and help me sleep. "Now, yer maw thinks poppyseed's too strong fer young'ns, so just keep this to yerself." It was still too hot to drink when she had me sit up and sip it with a spoon.

My cheeks burned like sitting in front of a hot fire. But the pain had dulled, and I wanted to talk. "Granny, are you Papa's mama?"

"Sorta. Your papa's paw, Greenberry Waldrop, was a-kilt out huntin' one day when your papa was a little bitty baby. My daughter, his maw, was so young. Anne left, got married ag'in, had her another fam'ly." Cool fingertips touched by brow and adjusted the poultice on my leg. "I took your papa like he was my own, raised 'im till he was a growed man and married your mama. He orter been a 'Waldrop,' but I raised him, so I called him 'Wright.'"

CHART OF MOUNTAIN MEDICINE

ALUM ROOT - astingent; used in diarrhea, dysentery; rinse for mouth sores, bleeding gums; helps stop bleeding; rids mucus, pus in bladder; bowel problems; female ailments; used in salves.
BALSAM - used in salves.
BIRCH BARK - teas; urinary and bowel problems; rheumatism.
BLACKBERRY WINE - stomach and bowel ailments.
BLOODROOT - astringent; also used for diarrhea and dysentery.
BONESET - herb for colds, grippe; acts as tonic and laxative.
BURDOCK LEAF AND ROOT - removes toxins from body; blood purifier; good for skin problems and arthritis.
BUTTERFLY WEED - used for poultices for skin problems.
CHIMNEY SOOT - stops bleeding in small cuts.
CORN LIQUOR - colds; grippe; pain; stress.
DANDELION LEAF AND ROOT - detoxifies poison from liver, lowers blood pressure.
FENNEL SEEDS - for gas, stomach acid; gout; cramps; eyewash; liver cleaner.
FEVERFEW HERB - migraine headache; arthritis; restores liver; female ailments.
GINSENG ROOT - cure-all; good for stress; slows aging process.
JOE PYE WEED - fever.
JERUSALEM-OAK SEED - intestinal worms.
MEAL AND ONION POULTICES - chest congestion.
PENNYROYAL - high fever; brings perspiration to promote circulation; toothaches; gout; skin problems; chest, lungs; also used as household disinfectant.
PEPPERMINT LEAF- tea; headaches; stomach acid.
PLANTAIN LEAF - cuts; skin infections; skin problems.
POPPYSEED - teas for colic; soothes; relieves pain and stress.
SAGE LEAF - stomach; digestion; hair tonic.
SASSAFRAS LEAF AND ROOT - purifies blood; skin disorders; stimulates liver; clears toxins.
SHAWNEE PLANT - female ailments.
SHEPHERD'S PURSE - diarrhea; female ailments.
SQUAW VINE - as a wash relieves sore eyes; for water retention in female ailments.
TANSY ROOT - female ailments.
WILD CHERRY BARK - loosens phlegm in throat and chest; helps asthma.
WINTERGREEN LEAF - stimulates stomach, heart, and respiration; clears bowels; for colic and gas.
WINTERGREEN SALVE - use on sores, bites; for aching joints.
WITCH HAZEL BARK AND LEAF - restores circulation; good for stiff joints; astringent for skin.
YARROW ROOT - for colds, grippe, fever; soothes mucus membranes.
YELLOW DOCK ROOT - purifies blood; tones system.

"My name's Selena Burzilla Wright."

"It shore is, honey, 'cept rightly you orter be Selena Burzilla *Waldrop*." I'd heard this story before but never quite figured all the connections.

"What's your name, besides 'Granny'?"

"It's Kate Stuart Wright. Your great-grandpaw, he was Monteville Wright."

"Then we are *all* 'Wright,'" I said. Granny clapped her hands and cackled. I wondered why that was so funny.

"Granny, can you read us a story from the wallpaper?" Our mud-daubed walls were papered with newsprint and magazine pages to insulate and give a finished look. Here and there colorful pictures were "framed" with scalloped strips. Mama had read many items over and over, till I knew some of them by heart.

Granny was sharp and learned quickly but could not read nor write, a fact she did not like to admit. "Well, now, this news is gittin' sorter old, and come fall cleaning time, we'll be a-pastin' up more on top of it. Let's see now, here's the *Ashville Citizen, Chicago Blade and Ledger, Saturday Evening Post,* and the *Comfort Magazine.*"

I ran my fingers over words on the wall, wishing I knew how to read. My favorite picture showed a hot air balloon rising from the ground. Two men waved from their basket gondola. Mama had said the men set a record in distance covered.

"Lay still now, and keep this poultice on your leg," Granny warned, "else it hain't a-goin' to work."

"How long?"

"Long enough." She took a seat in Mama's armless rocking chair near the small window and pulled Met onto her lap. In a throaty minor-key, hardly audible at first but crescendoing as the story built, she sang a song learned as a child:

"Lord Thomas, Lord Thomas, my only son,
You know I love thee well,
Listen to your mother's voice
The truth to you I'll tell, I'll tell,
The truth to you I'll tell.

"The Brown Girl has both houses and land,
Fair Ellender, she has none,
If you will take your mother's advice
You'll bring the Brown Girl home, home,
You'll bring the Brown Girl home."

Lord Thomas rode to Fair Ellender's gate
And jingled at the bell,
There was not one to let him in,
But Fair Ellender herself, herself,
But Fair Ellender herself.

She dressed herself in the finest silk,
And went out him to meet.
She shone like glittering gold, my dear,
She shone from head to feet, to feet,
She shone from head to feet.

"Lord Thomas, Lord Thomas, why are you here?
Why have you come to me?"
"I've come to ask you to my wedding,
For tomorrow it shall be, shall be,
For tomorrow it shall be."

She dressed in part of scarlet red,
In part she dressed in green,
And every town that she rode 'round,

They took her to be some queen, some queen,
    They took her to be some queen.

Fair Ellender rode to Lord Thomas's door,
    And jingled at the bell,
No one there would let her in,
But Lord Thomas himself, himself,
    But Lord Thomas himself.

He took her by her lily white hand
    And let her through the hall,
And sat her down at the head table,
Where quality was all, was all,
    Where quality was all.

"Lord Thomas, Lord Thomas, is this your wife?
    I think she's very brown,
Another like her you could not find
In all of London Town, Town,
    In all of London Town."

"Hush your flouting and hold your tongue,
    Don't throw your flouts at me.
I would not give your little finger
For the Brown Girl's whole body, body,
    For the Brown Girl's whole body."

The Brown Girl had a little pen knife,
    Both sharp and newly ground.
She pierced it through Fair Ellender's heart,
And the blood came trickling down, down,
    And the blood came trickling down.

"Lord Thomas, Lord Thomas, are you blind,
Or can't you ever see
My own heart's blood a-trickling down,
A-trickling down my knee, my knee,
A-trickling down my knee?"

He took the Brown Girl by her hand,
And led her to the hall,
He cut her head smooth off her shoulders,
And kicked it against the wall, the wall,
And kicked it against the wall.

"Go dig my grave both deep and wide,
And paint my coffin black,
And bury Fair Ellender in my arms,
And the Brown Girl at my back, my back,
And the Brown Girl at my back."

They dug his grave both deep and wide,
And painted his coffin black.
They buried the Brown Girl in his arms,
Fair Ellender at his back, his back,
Fair Ellender at his back.

Before the song ended, Met was sound asleep, her head dangling over Granny's arm, and I was sobbing out loud. With my light curly hair and blue-green eyes, I could have been Fair Ellender.

CHAPTER 5
The Visit

During this season between seedtime and harvest, we lived on what Papa managed to bring home every two weeks from his timber-cutting job, and sometimes ran out of food. Mama was too proud to ask Granny's help. Instead, as her mother had taught her during lean times when "only the Lord was there to provide," we looked to the hills and coves for tender shoots of vegetations, rising early to find them before birds and rabbits did.

In the eerie light of dawn, Mama dressed sleepy-head Met, and the three of us headed for fields of dandelion and pokeweed, and hidden crannies where jade sprouts of brier and henbit flourished.

"You's walking just fine now," Mama remarked as I marched ahead of her, swinging my basket. "'Spect you'll be good as new when school starts." Yellow circles marked the place on my leg where the runaway log had bruised it. Mama had worried the damage might be permanent and the long hike to school hung in the balance, so I tried hard not to limp. I gave a little skip to prove her right. More than anything else in my life, I looked forward to starting school.

As day dawned, Mama surveyed the hills, splotched in the deepest green. I came and stood by her while she held Met's hand, and we watched shards of light split the misty gorge, swords of brilliance cutting away darkness.

"I will lift up mine eyes unto the hills, from whence cometh my help," Mama quoted from a Psalm learned as a child at the Settlement school.

We scaled a rock-strewn slope in search of wild mustard, lambs-quarter, shepherd's purse, and narrow-leafed dock, and filled our baskets with the lacy greens. Even three-year-old Met recognized winter cress and wild lettuce, leaves succulent and crisp, spreading like rosettes in damp hollows. "Mama, Mama, wookee," she hollered each time she spotted a patch.

Soon, baskets overflowing, we headed home. There Mama mixed the greens, except for the lettuce, boiling them in a pot with a chunk of salt pork for seasoning. While they cooked, she formed corn dodgers and fried them in a skillet of bacon drippings. With that done, she then washed the lettuce, chopped it fine with onion tops, and scalded it quickly with hot grease and vinegar and served it up piping hot and tart.

"I like 'lettuce' best of all," I told her. The cabin walls reeked of it for a day or two, greeting us on entering with a pleasant tang.

One day while gathering, we came to a mossy glen near a cool spring. "Lookee—toadstools," I said.

"Don't pick 'em. They's p'ison."

"You pick 'em, Mama. Why cain't I?"

Met reached for the mushroom look-alikes, and Mama slapped her hand gently. "They's a difference. Some's good, some ain't. Only grownups knows how to pick 'em." I couldn't tell edible ones from the poisonous, but Mama knew the wild morel that grew in low coves. On rare days when she was lucky enough to find the cone-shaped fungi with tops that resembled honeycombs, we dined like kings.

My outings with Mama were love feasts, with piney hills stretching to eternity. The sun beckoned, "Come, bask in me," breezes were caresses, and springtime was ours alone. Often we strolled, arms interlocked. At times the wind swept us along. Bands of Painted Trilluim swayed, and we danced with them, circling, skirts held high till Met or I fell among them laughing and dizzy. Wild violets winked at such shenanigans with shy purple eyes. We cartwheeled into clover, then sat and pulled strands of it to weave tiaras for our queen and her two princesses. I wanted to stay forever in our emerald palace, but Met became sleepy, and Mama said we had to go. We picked black-eyed Susans to arrange in a Mason jar for the table.

One day while gathering, we came to a large flat rock, big as a giant's bed, with a lichen coverlet. The three of us took a seat on it, marveling at our sun-warmed bench. Mama took picture-story cards from her pocket that Papa had brought us, given him by a missionary at the lake site. Stories were printed on one side, and Mama read them to us.

"God made everything," she read from a card, "the sky, the mountains—even us." There was a Scripture verse for each story. One of the cards showed Jesus praying in the Garden of Gethsemane. The Scripture was Matthew 26:39, "My Father, if it be possible, let this cup pass from me. Nevertheless, not my will, but Thine be done." Jesus' face was very sad. On another he was hanging on a center cross looking heavenward, while thieves on either side writhed in pain.

My favorite pictured "the Ascension." Angels pointed toward a halo-crowned Jesus above ethereal white clouds. "Why is Jesus in the sky?" I asked.

"He's a-goin' up to heaven," Mama said. Her eyes were dreamy, like imagining how it would be.

"If you're good and do all the things God says in the Bible, someday when you die, you'll go there, too."

I looked up at a cloudless sky and wondered where God could be, why I couldn't see him seated on his big white throne. "Will you be up there in heaven, Mama?"

"Shore, honey. I love Jesus."

"I love you, Mama. If you're with Jesus, I want to be there, too." Wild phlox swayed with a soft droning of bees, and a mourning dove cried in the distance. We sat for a long time, huddled dreamily on our smooth rock pew. I could have stayed with Mama forever, just as we were, but there were eggs to be gathered, supper to be cooked.

Our chickens roamed free, so each day we had to search for hidden nests. Easiest to find were those beneath the house. The cabin was built close to the ground to keep out wintry drafts, and by lifting floor boards called "puncheons," left loose for the purpose, eggs laid there could be reached without going outside. Problems arose when a stray animal or snake crawled under the house, looking for shelter and a meal. Mama and Granny dealt with this in a time-proven way. When a snake was spotted through chinks in the floor, they quickly made a pot of scalding-hot lye water and poured it between the cracks.

Mother hens fared better than the rest of the flock. They were kept in small coops close to the house till their chicks hatched and were old enough to fend for themselves. When a setting hen went undetected and hatched her brood in the wild, the chicks seldom survived. Snakes lay waiting for her to leave the nest so they could dine sumptuously on the prized chicks—swallowing them whole! On hearing a mother hen's mad squawks, we ran to stop the theft, though likely as not, it would be too late. The nest would be in shambles, the baby chickens gone.

Since mountains were a natural habitat for snakes, France, Raymond, and I took care not to step on one as we ran barefoot along grassy knolls and ferned swamps or searched for hens' nests beyond plowed fields. One day in a stumpy spot near Uncle John's cornfield, I thought I'd found a nest of baby chicks. There was a flopping and rustling around my legs, so I stopped dead in my tracks. Looking down, I let out a scream at the top of my lungs. I was barefoot in a den of snakes!

"What's the matter, Sip?" France shouted from yards away, but I kept yelling till Uncle John came on the double from the cornfield, his sharpest hoe in hand.

He killed three big ones while the others scrambled into a clump of briars.

After making sure I was all right, Uncle John was

amused. "I swear if you hain't got lungs to beat anybody." He could hardly wait to tell everyone he saw how loudly I screamed. "Injuns on Big Cataloochee heard it and mistook it fer a war whoop," he swore, straight-faced as a circuit preacher. "Sippie brung on a two-day war 'twixt tribes."

No one had forgotten the letter from Alex, Mama's brother who lived in Asheville, about his planned visit by early June. Grandma, more than anyone, looked forward to her successful son coming to see his "maw." Yet preparations had not begun, not till a second missive arrived, giving an exact date. Tom picked it up from the mailbox at the Settlement where he had a part-time job loading and delivering lumber. Papa was away at his job, but Mama, Met, and I were at Grandma's to hear Tom's reading of the good news to Grandma.

"Hallelujah!" she shouted, raising her arms high. The "aristocrat" of the family and his city-bred wife were actually coming. With all the anticipation of a royal visit, things swung into high gear. Grandma's fall cleaning advanced six months, while sewing school clothes took a back seat. No one, including us children, escaped Grandma's all-encompassing plans.

Alex and his wife would sleep in the cabin behind the main house, she decided, where our family had lived following the fire. Only now the structure was crawling with fleas. Uncle Tom and Uncle George were hunters of the fox, with hounds ready for the chase. Allowed to sleep anywhere they chose, the hounds' favorite sprawling spot was beneath the small cabin. There they lazed on warm days, scratching themselves and digging holes in the soft earth. Their doggy duties were much appreciated—protecting the family from savage beasts and human thieves and ready for the hunt at their masters' command. No one paid them a lot of mind. Till now.

Grandma slapped her ankles free of the pesky insects. "Dad-blasted hound dogs." The problem loomed, a loose screw in the cogwheel of her plans—but not for long. She knew the remedy and had the ingredients. It was called lye soap—exterminator, house deodorizer, general cleansing agent. But supplies were low.

Grandma's lye was made by pouring oak wood ashes into an ash-hopper over a layer of straw and allowing rainwater to filter through. Oozing from a spout, the seepage slowly drained into a wooden tub, forming the solution used for soap-making and other household tasks. She added a small amount of the liquid lye to parboiled kernels of corn when making whole-grain hominy. It helped slough the outer skin.

For the tough job facing her now, Grandma used

lye already in the works to replenish her soap supply. Taking orts of pork, beef, and mutton fats and tallow, saved for this purpose, she tied them in a cloth bag then boiled it in an iron pot along with lye water. When the mixture thickened, the bag was discarded and the soft soap allowed to harden to the right consistency. This she ladled into shallow wooden boxes to cool overnight. She cut it into bars, and her powerful soap was ready.

The day Grandma chose for housecleaning, Mama rose early, scolding Met and me to hurry. Everyone was already busy when we got to her cabin, and Grandma was barking out orders. Beds were stripped, ticks emptied, washed, and stuffed with fresh straw. George filled the largest iron washpot with water brought from the creek, and Tom built a fire under it. As the water bubbled, Grandma threw in slivers of her strongest soap and a bunch of pennyroyal weed. With bucketfuls of the boiling-hot liquid, she scalded all the woodwork in her house and the cabin to be occupied by Alex and Loulie. Bedsteads, shelves, and floors were doused. The odorous blend of herb-scented suds piqued our nostrils, wafting all the way to the creek bank.

Routed from their holes, the hunting dogs whined nervously and took off for a new spot in a clump of bushes. But there was no escaping Grandma's zeal. Tom and George yanked the squealing hounds out and held them one at a time while she sponged them with a cool pennyroyal bath. Then she doused their sprawling spot with the same solution.

Relieved of incessant scratching, the dogs began to romp like puppies. With barriers of chicken wire, Grandma made sure they did not creep back beneath the small cabin.

Tom brought from the loft stacks of newspapers and magazines he'd scrounged and saved for re-papering walls. Pictures and bric-a-brac were removed, cleaned, and laid aside, while old wallpaper was peeled off and new hung. Mama and Grandma pasted important news items and colorful magazine pictures at points of interest along the newly-papered walls. They cut loops and scallops for edging shelves and mantel.

Young Aunt Effie, Uncle George, and I lugged buckets of sand from the shallows of Jonathan's Creek, and Mama used it to scour pots and pans. After cleaning the fireplace, she used the remaining sand to scrub floors to a smooth whiteness.

"I could make up biscuits on them floors," Grandma said, admiring Mama's job. "They's that clean."

"I reckon you'd have some mighty gritty biscuits." Mama laughed as she swept sand through cracks and out the door.

Wooden tubs and kegs were scoured, readying for kraut-making time. Stone crocks were washed and stored to be later packed with apple peels for fermenting into vinegar. Fruit jars were brought out and counted, making sure there'd be plenty for summer canning.

Old fly swatters were thrown out. George showed me how to make new ones by tying streamers of cloth and newsprint to strong slender canes. "It's easy, Sip," he said. "Just make shore yer sticks is long enough. Flies is right smart critters." Without window and door screens, "shoo-fly sticks" were a necessity. At mealtime one was twirled at intervals above the table. When someone was sick, a bedside vigil always included a constant waving of the cane above them. Mama usually protected Met from flies during naptime by placing a thin cloth over her face, but after Grandma's lye soap and pennyroyal treatment, the pests disappeared completely and were slow to return.

In the back cabin, at Tom's suggestion, Grandma added a thick "bed-quiet" between cords and straw tick. "Alex is more'n apt used to sleepin' on bedsprings," Tom explained. "Them cords is liable to bother 'im."

Grandma snorted. "Fiddle-faddle, Tom-boy. If folks 'round my house slept any better, Old Gabriel'd need a louder horn to rouse 'em come Judgment Day."

"Git on now, Maw. Way you talk, I'd swear you was meaner'n a devil—'ceptin' I know better."

Grandma added a thick layer of quilts over the cords then put a feathertick atop the straw one.

Tom laughed at the fat, pillow-like bed. "Dang. Alex and Loulie's liable to git plumb lost in there."

According to his letter, Alex would hire a hack at the livery stable when he reached Waynesville. They'd drive to the cove, arriving about noon the first Monday in June. With the cleaning complete and both cabins reeking of pennyroyal, Grandma picked Saturday to do her cooking. "The Lord's Day's 'twixt, for restin' up," she explained, but we knew there'd be no rest for the weary. That's when last-minute chores would get done.

Anticipating her cherished son's visit, at hog-killing time Grandma began his favorite dish. She took pigs' hooves, stuck them in hot embers to loosen, then pried off the feet. She cleaned them carefully and packed them in salt. Afterwards the feet were soaked in fresh water a day or so, boiled till tender, seeped in spiced vinegar, and packed in jars. Now it was time to bring them out along with a "poke-full" of her shelled "October speckled-beans" set aside just for Alex.

"They's his pick of all beans," Grandma said. "I recollect how he'd squall fer 'em when he weren't no bigger'n Met here." She made fruitcake—stacked layers filled with dried spiced apples.

For Alex and Loulie, cream would be skimmed

from the top of the milk can, whipped, sweetened, and served atop the cake.

Papa's work at the lake site was at a temporary halt, and he got home in time for he and Tom to "git some huntin' in" before company came. They bagged six partridges and four rabbits for the planned feast, to Grandma's delight.

Early Monday, everyone on the mountainside—Grandma and her clan, Papa, Mama, Met, and me, even Granny and Uncle John's two boys, France and Raymond—was present, dressed in our finest, practicing our manners.

"No sir, Uncle Alex." "Yes ma'am, Aunt Loulie," I rehearsed with my rag doll. Met eyed me curiously.

"'At's Liddy," she said. At three she had not learned how to put on airs.

Staying clean and behaving for hours was a strain on us children, so when creaking wheels and horses' hooves sounded from the narrow trail that ran along Jonathan's Creek, my cousin France bolted toward the approaching carriage. Young Aunt Effie lit out behind.

"Come back! Come back 'ere, ye young'ns!" Grandma shouted. At that, the dogs began yelping like crazy, bringing Papa and Tom out to see what the devil was happening. France stopped short, staring at the hired hack as it rolled into view, bearing the special pair. I grabbed Mama's skirt where she stood holding Met in her arms. We formed an uneasy receiving line for this one we'd not laid eyes on for a year and his wife, whom we'd never met.

Alex reined up and jumped down from his seat as Papa edged toward the rig. "Jim, you ole booger," Alex shouted. Alex lifted his wife to the ground, came over, and extended his hand to Papa. "It's good to see you. And Tom, just look at you—you're a man now." Tom beamed as Alex grabbed him in a brotherly embrace.

"G-good to see you'ns, too," Papa stammered, removing his hat. "I see you've brung yer pretty little wife fer us all to meet."

"He couldn't have kept me away." Loulie did not appear the least bit shy.

Why did Papa call her "pretty"? I wondered. She wasn't pretty at all. My good-looking uncle Alex, apple of his mother's eye, had picked himself an ugly wife. Her chin was prominent, nose long and thin, and her red hair frizzed around her store-bought bonnet. She smiled at me, and her nose crinkled into a sea of freckles.

"You'ns git on in and see Grandma," Tom said to them. "Jim and France'll tote yer bags. Me and George'll look after yer hoss."

Everyone scurried to the cabin door where Grandma stood, arms outstretched. "Gawd love my han'some boy!" she cried, tears welling in her eyes.

With that, Alex swept her off her feet with a giant hug, depositing her inside. Robust and tall, with blonde hair and steel blue eyes, Alex towered above us all.

"Maw, he hain't no 'boy' no more," Papa pointed out.

"He's a Robards fer shore," Grandma said. "Took after my papa's side of the fam'ly." Alex bore only slight resemblance to Mama and Tom, both of whom were short with dark hair and eyes and skin that tanned easily. "I orter named you 'Alexander Robards,'" she said, leaving Alex's embrace. "I swear you look more like my papa ever'time I lay eyes on you."

Alex swung Mama around like she was a child.

Grandma beamed, watching them. "Now take Rachel, Alex—she's me over again." Mama was pretty, and everyone knew it. Her cream-tan complexion was smooth and unblemished, her eyes doelike, her hair silky and dark. Hard work kept her petite figure firm. Looking at Mama, there was no doubt that once Grandma had been pretty, too. Now Grandma was slightly humped, the once-jet hair streaked with silver, and her olive skin crinkled like old leather. But the eyes remained bright and sharp as a hawk's, missing little.

Alex put Mama down and picked up me and Met, one on each arm. Grandma looked at Loulie, who stood watching it all. "Gawd bless you, honey." She hugged her daughter-in-law in embarrassment at having ignored her. "I hope you'ns is proud of this here feller as I am."

"Oh, he knows how I feel." Loulie graced us all with a broad smile. Her brown eyes sparkled.

Alex deposited Met and me in front of a large satchel. "Come on, everyone, let's open these presents." He reached inside and pulled out wrapped gifts. "Adults come first."

With a broad toothless grin, Grandma tore off paper to find a pale blue fascinator. She draped it around her shoulders. Mama's gift was a white ruffled petticoat. She held it up, giggling like a child on Christmas morning. The men, including George, all received red-striped galluses, and for all of us there were loaves of bakery bread—the first I'd ever seen.

Loulie gave out gifts to us children. There was a harmonica for France, waxed-cloth picture books for Raymond and Met, and storybooks for Effie and me. After unwrapping my neatly tied package, I gazed at the storybook, unable to believe it was mine alone.

"This book is very special," Loulie said to me and put her arm around my waist. "I picked it out for my brother's little girl last December, because she loved more than anything for me to read her stories. My brother wanted you to have it. You see, his daughter died of diphtheria before Santa Claus came. Mirium was *exactly* your age."

I had never received such a gift before, even at Christmastime. My book was glossy and big, with stiff pages—each encircled with colorful garlands of flowers. I forgot the manners I'd practiced for days.

Mama broke into my trance. "Sippy, what do you say to Loulie and her brother? Sippy, say 'thankee' to Loulie!"

"Oh! Th-thankee," I stammered. "And thankee to yer brother." Loulie caught my hand and squeezed it. How could I have thought her ugly? She was like Cinderella's fairy godmother, kind and beautiful. I was glad Uncle Alex had picked her for his wife.

"You'ns, come on to dinner," Grandma called. "It's way after twelve. I reckon these here folks is hungry after ridin' so fer."

"I'm hungry for whatever that is I smell," Alex said.

"We got rabbits and partridges," Tom stated proudly. "We knowed you'd be a-wantin' some wild meat."

"I sure do," Alex admitted. "And I want to do some hunting myself, while I've got the chance. I'll just bet these women would like us menfolk out of the house for a while."

"We'll head out first thing in the morning," Tom said. "I'll git you up real early."

Before daybreak the next day, the men were up and out while the women lingered over coffee cups till the sun was high. "My goodness!" Mama fretted. "Look what time it is. We orter git somethin' started fer dinner."

"Don't bother about that," Loulie said. "The men aren't here, and there's nothing I'd rather do than just sit talking to you and Mother. We can snack on what's cooked and have dinner when the men get home. I've got stories to tell I'll just bet the children have never heard."

Loulie told us how she'd developed her love for books while serving as nanny to the offspring of a wealthy Asheville family, having access to their fine library, filled with classics. Her favorite task had been telling the children stories.

"I want to hear your stories, too," Mama said. "Hit's been a long time since I heard a new one. I'll git these young'ns tended to, and we'll all set and listen." Mama had only completed the third grade at school, but she had a love of the written word. Both Grandma and Granny enjoyed nothing better than hearing her read aloud—old school textbooks, readers, Bible story cards, anything she found. I'd learned most of her stories by heart.

We formed a circle and sat in rapt attention while Loulie began. Her crafted stories from Dickens, Irving, and Craik were told with vivid facial expressions. Mama and I blinked back tears, and Effie hid her face in her hands through *The Little Lame Prince*.

Loulie gestured like a stage player, and Grandma laughed out loud at the plight of *Ichabod Crane*. Near the end of *A Christmas Carol,* Grandma clapped her hands in glee when a reformed Scrooge extended his Christmas kindnesses.

"Shucks a'mighty," Grandma exclaimed, and we wondered at such a response to the story's happy ending. But Grandma was peering out the open door. "Just look where the sun's at. Them men'll be a-comin' to an empty table if'n I don't git hoppin'."

When the men came in from the hunt, sweaty and smelling of dogs and open fields, the meal was ready, thanks to Mama and Loulie's help. "Yer supper's a-waitin'," Grandma announced proudly, wiping her hands on her long apron tail and huffing from the hurried fixings.

"Just git yerselves washed up and you kin set right down."

"Did you fellows have any luck?" Loulie asked.

"Bagged a couple of rabbits," Alex replied, filling his plate.

Papa grunted. "Alex ain't satisfied. He wanted to fetch some fine birds, enough fer a meal."

"We'll go ag'in tomorrow," Tom said. "I know a place nigh the river where they feed. If'n we git there time the sun's up good—'at's their feedin' time—and we might just git us a bunch."

After a hearty supper of beans with pork backbone, steamed sauerkraut, crackling-bread, and dried peach jacks with whipped cream, the men sat close to the fire, coffee mugs filled, legs sprawled, and stomachs protruding. Tom put down his mug and pulled out his tobacco pouch to show Alex his nimble trick of rolling a cigarette with one hand. Then they reminisced about hunts of the past from squirrels to bears, till it was time to retire for a night's sleep before the next day's hunt.

The women chatted in low tones as they cleared the table and washed dishes. I looked at my new book, wondering who the pretty princess was and why she looked so sad. Maybe tomorrow Loulie would read me the story. I ran my fingers over the book's sleek pages, savoring the smell of newness.

Next morning the men were on their way down the mountain to an old cornfield near the river before Grandma got up. When she rose, she took a long look toward the eastern horizon. "Uh-oh," she mumbled. "Bad weather's a-comin'. I knowed this here pretty weather weren't about to last. Hit's gitten' ready fer a change."

"I'm bound to git home and git clothes washed a'fore it does," Mama said. "Hope you'ns don't mind, Loulie."

"No, no. But do let the children stay here, out of your way. I love keeping children, and Met has caught a cold."

"I've got Balm of Gilead mixed with tallow I rub these young'ns with," Grandma said. She got a baking powder can of the salve from the fireboard and made a poultice for Met's chest then made soothing mint tea for her to sip while Loulie read from our books.

By sundown, clouds were forming in the northeastern sky, and unseasonably cool winds whistled through the cove. The men arrived tired but pleased. Alex had six partridges and three rabbits, dressed and ready for Grandma's skillet. "We'll be leaving first thing in the morning," he said. "I don't know what this weather may bring, and I need to get that rig safely back to the livery stable."

"Shore hate to see you'ns go," Grandma said. "But that sky tells me we're in fer a lot of rain."

After supper, Tom dragged out a large wooden tub from the lean-to. Mama heated several pots of water, poured it into the tub, and the men all took a hot bath before going to bed. Next day they were up and had the buggy packed and ready to move out by sunup, while Grandma made a fire to fry bacon and hotcakes. Alex and Loulie would not leave without a hearty breakfast, not from Grandma's house. There was a round of hugs, kisses, goodbyes, take cares, and the couple climbed into the loaded carriage.

"Wait! Wait up!" Grandma shouted, and Alex pulled back on the reins. She ran from the cabin door, holding a Mason jar high. "It's pickled pig's feet fer you'ns to take with ye." She huffed to the hack and handed the treat up to Loulie. "They'll make a nice snack on the train ride."

"Thanks, Maw. I'll think of you every time I eat one," Alex promised.

With that he gave a loud "gee up," and they were on their way, arms waving high as the horse and rig disappeared from sight around the bend of the trail.

CHAPTER 6
Mountain School

I was seven years old and had looked forward to starting school since I could remember, but it was only after the visit by Uncle Alex and Aunt Loulie was concluded that we realized it was time. During the housecleaning project, Grandma had retrieved old textbooks from the loft. Used by my parents and others, the books were carefully preserved treasures. Now they would be strapped to the backs of France, Raymond, and me for another season of filling young minds with dreams and knowledge.

The one-room log schoolhouse was built high atop Utah Mountain, affording children from each side equal opportunity to attend. France knew the way well. I'd been there once but would never forget that cold Lord's Day. Mama and Papa had taken me with them to a meeting led by a circuit evangelist. The sermon ended and everyone began singing "Let the Lower Lights Be Burning." Some souls were crying and walking the aisle to get saved. Others had fallen to their knees to pray, while a few, unmoved, just waited around to shake the minister's hand. Suddenly from somewhere outside came a loud commotion and horse's neighing. The singing and praying took on a hollowness as the preacher and some of the men got off their knees to check their animals. Soon the minister was back, breathing hard, and asked to make an announcement. An "errant sinner in great need of repentance" had turned his mount loose. According to Papa, the irate evangelist "nearly lost his religion" that day when he had to walk back to town.

Suspiciously, fourteen-year-old Willie Muckle had been seen slipping from a back pew and out the door just as the preacher gave the "invitation." Case Muckle defended his son, claiming Willie left to go hunting, same as he did every Sunday.

On that first school day, the puncheon floor of the one-room schoolhouse fairly quaked beneath brogan-clad feet as we marched in, shoving and teasing. Mr. Price, the teacher, sat on a slightly raised platform behind a small pinewood desk. He rose from his railback chair. Tall and slender, he wore a striped shirt with a white collar and black string tie.

He stared at us, unsmiling, and gave one loud rap with a wooden mallet. Immediately we all took seats in rows of split-log benches.

Mr. Price appeared about the age of my father, but his smooth face and hands revealed that he had never had to work in fields or cut timber for a living. His polished boots and neatly-pressed trousers affirmed his place in life. We began with the Lord's Prayer. Afterwards Mr. Price prepared a list of the eighteen of us, ages seven through sixteen, in alphabetical order. He would use it each morning for roll call.

When we stood for the pledge to the flag, we had to remain standing while he seated us according to size and need. The big boys were placed in back, near the door, so they could prop it open, close it, or refill the water bucket at his request. Though it was summer, by the time school closed for winter, mornings would be frosty, and the older boys would have to stoke our pot-bellied stove before learning could begin.

Mama had made me two school dresses, allowing each to be worn once during the time of Alex and Loulie's visit. From the same bolts of calico, Granny had stitched shirts for France and Raymond. Mr. Price took note of our clothing and thought Raymond and I were twins. Raymond hated girls. He was insulted.

"I hain't got no sister," he boasted.

"Raymond, say 'I *have no* sister,'" Mr. Price corrected. He came and stood, peering down at the front row where Raymond and I were seated.

Raymond glowered at me and hissed, "I don't have no sister." Truth was, a real sister could hardly have looked more like him than I. His curly mop, shorter than mine, was the same dark blonde, his blue-green eyes from the same ancestor.

For France, Raymond, and me, walking the rugged miles to school was not a chore, but a daily journey of high adventure. Soon after daybreak, the cousins came by for me, and we began our trek like pilgrims toward a shrine. Every bird call was an Indian brave, every animal ferocious, the woods were an unexplored jungle, and our trail led to never-neverland.

Shouting threats from a high knoll and listening to the echo was a favorite game: "I'll knock your head off," France yelled fiercely on a hazy morning, his ten-year-old courage impressing Raymond and me.

"I'll knock your head off," the vile words came back just as boldly.

"Just come out and try," France hollered.

"Just come out and try," the echo shot back.

"D-double dare you!" France raised a fist defiantly.

"D-double dare you!"

Mr. Echo never came forward to accept France's final challenge, and as always the mock battle was won by default.

We set deadfall traps for birds and other small game on the way up the mountain and checked them on the way home. One day France thought we'd found a pheasant hen's nest, till a *polecat* stopped us short. Mama polecat sat by the entrance to her burrow. When she saw us she stomped her feet, raising her tail high; even Raymond and I knew about her "weapon." "Let's git!" France hollered, but it was too late. The dreaded odor lifted as we took off running.

Soon France threw out an arm, bringing us to a halt by a patch of purple-topped weeds. "If you want to smell good," he said, "just grab some of this horsemint and rub it on your legs." He'd learned this antidote from Granny. We pulled bunches of the pungent plant and rubbed it on our shins. When we got to school, Mr. Price circled us, sniffing suspiciously and, despite the coolness of early morning, asked Luke Gordon to prop the door open wide. At recess the three of us ate alone.

Always we piddled along the trail, lunch pails dangling from a stick, yet we were never late. An early start was the key, plus our eagerness not to miss activities that only school afforded.

"Recess for lunch!" At noontime when Mr. Price

spoke those magic words, we scrambled out to spread our food picnic-style on a large flat rock. Our fare varied with the season—apples or peaches, fresh or dried; kraut; dried beans or pumpkin; fried salt meat; sometimes chicken or wild meat. There was buttermilk, clabbermilk, sweet milk, or bark tea in a fruit jar. I learned to save a space on the rock for Aunt Mag's children from the other side of the mountain. Aunt Mag was "the 'champeen' puddin' and dumplin' cooker of Utah Mountain." If I got lucky, these cousins would share her goodies. We ate hurriedly on pretty days, saving time for games—unless a train's doleful wail sounded from the knob clearing. Then we'd scramble to the rail fence to watch it emerge from a distant tunnel, black smoke curling from its stack into blue-gray mountain mist.

"Here we go 'round the mulberry bush, mulberry bush, mulberry bush—here we go 'round the mulberry bush so early in the morning." Girls my age liked this game best of all: "This is the way we wash our hands, wash our hands, wash our hands—this is the way we wash our hands so early in the morning," and we made the motions of washing our hands, then our face, then brushing our teeth, till we could not think of anything else to do "so early in the morning."

Scrambling to seesaws the older children had built by placing planks over a wooden fence, we teeter-tottered till something else beckoned.

Sometimes we played tug-of-war, tap-hand, or blindman's buff. In blindman's buff, a blindfolded player, armed with a cane, stood in the center of a ring. The other players joined hands and moved around him until he tapped his cane on the ground. Then they stood perfectly still while "Blind Tom" pointed his cane at one of them. The player thus indicated had to say "Good morning, Blind Tom." Blind Tom would address five questions to the person at whom he pointed. Each question had to be answered. If the blindman guessed the name of the player, the "victim" must take his place and become "Blind Tom."

Older girls liked tap-hand. As players moved around in a circle, the person who was "it" tapped the hand of anyone she or he chose and could walk with that one around the ring or anywhere else nearby. Aunt Mag's oldest daughter, fifteen-year-old Lottie, tapped the hand of tall Luke Gordon. I followed them down to the cool spring where "lovers" liked to meet. There Luke toasted Lottie with water from the big gourd dipper.

"Here's to one, and only one, and may that one be she, who loves but one and only one, and may that one be me."

I stifled a giggle, but France broke the spell completely when he came up just in time to give his silly toast all of us knew by heart.

"Here's to you as good as you are, and to me as bad as I am. As good as you are, and as bad as I am, I'm as good as you are as bad as I am." So saying, he put the dipper to his lips, took a tiny sip, and threw the rest of the water on freckled-faced Annie Gordon, Luke's sister. France was up the hill and out of sight before Annie could catch her breath to chase him. All afternoon she sat fuming, staring at France, while he acted innocent of the telltale wetness on the bodice of her ruffled pinafore.

Early in July Mr. Price brought a ball and bat to school. The older boys and some of the girls chose sides, and the game of tap-hand was no longer played—or left for girls only. Lottie didn't like baseball. She sat pouting on a log bench, waiting for lunchtime to be over, while Luke became star pitcher and played every game. When Mr. Price appeared at the door yelling, "Books!" she grabbed Luke's hand and spent the afternoon seated close to him, whispering in his ear, while the rest of us read in hushed tones.

Mr. Price began "lessons" with the older children who read best, continuing through age groups until all had taken a turn reading aloud. Studying then resumed in soft whispers.

Aunt Mag's son, Robert, was a bright student. He was also a showoff. One day, after being called on to come and read, he decided to gamble on our teacher's not paying attention to the good readers. After his recitation, he proceeded with an ugly rhyme he'd written onto a scrap of paper:

> When I was just a wee lad,
> Guess what I could do?
> Kick some ass and talk some sass,
> Just like the grownups do.

There were titters and a few gasps from those of us listening, and everyone wondered if teacher had heard it. I buried my face in my reader, embarrassed to look at Robert. Mr. Price had heard. He snatched away the paper, tore it to bits, and made Robert stand in a corner facing the wall until recess. Then Robert had to clean the blackboard and erasers before going outside to lunch.

Beginning readers like me used bookmarks, called "thumbpapers," to highlight lines as we read. These were made from seed catalogue cut-outs of apples, peaches, cabbages, or any pretty fruit or vegetable. Older children made fancy and creative thumbpapers to mark their places, saving wear and tear on textbooks. They were prized pieces and often traded or collected like valuable stamps.

My reader was *The Graded Classic First Reader*, with stories of "The Little Red Hen," "Tom Thumb," and "The Old Woman and Her Pig." Young Aunt Effie helped me with my reading, but the tutor I liked most was Nellie Sue Muckle, a cousin on Papa's side. Nellie Sue had long brown hair, which she wore in a single braid.

Sometimes she loosed it, allowing it to cascade over her shoulders and down her back. Wavy tresses would be anchored behind one ear with a silver comb. Nellie Sue was pale of complexion, her eyes large and dark, and her skin smelled of rose water. I thought she looked like Mary, the mother of Jesus, pictured on one of my Bible cards. With quiet patience she taught me phonics, her tapered fingers touching mine as I moved my thumbpaper along printed words. Softly she turned the pages of my reader in a shared world of fantasy.

"Read this sentence, Sippy," she whispered, guiding my fingers with hers, pronouncing strange words when I stumbled. If I repeated them correctly, she placed her warm hand over mine and smiled. Nellie Sue's handwriting was immaculate, prettier than anyone's, and she always made As. She was teacher's pet, and everyone knew it.

On a warm hazy day when wild lilies bloomed, crimson heads drooping like shy damsels in red hats, I shooed away bees and picked a bouquet to give Nellie Sue. It was recess, and she was inside helping Mr. Price prepare the board for the afternoon arithmetic class. Everyone else was outside playing games or eating lunch. I tiptoed in, flowers behind my back.

In a corner Mr. Price stood with his arms around Nellie Sue. He was kissing her on the lips. Noticing me, he quickly pulled away, and before Nellie Sue looked, I ran out the door. I threw my lilies beside the stone steps and, as fast as my legs would go, ran to the spring where I sat down on a stump, jealous and confused. The only man I'd seen kiss a woman like that was Papa kissing Mama when he'd been away for a long time.

That afternoon Nellie Sue stayed after school to help clean slates and grade papers. On our way home, I did not feel like playing games. France kept asking me what was wrong, but I would not tell him or anyone else.

CHAPTER 7

Cloudburst

As did other mountain women, at times Mama and Granny hired out to work in fields or do housework such as washing, ironing, and scrubbing floors for the Kingsleys and other well-to-dos. Payment might be old clothes, cornmeal, scrap meat—anything to help out.

One day they both were hired along with others to help a farmer process sorghum into molasses. Mama had been getting sick, throwing up in early morning, but did not tell Granny. She warned me not to say anything because she needed to work. At the farmer's field, I watched his old mule pull a heavy shaft 'round and 'round as juice oozed from cane stalks, and the women tended the turning bar. Soon a fire was built beneath a huge pot, and the extracted sap was slowly simmered. We children watched the boiling process, fidgety, but staying clear of the fire and "not causin' trouble." We could hardly wait for the sweet reward for being good. Foam was skimmed from the top of the pot, and as soon it cooled, we ate our fill, sucking the tasty goo from our fingers like licking lollipops.

When the sweet syrup was cooked to the right consistency, it was divided into jugs and buckets, each helper getting a share. For Mama, Grandma, and Granny, molasses was not only an important mealtime staple and cooking sweetener but a base for making palatable tonics of bitter hard-to-take medicines, such as vermifuge and sulfur.

In late summer France and I worked in Uncle John's fields, helping him get caught up. He was leaving for a few days to meet with his Spanish-American War buddies in Waynesville. While he was gone, Granny, France, and Raymond went to visit another of her sons, Uncle Lowery, and his wife, Aunt Mag, on the other side of the mountain. With our nearest neighbors over two miles away, Mama, Met, and I were lonely during this time. We looked forward to Papa coming home more than ever.

On Saturday Mama felt so strongly he'd be home that day she decided to cook his favorite foods—egg bread, fried onions, and steamed cabbage. For the bread she used the last of her cornmeal. Papa would bring more when he came. By noon Sunday, he still wasn't there. Persistent morning sickness depressed her, and she worried something might've happened to Papa.

"They's lots of sickness in town," she said. "They's a spreadin' sickness goin' on, and your papa mighta caught it." By now it was late Sunday. Her prepared meal had been eaten, with leftovers thrown to the dogs.

"I'm hungry, Mama." I'd waited as long as I could before saying it.

"Me hun'ry, too," Met chimed in.

Mama poured two cups of warm milk. "Drink this, and soon's I fix this corn, I'll make us some bread." She grated half-ripe ears pulled from stalks that morning and made "sticky bread." We drenched it heavily with molasses. The humble meal satisfied. "Hunger's a sauce for any food," she quoted.

I cuddled Liddy in my arms while Mama sat in her rocker and pulled Met onto her knee. "When'll Papa be home?" I asked.

"He'll be along soon. Come on, I'll sing one of yer papa's songs, and we'll pretend he's on his way. You can swing Liddy whilst I swing little sis."

FLORA ANN SCEARCE

"Fly around my pretty little miss,
Fly around my daisy,
Fly around my pretty little miss
You almost drive me crazy."

"Am I pretty little miss, Mama?" I wanted to know.

"Oh my, yes. You've got pretty blue eyes and pretty curly hair."

"Fly around my buttercup,
Fly around my daisy,
Fly around my buttercup,
You almost drive me crazy."

"Is Met pretty, too?"

"She shore is. Both my gals is pretty—"

> "Fly around my pretty little miss,
> Fly around my honey,
> Fly around my pretty little miss,
> You'll be sixteen on Sunday."

"Are you sixteen, Mama?"

"I was sixteen when you was born. 'At was seven long years ago."

Papa still wasn't back when Granny returned with the boys. She sent France and me to the Settlement store for salt, thread, and matches. Mama needed sugar as well as cornmeal, and each of them sent a chicken to pay for the items. They tied the legs of the chickens together so they couldn't run if we laid them down.

As we ran toward the trail, each with a chicken under our arms, Granny yelled, "Don't you'ns tarry. They's black clouds on the horizon."

France and I stopped halfway down the mountain where a vine hung from the twisted limbs of a large oak tree.

"I double dare you to swing over that snake nest." I pointed to a pile of leafy debris beneath the tree.

Placing his chicken on the ground, France made a running leap, grabbing the vine high. "Whee-e-e!" He veered back and let go amid a flurry of chicken squawks.

"Them snakes done heard our chickens hollering. They's a-comin' to get 'em now."

"I d-double dare you to take a swing," he said.

"I hain't a-scared." I took the vine and timidly swung a few feet.

"Scaredy-cat, scaredy-cat."

"I d-double-dog-dare you to swing and let go over them snakes," I challenged.

"D-double-dog-dare, steal-a-hog-and-eat-the-hair." France took the vine and swung wide, jumping into the pile of brush. "Yee-e-e!" He scrambled to his feet and high-tailed it back.

"Weren't no nest," I said, belittling the feat.

We came to the "Stock-Law" gate, lawful boundary for a cattle range. Both of us took three swings while the other pushed the wide-hinged turnstile, then we re-fastened it carefully.

At the foot of the mountain, we ignored the log bridge across the creek and opted to splash through cool knee-deep water. Nearing a large farmhouse, we adjusted our chickens beneath our arms and began a sedate walk down the middle of the road. As we passed, I stared at the house.

"When I get growed-up, I'll live in a house like that'n," I said.

"Who you expectin' to marry what can give you a house like that?" France sneered.

"A bossman." I tossed my head high.

He laughed. "Hain't no bossman a-goin' to marry no mountain-hooger."

I shifted the chicken to my other arm and pouted all the way to the Settlement.

Mr. Kingsley was not in the store. Someone we did not know, younger with dark hair and eyes and a long thin nose, stood behind the counter.

"Where's Mr. Kingsley?" France asked.

"My father passed away. I'm *Caleb* Kingsley. This is my store now. And who are you?"

"I'm France Wright, and this here is Selena Wright."

"Are you Granny Wright's grandchildren?"

"Yessir. She gave us these chickens to trade fer what's on this list." France handed the list to the new owner.

Caleb Kingsley weighed the chickens and put them in a coop. One by one he placed items in a sack. "You got more coming," he said. "What else do you want?"

"Granny figured that. She wants tobaccy fer her pipe."

"I don't sell tobacco to children, but I know Kate Wright well, so I'm letting you have it this time. Tell Granny I want to keep her business."

"Thankee," France said.

Caleb Kingsley took a jew's-harp from a shelf of toys. "This is for the two of you. You can share it."

"Thankee, thankee, Mr. Caleb!" France took the small instrument and played a made-up tune on the spot.

We left the store just as a clap of thunder sounded from the west above the mountain. Clutching the sack, France commenced running up the middle of the road with me right behind. As we neared the two-story farmhouse, black clouds were churning directly above us and lightning zigzagged with a loud crack in sky-splitting patterns. A woman appeared at the door of the house. She motioned toward us. Thunder rumbled and the earth shook as rain descended in torrents. We scrambled up her steps to the porch.

"What on earth are you children doing out in this storm?" she asked. "Stay right here till it's over."

All sounds were muffled by the roar of the rain on the tin roof. I leaned back in the porch swing as the steady beat of rain numbed my senses. It seemed to go on and on, and I wondered what Mama would do if night came and we weren't back. *God is up there somewhere,* I thought. *He knows we need to get home.* "Help us get home before dark," I prayed. I closed my eyes, very tired …

"Wake up, child, wake up. The storm's over." Someone was shaking me gently. It was the woman who lived in the two-story house.

"Thankee," I said.

France picked up his bundle, and we headed

down the drenched road till it ended in a flood of churning foam. Ahead the once rippling stream was a roaring cataract bounding down the mountainside. Boulders marking the creek bed were now swirling eddies, and the foot log was gone. Venturing as close as we dared, we peered across the muddy waters to the far side. There stood Mama, her face distraught, her clothes soaked. I began to ford the stream.

She cupped her hands, shouting, "No, Sippy! No! Stay there. Wait fer this water to go down." She took a seat on a tree stump. Between us the water gushed headlong over rocks, carrying tree limbs and debris.

It seemed hours till waters began to recede and boulders marking the creek bed reappeared. Step by step Mama instructed how we should cross the roiling stream.

By the time we got home it was completely dark. Exhausted, I went straight to bed. "Mama," I called from the warmth of my favorite quilt, "old man Kingsley died."

France forgot all about the jew's-harp gift till the next day.

CHAPTER 8
Death in the Hills

In September Papa came home without a job. The work at Tuscola had stopped before the lake was completed. Papa decided not to look for another job until crops were harvested. Uncle John needed help, and Mama was no longer able to work in the fields. France, Raymond, and I helped by pulling fodder, and Met carried water to those needing a cool drink, but only another strong back would get the job done.

Mama and Granny had plenty to do—drying, canning, preserving fruits and vegetables as they ripened. And, mysteriously, they began sewing tiny clothes, only to tuck them away when curious children entered the house. I knew Mama's fat stomach meant another baby was on the way, and France always knew more than a ten-year-old should, but

Raymond and Met were unaware. No one talked about it. That was not the mountain way.

As days cooled, Papa and John headed to the forest to snake out logs for firewood. There could never be too much on hand for bitter wintertime. When, like clocks, their stomachs told them it was noon, Granny had a hot meal waiting. She called this meal "dinner." And it always came in the middle of the day.

"Um-umm!" Papa sniffed the air as he entered the house. "I do believe Granny's got shucky-beans fer dinner."

"Nope, they's *leather britches*," she countered, using the term she preferred. "Dried 'em myself."

Papa nudged Uncle John as he helped himself to a man-sized plateful. "Well, these here leather britches shore do taste like shucky-beans."

"Mighty good vittles to split logs on," Uncle John said. He crumbled crispy fried salt pork over his beans.

"And after that, it's mighty good vittles to go a-huntin' on." Papa winked at John.

Mama caught the exchange. "Some wild meat shore would taste good. What you'ns a-goin' to hunt, John?"

"Ever eat rattlesnake meat, Rachel?"

Mama looked surprised. "I reckon I hain't never."

"Then you and Granny better git to studyin' up on how to fix it. Jim and me done found us a den full of 'em, and we know a man in town what pays fer 'em brought back alive."

Granny's mouth flew open. "What in tarnation fer?" She slapped Raymond's hand when he pointed to an earthen bowl of steaming ginger-spiced pumpkin.

"He dopes 'em up, pulls out their fangs, and puts 'em in a show fer to make money off'n," John replied.

Granny shook her head in amazement. "Now what dang fools'd pay fer that?"

Papa and John left early the next morning prepared to bring a rattlesnake back alive. They wore leather boots and gauntlets. Armed with a gun, a cant hook for overturning rocks, a stout forked stick for pinning a serpent's head to the ground, and a box to put him in, they took off on the strange safari. Watching hunt preparations, the hound dogs yelped wildly—only to be left in their pens, whining and confused. Ever sensitive to signs of danger, Ole Blue slinked back to her place of vigil by the cabin steps.

Later that day France came yelling from his lookout station by the creek. "They's got one! They's got one! They's a-comin' with the box.

Mama grabbed Met's arm. "Git in the house now. Sippy, git in and keep her in." She and Granny stood just outside the door.

"Mama, you come in too," I begged.

"I'll be in afore long."

I went to the window to keep watch. What they'd caught was a three and a half foot long diamondback rattler. As soon as Mama and Granny got a peek, Papa and John went to a far corner of the yard and transferred it to a larger box, where it would remain till the man from town came for it. The special box had a glass lid for viewing, and Papa said it would be all right for Met and me to come outside and take a look.

I was frightened, though I wanted to see it. "Will you hold me up?" I said to Papa. From the safety of his arms, Met and I each took turns looking through the glass. Afterwards Mama gave us strict orders to stay away from the box. Even Papa was uneasy. He kept the yard gate fastened so no animal would wander in and upset the snake's home.

Days passed, and the man from town never came. Soon rules were relaxed. We began treating the snake like a pet. We dubbed him "Jack of Diamonds" and fed him by stuffing bugs, worms, spiders, and butterflies through air vents in the box.

One morning after feeding the snake, France began rapping on Jack of Diamond's box to make him coil and strike. I peered in just as the rattler struck the glass window. Granny heard my screams and came running from the cabin.

"Scaredy-cat, scaredy-cat," France teased. It wasn't so funny when Granny broke a limb from a peach tree and switched his legs. He danced a jig all the way to the cabin door. I stifled my mirth; I could be next.

On a moonless night, Blue's sharp bark woke us all, and the sound of hooves could be heard near the cabin. Papa bolted upright. "Somebody's done left the dang gate unhitched," he said disgustedly. He lit a lantern by the bed and reached for his trousers.

"It was locked at sundown," Mama reminded. "Don't go out there now. You cain't see nothing. It's too dark."

Papa knew she was right. He waited till dawn was graying across the eastern sky. He pulled on his leather boots and gloves, loaded his gun, and went to fetch John. Both grabbed pokers.

There were no cattle anywhere to be seen, though drops of blood were found in front of the open gate. The glass on the snake box was broken—Jack of Diamonds was gone!

"Danged if I can figure what happened," Papa said.

John stratched his head in puzzlement.

All of us had to stay in for days while Papa and Uncle John mowed every weed, burned every stump, dug out every hole, and overturned every rock near the house. There was no snake anywhere. Later Papa found a half-grown bull with a bloody leg, but it was proved only a cut when it soon healed. No one ever admitted to leaving the gate open.

For months we lived in fear the snake lurked nearby, waiting to wreak vengeance on his captors. Tales about Jack of Diamonds' fate spread over the mountainside, down to the Settlement, and as far away as Waynesville, growing more incredible with each repeating. A few of the curious came up to take a look at the broken viewing box.

December came with a hard freeze, causing Jonathan's Creek to creep beneath a mantle of ice and Granny's house to quake from children playing indoors. Smoke straggled and puffed from the chimney as the fireplace backlog blazed or smoldered day and night.

Mama and Granny stitched gray cotton flannel underwear, tucking the prettier cream-colored flannel out of sight of prying eyes. "Who's that fer?" Raymond asked, still oblivious to what Mama's enormous belly and waddling walk meant.

"It's cat's fur to make kitten britches," Granny said, knowing her words were bristling to a seven-year-old.

"Aww-ww."

One icy-cold morning we heard horse's hooves with Ole Blue's standard announcement. John had gotten up early, stoked the fire to a roaring, snapping cabin-warmer, and gone out to milk the cows.

Papa started out the door but came back when he saw the rider. "It's Case Muckle's boy, Willie."

France and Raymond dashed for the door, almost tripping Granny. She shoved them both from her path. "You'ns is a-goin' to git yer noses knocked off if you keep stickin' 'em in my business." Raymond fell to the floor squalling, but France nudged past her for a look.

"It's Case's boy, shore enough," Granny affirmed as the rider came into view. "They's bound to be somethin' wrong fer that lazy scalawag to be out and around so early." She stood at the open door.

The boy dismounted. He came up and extended his hand. "Howdy, Miss Granny. Paw sent me to …"

"Come in, boy, come in and warm them hands," Granny interrupted. "They's cold as frog legs."

"Yes'm." He came inside, blowing on his hands, and headed for the fireplace, stomping his boots as he went. "Now what is it yer paw wants?"

He backed up to the fire, hands behind him.

"It's Nellie Sue. Paw sent me to fetch you real fast. We's afeared she's dyin'."

Granny drew back. "What in tarnation's wrong with 'er? She's pert as a cricket last time I see'd 'er."

"Yes'm. She done took somethin' to kill 'erself. Drunk 'pizen' tea and drunk laudanum on top of it."

"Thun-der-ation!" Granny slapped her sides. "What fer? She plumb crazy?"

"No'm. She done it 'cause Paw said he'd beat 'er to death if she didn't tell who it was what ruint 'er."

"That dad-blasted infernal fool." Granny spit, missing the fireplace by inches. "If Case warn't my blood cousin, I wouldn't budge one inch to go. But it's my bounden duty to help." She grabbed her cloak and fascinator while France and Raymond stood gawking like statues. "Rachel, take care of these young'ns fer me."

"Shore, Maw, shore. Don't fret nary a bit about things 'round here."

We watched Granny straddle Willie Muckle's horse. She held fast to his back as they went over the hill and out of sight, the tail of her gray fascinator trailing like a flag in the wind.

"Shut the door now. Finish yer breakfast," Mama told France and Raymond. "Yer papa's a-goin huntin', and you'ns is a-goin to help me keep house fer Granny till she gits back." Mama washed dishes nervously while Papa and John made obvious attempts to get our minds off Willie Muckle's news.

"Yep, we'll be a-gittin old Santy Claus a mess of

wild meat," John promised. "He always stops here on his way down the mountain. He just cain't git no further till he's bound to git his snack of wild meat."

Papa grinned at Met. "I don't know what the old feller'd do if'n he couldn't find no wild meat here. They's just no tellin'." Met giggled.

"Git Santy a big fat 'possum," I told Papa.

"Git 'im two big fat 'possums," France said, always topping me. Raymond spun on the floor like a top.

Granny was gone three days. All she said when she got back was that she could not save Nellie Sue and that Case needed Papa and John to come help bury her. So saying, she took to her bed with the grippe.

"Rachel," she said, wheezing as she crawled under her warmest quilt, "send Case and Surry a jug of my blackberry wine. It'll help settle their shaky stomachs, pore souls."

I moped for days, hardly able to eat. I pictured Nellie Sue in a pine coffin-box, her eyes closed in death, the long tapered fingers that guided mine clasped across her bosom. Some mean man hurt her, but how? Why? And why would she want to kill herself?

Granny was so used to doctoring others that she was a hard case to deal with. She kept everyone at her beck and call. Mama applied hot meal and onion poultices to her chest, dosed her with rock candy whiskey syrup and boneset tea with ginger and molasses. As often as Granny called for it (and it was often), Mama poured her a shot of straight corn liquor.

When she got better, things got worse—"Fetch this," "Put that down," "Pick that up," "Open that door," "Shut that door," "Stop that runnin'," "Run and git my liniment," "Speak up," "Hush up."

After a good night's sleep, Granny sat up one morning and informed Mama she was ready to tell her about Nellie Sue.

"It was just awful," she said. "That pore little gal would've been sixteen come Sunday. She just weren't a-goin' to live. I brung 'er back once, but she couldn't speak. Tried to, but ever'time she opened 'er mouth, she heaved and puked. Spite of all in Gawd's name I could do, she just plumb give up and died."

Granny fell back on her pillows and blew her nose then asked for a swig of whiskey syrup and continued. "Case was a pitiful sight to behold. First he cussed like a sea captain, then he cried like a whupped child. He told how fer days he'd done ever'thing he could to make Nellie Sue tell'im who'd a-been the daddy of her young'n. She'd done said the feller was a married man, said she'd *die* afore she told his name. When she said that, Case went out and got his hoss-whip. 'At's when she took off running down the hill to

Aunt Callie Dock's, and Case just let 'er go." Granny stopped to blow her nose. Mama started crying. "Next day Aunt Callie Dock come a-runnin' and told him what Nellie Sue had done. He went and carried 'er home in his arms and sent fer me. Case said if'n any human could save 'er, I could. But, honey, I couldn't." Granny commenced coughing again and reached for the whiskey. After taking a swig, she lay back, chest heaving, and closed her eyes.

Mama wiped her eyes on her apron tail. "Well, I don't see why Nellie Sue'd rather die than a-told the feller's name. If'n he's already married, Case couldn't a-made 'im marry 'er nohow."

"Oh, Lordy, Rachel. Case done laid his hand on the Good Book and swore to Gawd he'd kill whoever 'twas if it took 'im till Doom's Day to find 'im."

Mama reached out and pulled me close to her. "When I think on my own gals, I cain't say I blame 'im fer wantin' to kill the rascal."

"I hain't blamin' 'im. I'm a-feared, a-feared Case'll git *hanged* fer it if he does."

Mama whispered, "God forbid."

I looked at Mama's tear-streaked face and vowed I'd *never* do anything to make her as sad as Nellie Sue had made everyone. I wanted to ask questions, but Granny did not like for children to "stick their noses in grown folks's business." I sat on the floor and began cutting pictures from an old seed catalogue. I would make a pretty thumbpaper to place on Nellie Sue's grave.

Granny had settled beneath her quilt, exhausted from her account of Nellie Sue's death. She was snoring loudly when France came and shook her arm. "Granny, just what was it that feller *did* to Nellie Sue?"

Granny bolted upright and shook her finger. "Git that boy out of here!" she bellowed. "Shut him in the lean-to till he learns to keep his nose out of other folks's business."

Mama took France's arm and led him outside quickly where he stayed till Granny was back asleep. He never brought the subject up again.

Late the next day, Papa and Uncle John returned from burying Nellie Sue. Both talked about Case's planned manhunt. "He's liable to kill the wrong feller, 'het up' as he is," Papa said. "You know how folks is. They's a-goin' to tote tales and tain't always the truth."

"That's right," John agreed. "They shore could git somethin' started on the wrong man, git 'im killed."

"Wrong feller or not," Granny said, "you'ns just keep them mouths shut about Case's trouble. I don't want to hear no more about it."

"Yes'm," Papa pretended meekness. "Only thing I want to say right now is—I'm hungry as a hound dog. I'd shore like to have some of them vittles I'm a-smellin'."

"Me, too." John rubbed his stomach and groaned. "I'm so hungry my belly thinks my throat's a-been cut."

"Shucks a'mighty," Granny scolded. "Afore you'ns starve plumb to death, git in yonder and fill them bellies with hog haslet, corn dumplin's, and sauerkraut Rachel's done fixed."

CHAPTER 9
Little Noble

Granny's grippe launched a small epidemic. Before winter was over, all except Mama and me took turns taking to bed with it. Papa still felt "weaker'n a worm-eaten hound dog," when a week before Christmas I realized he and Mama had gotten up in the middle of the night to go to Granny's. Frightened, I lay waiting. Moments later, Uncle John appeared at the door with a sound asleep Raymond in his arms. France was right behind, tousled and half-asleep. Uncle John deposited Raymond on the bed next to Met and, when he saw I was awake, placed a finger to his lips then hurried back out.

"What is it?" I asked France.

"Sh-hh," he whispered. "It's your maw. She's a-goin' to have 'er baby. Wanna go listen?"

Quietly, I stuck my bare feet into unlaced brogans and snatched my cloak. France got the lantern, and we trudged to the big cabin. Shivering in the cold, we took turns cupping an ear to the door, while the other held the light.

Inside, Mama moaned and called for Granny to help her. Soon the voices grew louder, more anxious.

"Push, Rachel, push. Now grab some breath." Granny sounded harsh, demanding, as she did when scolding France to get his chores done or else. Then I heard her say to Papa, "T'won't be long now, Jim." Mama was growling like an angry bear.

France cast sidelong glances my way. "Don't sound like no baby," he said. "Sounds like somebody a-dyin'." I knew he was remembering his own mama, who died in childbirth.

My mama must not die, not when I loved her so much. "I'm scared, France. Oh, Lordy, I'm scared." I wanted to burst inside and run to her. I began to cry.

"Hush up," he whispered. "Wait—I hear somethin' else." He nudged me, his ear pressed to the door. "Listen."

I put my ear to the door again. There was a strange new sound—a whimpering. Soon it became louder, drowning out the other noises. "Eee-ah! Eee-ah! Eee-ah!"

France turned to me, his eyes wide. "Aunt Rachel's

done got herself a baby." He tittered just like Annie Gordon did at school when a boy tagged her.

I started giggling, too, and couldn't stop.

"Hush!" he said, putting his hand on my mouth. "They'll hear you." He took my arm and drew me back toward our cabin.

There we scurried inside and jumped in bed, pulling a quilt over our heads—and waited. No one came. With warmth, my courage returned. "I'm a-goin' back where Mama is," I whispered in France's ear. "You can come if you want."

Ever ready for a challenge, France said, "If you go, I'm a-goin'."

Hurriedly we slipped back into the dark. This time I rapped hard on the big cabin's door. "Mama! Mama! It's Sippy. I'm cold." Even if Papa got mad, I would not leave till someone let me in.

Papa opened the door. "F-France and Raymond came to our cabin," I stammered. Beyond him I could see Mama lying on Granny's bed, very still, her eyes closed.

Papa wasn't mad; he seemed oddly amused. "Come 'ere," he said. "I want to show you somethin' real purty." I followed him to Granny's bed. He pulled back the covers. "Take a look at our *big boy*." A tiny baby, wrapped in cream-colored cotton flannel, nestled on Mama's breast.

How could Papa call him a big boy? I wondered. The baby was smaller than my rag doll, Liddy.

And how could something so little make the shrill screeches we'd heard through the door? France came over hesitantly and stood beside me.

Mama's face was drawn, her hair tangled, but she opened her eyes and smiled, then turned the baby so France and I could see his small countenance. "Santy Claus just weren't a-goin' to wait fer Christmas to fetch my gift," she said. "But he knows you young'ns has been good. He'll be back Christmas Eve and put somethin' in yer stockin's."

I was so excited about my baby brother that Christmas didn't seem important. Everything revolved around little "Noble," whom Papa named for a friend he'd made while timber-cutting at the lake site.

"A right smart rascal," Papa said about the original Noble. "Good-lookin', too. Noble Garrett Wright oughta grow up and be just as smart."

Granny didn't like the name. Thought it was "too fancy-soundin'," but Mama sided with Papa, so Granny was overruled.

On Christmas Eve, since Mama was still at Granny's house, we hung our stockings there. Daybreak the following morning, I paused long enough to slip bare feet into my shoes before racing into new-fallen snow to the big cabin, more to see Mama and baby Noble than to discover what Santa had left. But my stocking, misshapen and bulging with its contents, stood out from the others where it leaned against the hearth. A china doll's head poked out, her eyes staring at me in my winter shift and unlaced brogans.

I ran and picked the stocking up. "Mama, Mama, a chiny doll!" I carried the stocking to Mama's bed. Little Noble lay beside her, for all the world like a doll himself, in his flannel gown. Pulling my doll from the stocking, I laid her next to him. When her eyes closed, I clucked, surprised.

"Sh-hh." I put a finger to my lips. "The dolly's a-sleeping."

Mama smiled. She kissed a purring Noble and sat up on the edge of the bed. Wrapping a quilt around her shoulders, she slid to the floor and, with an air of mystery, took my hand. She led me out the cabin door. On the lower step she paused and pointed to the snow in front of us. "Lookee there, Sippy." Beside my own tracks and a set of big-booted ones, were tiny doll tracks leading to Granny's door.

I was entranced. "How could my dolly walk in the snow?"

"Santy Claus has magical powers. He held her hand as she walked in the door."

I knew it had to be true, because Mama did not tell lies. We walked back inside, and I examined my doll's shoes, still slightly damp from her walk in the snow. Her head, hands, and feet were real china. The dark eyes were large and pensive. They reminded me of Nellie Sue Muckle's. Like hers, too, the doll's fingers were slender and beautifully tapered. Painted lips parted in a pouty bow and brown curls clustered below a green velvet bonnet. The doll's skirt matched her bonnet, and lace trim cascaded from a white high-necked blouse. She was perfection.

"Her name's 'Nellie'," I announced emphatically. "Nellie" meant "beautiful" in my mind.

Mama leaned back on her pillows. She put Noble to her breast and was quiet for a long time. I wondered if she objected to the name I'd chosen. Finally she spoke. "What about Liddy, yer rag doll?"

"Nellie and Liddy will be sisters," I said, "like me and Met." Yet button-eyed Liddy no longer held my interest. I made her a bed on our rag heap then gave her to Met, who was still too young for a real china doll.

"Be sure and say 'thankee' to yer papa," Mama said. "He caught lots of wild meat fer Santy to feast on. I reckon that made the old feller right generous."

"I reckon Santy likes 'possum meat." I remembered Papa's grubbing for ginseng root all through October and November and his many trips to town. *It must all be connected*, I thought, though I didn't know how. Nellie was my very best Christmas gift ever.

By the time France, Raymond, and Met were up, emptying their stockings of toys, candy canes, and oranges, Granny had re-stocked the fire and was rattling pots and pans. She'd invited Case Muckle's family to dinner.

"After all," she said, "Surry won't be of no mind to cook none." Soon pots were boiling, trails of steam rising, and the smell of beans and turnips blended with orange peel and peppermint.

Mama got dressed for the first time since Noble's birth, combing her long hair and twisting it like a halo around her head. Afterwards, with Noble clasped in her arms, she reminded me of "Madonna and Child" on one of my Bible cards.

Anticipating company and Granny's big dinner, France and I kept an eye out for the visitors. Each wanted to be first to give them news of the baby. Granny was happy to get France off the floor, along with his new spinning top.

"Dad-nabbed top's a-goin' to trip me up yet," she complained while boiling a hefty pot of coffee for the menfolk.

With Case and Surry Muckle astraddle, their old gray horse soon rambled into the yard, his sway back appearing to sag beneath the burden. France and I rushed out the door.

"We got us a baby; we got us a baby!" we both yelled before they could dismount.

Surry pretended disbelief. "A shore-nuff baby?"

"Yeah, but he hain't France's brother, he's *mine*."

"Well, now, that's fair," Surry said, "seein' as France is already got one."

She threw a lanky leg over the beast and slid to the ground, while Case steadied the animal then tied him to scraggly sassafras tree.

"Come in, come in," Papa and John shouted from the doorway.

First thing the Muckles wanted was a look at the baby, and Mama held little Noble up for inspection.

"I swear if he ain't the spittin' image of Jim," Case said.

Surry partly agreed. "'Cepting he's a heap like Rachel, too."

"I expect he's more'n apt Monteville Wright all over ag'in," Case declared, catching Granny's eye.

Granny nodded, grinning proudly. "Just so's he don't have Grandpaw's bullheadedness."

Case guffawed, wagging his head.

Mama handed the tiny bundle up to Papa, beaming all the while. "I want'im to have red curly hair and blue eyes like Jim," she said.

"Tall and long-legged, too?" Surry asked.

"Just the same," Mama said. "Just the same." She told Case and Surry about the squabble Papa'd had with Granny over Noble's name. "Granny wanted to name him after his father, grandfather, and the president of the United States—he'd of been 'James Monteville Theodore Wright' and be called 'Jimmy,'" she said.

"Mighty big name fer a mighty little feller," Case allowed. "'Noble Garrett Wright' is just fine."

"Let me help with them vittles," Surry said, after placing folded quilts in a chair for Mama to sit on. "Case'll set yonder with the men. They's got a fire a-goin' in t'other cabin."

Next to full-bodied Surry, Mama looked like a little girl playing with her baby doll. "Whyn't you set here with me and rest yerself, Surry?" she offered. "Maw's about got her vittles ready. She's done cooked fer days."

"Oh, Lawsy, Rachel. I cain't rest 'less'n I'm busy at somethin'." She grabbed a spoon and began stirring a pot of beans steaming on the hearth.

"If'n you must help," Granny said, "then set the table. Rachel's got somethin' purty to put'er mind on. I just want you and Case to git yer minds off'n yer troubles whilst you's here." She handed Surry a muslin tablecloth.

Surry stretched the cloth across the table and smoothed away wrinkles with thick brown-splotched hands. "Gawd knows, Kate, I wish Case'd git his mind off'n killin' that feller what ruint Nellie Sue." She took a clean rag, wiping plates to set places for the grown folks. "He scares me plumb pale in the face."

"Now, Surry," Granny said in a calming voice, "Case don't know who 'twas. He just talks big. Makes 'im feel like he's doin' right by his little gal."

She paused to pat Surry's shoulder. "Let 'im talk, honey, since he don't rightly know who he's a-talkin' about."

"Maybe Jim and John'll git his mind off'n it," Mama said. "They's two big talkers, if I ever knowed any."

Papa got his pipe out, filling it from his cloth tobacco pouch as the men strolled to the other cabin, happy to get out of the women's way. Case brought up immediately what was on his mind.

"I got me an idea what that damned rascal looks like," he declared out of the blue.

John winked at Papa. "What damned rascal?"

"The damned rascal what ruint Nellie Sue, that's who." Case was working himself into a lather.

"Where'd you git the idea?" Papa asked. "How's he look?"

"Well, first off—he's married. She told me that much 'erself. He ain't old—I figure in his twenties. He's bound to be a good-looker, else she'd of paid 'im no mind, a good talker or else he couldn't a-talked 'er into what he done. He lives around here, or she wouldn't of met 'im in the first place. *That's* the feller I'm a-goin' to kill."

"Case, if you'ns crazy as hell," John exclaimed. "You know what you just did? You just dee-scribed Jim here! Shorely you didn't aim to do that."

Case stared at Papa like he'd never noticed his

looks before. "I hain't aimin' to accuse a soul 'ceptin' the scoundrel what ruint Nellie Sue," he said. "If'n it turns out to be Jim—shore, I'd kill 'im."

John shook his head in disbelief.

Around folks they knew, Papa and Uncle John's favorite topic was politics. In Mama's words, Papa "would rather talk politics than eat when he was hungry." She admitted that said a lot, considering his appetite. Papa tried to keep himself informed. He picked up newspapers each trip to town, reading them front to back. *The Asheville Citizen* reflected his conservative viewpoint, and he quoted often from its editorials, seldom disagreeing.

Case was a different story. Bald and wiry, with a bantam rooster temper, Case could barely read and write his own name. Taking it for gullibility, Papa and John were quick to unleash their political beliefs on him, waxing loud and long. Both staunch Republicans, they lauded Teddy Roosevelt.

"Tell you the truth, Case, old Teddy's fer the pore man ever'time," John said. "Long as he's up there in that White House, we's all a-goin' to fare better."

"Yep," Papa agreed. "It shore hain't no fault of his'n I'm in the fix I'm in. 'Sides, I got a job a-waitin' right now where I'll make good money, soon's I can git to it. Trouble is, it means a-movin' my family."

Case appeared unimpressed about what was taking place in the White House, but when jobs were brought up, he jerked to attention like a hound dog to a fox call. "Where's that job at, Jim? Nigh here?"

"Well, 'tain't so nigh. 'Tain't so fer neither. It's nigh Asheville. But first I have to see a feller name of Rance Hoaghan. You might know 'im, Case—old man Kingsley's son-in-law. Kingsley died, you know."

"Uh-huh." Case looked dubious, so John picked up on it.

"Sawmillin's just played out 'round here, Case," he said. "That feller Hoaghan claims they's plenty of fancy timber over in Buncombe, timber the big builders in the lowlands is askin' fer."

Case eyed Papa. "When you'ns a-goin' to leave?"

"Soon's my brother, Harve, comes next month. I'll go back with him as fer as Waynesville. Then I'll hobo a ride to Asheville. When I git back, I'm aimin' to sell my cow fer money to buy the fam'ly train tickets."

"I reckon Maw'll shore miss havin' Rachel nigh her," John commented. "Then they's her own maw down in the cove. Rachel hain't never lived no place 'ceptin' this here mountain."

"I hate to take her so fer away," Papa admitted. "And I thank you'ns fer all yer help, John, but a man's got to make a livin' fer his fam'ly." Papa placed his hand on my head where I sat close to his chair. "After

I git money ahead, we'll come back fer visits like Rachel's brother Alex does."

All this seemed remote to me. I'd heard Papa talk many times about jobs in far-off places. But we still lived on Utah Mountain.

"Lawsy, Jim," Case told Papa. "Money hain't ever'thing. After all, the Good Book says it's a *sin* to want money."

Papa laughed. "'Tain't exactly what it says, Case ..."

"Dinner's ready, dinner's ready! It's on the table." Surry stuck her head in the door, cutting short another of Papa's favorite opportunities to best an illiterate—a good biblical argument. "Ever'body bring yer chairs and come on," she said.

Granny seated the grownups at the table, with John at the head. We children found places on the floor, and our plates were handed down with instructions not to speak unless spoken to. Table conversations were adults-only.

"I shore wish my Harve coulda been here to eat with us." Granny sighed like she'd uttered a prayer. "These is his favorite vittles." Harve was the son who lived in Waynesville clerking at the hotel there. "Harve's got such a big job, he just cain't git away."

Case nodded agreement. "Takes book larnin' to hold down such jobs Harve's got, but they shore pay a feller good wages."

"My Harve's got the book-larnin', all right," Granny stated proudly. "He went all the way through sixth grade; you just couldn't stop that boy. No siree, Harve aimed to git hisself some top-of-the-pot larnin'."

"Yeah, Maw," John added. "Come hell or high-water, that Harve went to school. 'Sides that," he turned to Case, "that booger even learnt *me* to read. He orter been a teacher."

"Well, John, they's all sorts in this ole world," Case philosophized. "Now take my boy, Willie. He just hain't the kind what cares about school. He'd a whole lot druther be out rabbit-huntin', free as a bird. That's just the sort he is."

"Surry done told me he druther go rabbit-huntin' than come fer dinner today," Granny said. "Now that's a boy what loves to hunt."

"Well, Granny, I figure long's he's out rabbit-huntin' he hain't doin' nobody no harm. As fer 'im a-goin' to school, I say it's a waste of time to send 'em if'n they hain't got a mind fer larnin'." Case took a large helping of turnips mashed with butter and a wedge of skillet-baked cornbread. Granny beamed at this compliment to her cooking. She refilled Case's coffee mug and passed him a pitcher of milk.

"That might be so," Papa spoke in response to Case. "But I remember when my folks had to near 'bout hoss-whup me to git me to school. Now I wish to Gawd I'd a-gone further. When my maw remarried and left, I just never went back. 'Course I'd learnt a good deal, and learnt a good deal since. But I shore need more book-larnin'." He helped himself to seconds of braised rabbit in brown gravy, shucky beans with pork ribs, and brine-pickled cucumbers. "Maw, you done out-did yerself today," he said.

"She shore did," Surry agreed. "She knowed my favorites—this here stewed chicken and dumplings and homemade sauerkraut. And it's a long time since we'uns had wheatbread. I swear, Kate, I cain't see how you cooked such a feast while midwifin' fer Rachel."

As if to confirm all the plaudits, Granny rose, stepping gingerly over children to bring to the table the best of her culinary feats—desserts of dried apple turnovers, pumpkin stack-pie, and molasses gingerbread. These she served with foaming sillabub and bark tea sweetened with honey.

After sampling each, Papa got up, stretched his lanky frame, and belched loudly. He punched down logs in the fireplace and added more wood. As the women cleared the table, we children picked up our plates to make ready for gathering around the fire. It was time for music and games, the time we'd waited for all day.

John had already brought his banjo from the loft, and he plunked a few notes while examining the strings. Case took up Papa's fiddle and began tuning it.

"You'ns plays a better fiddle than me," Papa told him. "Me and Rachel'll lead the singin' whilst you play." Granny brought out a mouth organ for Surry, while she herself twanged on France's jew's-harp.

"Jim, come sit here by my chair," Mama said. "I got to suckle this baby to sleep whilst we's a-singin'."

John nudged Granny. "Might as well start off with the one Maw likes," he said. He strummed banjo strings, searching for the right key. "It'll be 'Sweet Deliverance.' Rachel, heist it to the right pitch fer us."

Mama raised her voice clear on the note she'd chosen, and the rest of us joined in:

> "I saw a wayworn traveler
> In tattered garments clad,
> And struggling up the mountains,
> It seemed that he was sad;
> His back was laden heavy,
> His strength was almost gone,
> Yet he shouted as he journeyed,
> 'Deliverance will come.'
> Then palms of victory, crowns of glory,
> Palms of victory I shall wear."

Surry swayed, lifting her skirt and dancing to the center of the floor. Her long drawers were exposed above black-stockinged legs.

> "The summer sun was shining,
> The sweat was on his brow.
> His garments worn and dusty,
> His step seemed very slow;
> But he kept pressing onward
> For he was wending home,
> Still shouting as he journeyed
> 'Deliverance will come'
>
> Then palms of victory, crowns of glory,
> Palms of victory I shall wear.
>
> I saw him in the evening,
> The sun was bending low.
> He'd overtopped the mountain
> And reached the vale below.
> He saw the Golden City—
> His everlasting home—
> And shouted loud 'Hosanna,
> Deliverance has come!'
>
> Then palms of victory, crowns of glory,
> Palms of victory I shall wear."

As the last note faded mournfully, Granny, overcome by spiritual ecstasy, clapped her hands and shouted—"Hallelujah! Hallelujah! Amen, Lord Jesus!"

Surry kept singing, though everyone else had stopped. "Glory! Glory! Glory!" she shouted. A straggly twist of graying hair pulled free, floating around her ruddy face like a loose turkey feather. "Praise Gawd, Nellie Sue's a-waitin' fer me up yonder." She closed her eyes, arms extended heavenward. "I'm a-comin', honey! Hold on. Hold on. Mama's a-comin'."

Frightened, Met ran to the back of the room as far from Surry as she could get. Raymond followed, cowering in a corner, his face in his hands. I crouched next to Mama and watched France. He was clapping and laughing out loud, like Surry was doing this just for him.

In the midst of it all, Surry's body began quaking, great sobs breaking from deep inside. Granny went to her, embracing and rocking her back and forth. "It's all right, honey. It's all right."

I buried my head in Noble's blanket.

Mama seemed unmoved by the performance. She got up and laid the sleeping baby on the bed then took my hand. "John, whyn't you pick somethin' these young'ns can sing?" she said. "France, tell yer papa what you'ns want to sing." Getting Met and Raymond to take part would not be easy.

"How about 'Johnny, Won't You Come'?" France offered. Uncle John struck a loud rollicking tune, and most of us starting singing:

> "Coffee grows on locust trees
> Branches flow with brandy,
> Boys are made of a lump of gold
> And girls of sugar candy.

Oh, Johnny, won't you come?
Johnny, won't you go?
Johnny, won't you pick it
On your old banjo?

Johnny loves a pretty little miss-
He cannot spell her name,
But he writes x's on her slate,
And she writes on his the same.

Oh, Johnny, won't you come?
Johnny, won't you go?
Johnny, won't you pick it
On your old banjo?

Poor Johnny wrote some x's
On her slate one day at school.
The teacher thumped him on his head,
And sat him on a stool.

Oh, Johnny, won't you come?
Johnny, won't you go?
Johnny, won't you pick it
On your old banjo?"

By now Raymond and Met had crept from their hiding places, but France had become bored with the lengthy song. "Let's play games," he suggested.

"Well and good," Papa said. "But it's Christmas Day, so first we orter close our singin' with a Christmas song." "Away in a Manger" was the only one everyone knew, and in the course of the song, even Surry joined in, apparently recovered from her grieving spell. When all verses were sung, we commenced the games.

Granny took a basket of roasted chestnuts and gave each player a double-handful. In her game, a player shifted chestnuts from pockets to hand to pockets, holding a chosen number in his hand. To his opponent he said, "Hold goal." His opponent answered, "Hand-full." The player then asked, "How many?" If the opponent guessed the exact number the player held, he won them. If he guessed less than was held, he paid as many to the player as it took to make that number. If he guessed too many, the amount over was put in the "goal pot," which was drawn for at the end of the game.

The rest of our time was saved for tall tales, riddles, rhymes, and tongue-twisters. Uncle John went first with his best tongue-twister: "How much wood would a woodchuck chuck if a woodchuck could chuck wood? He would chuck, 'e would, as much as 'e could, and chuck as much wood as a woodchuck would, if a woodchuck could chuck wood." Everyone applauded.

"I'm a-goin' to say mine, if'n I can," Mama said. She took a deep breath. "She sells seashells on the seashore. The shells she sells are seashells, I'm shore. So if she sells seashells on the seashore, then I'm shore she sells seashore shells." Mama messed up but kept laughing and trying till she finally got it right. None of us had ever seen seashells, but I imagined selling shells would be a heap easier than selling berries.

"They's a cloud a-risin' f'um the east," Case announced after a trip to the outhouse. "'Sides, me and Surry's got cows to tend afore dark."

"Let me take one more peep at this 'ere purty little thing afore we leave." Surry pulled back the cover and touched little Noble's soft hair. "I do declare he's the best baby I ever see'd."

"Thankee," Mama said.

"Ta-ta, purty thing." Surry sniffed loudly. "I wish to Gawd Nellie Sue had lived to've had her'n." She wiped her eyes with a handkerchief then got her pink fascinator and wrapped it tightly about her head.

Pointed shards of afternoon sun broke through the deep green spires of Piney Ridge as Case and Surry Muckle mounted their horse for the trip across the hills to Shakers Knob. Patches of snow stretched here and there like bedsheets out to dry.

John chuckled as the two disappeared down the trail. "If'n that old bag o' bones hoss of their'n don't fall from under 'em, they'll make it home afore dark." He slapped Papa on the back as they walked back inside.

Papa sniggered. "At old mule of mine that fell dead in his tracks looked a heap better'n that critter."

Granny had taken her hearth broom and was

busily sweeping up nutshells. "I hope to Gawd Case fergits about wantin' to kill Nellie Sue's feller," she said. "He appeared in good humor afore he left."

Papa grinned at her like a Cheshire cat. "Surry shore liked our singin', Granny. What happened to 'er? 'Sweet Deliverance' a mite too high?"

John snorted. "Shucks, Jim, after Surry got two-three mugs of Granny's wine in 'er, she weren't carin' how high-pitched it was."

"Hush yer mouth, Johnny Wright!" Granny shook her finger at him. "And git me some kindlin' wood afore it's plumb dark."

Mama gathered up Noble to nurse, winding him tightly in a blanket. "Well, I'm glad Surry got 'er mind off'n 'er troubles fer a while." She kissed the top of his head. "Maybe she'll sleep good tonight."

I picked up my doll, kissed the top of her bonnet, and cradled her in my arms, thankful Mama hadn't told Surry I'd named the doll after Nellie Sue.

CHAPTER 10
Aunt Callie Dock

January started out fair and rather warm, until one day when the sky turned a peculiar tan. Howling winds whipped up suddenly, chasing a parade of dark clouds across the sky. Snow began to fall with a vengeance, thick and fast.

"I knowed it was a-comin'," Granny declared, surveying the scene from the cabin door. "The Twelve Days is over and it's wintertime. Christmas had a good time to come, and a good time to go." She closed the door and went to the hearth. Sticking a hickory twig into red embers, she lit her pipe and puffed several times then spat into the flames.

Granny took inclement weather in stride, just as she did hard times. She'd always seen it colder, hotter, rainier. According to her, winds blew harder in the old days. Snows came deeper—lasted longer.

For Mama, when winter snows blanketed the hills as far as the eye could see, the security of cabin walls was eroded, and she thought of all the things that could happen. "It's sorter lonesome," she told Granny as she rocked little Noble back and forth in the high-backed rocker.

"Christmas over, no more company, now this storm." Frowning, she pressed Noble's brow to her cheek. "And this pore baby's ailin'—cried all night."

"That young'n's got the colic," Granny said, "just like Raymond did from the day he's born till he's three months old. Hain't nothin' a-goin' to ease it 'ceptin' poppy-seed tea." She knew Mama didn't like giving the strong potion to children, so she stressed her point by rising, knocking ashes from her pipe into the fire, and placing it atop the fireboard. "If'n you're a-mind to, I'll git my bag outten the loft afore bedtime and show you how much to give 'im. Don't take much fer a baby young'n." Granny got her quilting basket from the corner and set it next to her chair.

"I aimed to help you git her maple leaf quilt top together," Mama said, "but I just cain't do nothin' with this pore little thing a-bawlin'. I walked the floor with 'im all last night. I's a-feared he'd wake up Raymond and git 'im to coughin'."

Granny laid out piecings in her lap, smoothing and pressing them with strong fingers. "Raymond just keeps on havin' the croup," she said. "I cain't find nothin' to cure 'im of it. Ever'time he gits a spell, I tie his dirty stockin' 'round his neck and grease 'im up good with sheep tallow and lamp oil. It helps, but 'taint cured 'im." Squinting at a purple and yellow square, she examined the stitches and sighed loudly. "Oh, Lawsey, that Raymond's sich a slow growin' little feller. I cut a notch in the chimney corner a long while back. He ain't never outgrowed it yet. Takes after his maw, Gawd rest her soul. He ain't never a-goin' to be much size."

"Cuttin' that notch is the only cure I know of," Mama said. "When he outgrows that notch, he'll be all right." She placed Noble against her shoulder and patted his back gently. I knew Mama's sadness was not just because of Noble's colic or the prospect of our being snowbound. Papa was gone, and she didn't know for how long.

"It's awful lonely," she said, as if reading my thoughts. "Jim gone; us snowed in." Mama was afraid we were a bother to Granny, but her fear of our staying alone in the other cabin was greater. Papa had left for Waynesville to see Rance Hoaghan about the timber-cutting job. He planned to stay with Harve and his family until something was worked out. With bad weather, he could be gone a long time.

Granny delved into her basket, pulling out brightly-colored strips. "First thing you know, Jim'll be home braggin' about what a good job he found," she said. At her feet, Met and Raymond fought over discarded scraps, fitting them together like jigsaw puzzle pieces. On the drab puncheon floor, the crazy-quilt design grew in all directions.

Their game didn't interest me. I was lonely, too. Early that morning Uncle John had mapped out a course across frozen hills to track rabbits. France begged to go with him and John finally relented. They took along Ole Blue and Bossdog, John's best hound.

"Best kinda huntin' weather," Uncle John had commented, observing the pristine whiteness from a frosted cabin window. "Critters is all holed up, right where we can git 'em." He advised France to wear all the clothes he could find to put on. They'd check deadfall traps before returning and be gone all day.

France and I had tracked rabbits many times, smoking them out of hollow logs. We'd tended deadfall traps. I'd long ago graduated from my fear of stepping on bugs or touching dead animals. I did not cower inside the house when Papa killed chickens anymore. Instead I forced myself to watch the process as they flopped and flopped after their necks were wrung. Still, I wasn't surprised Uncle John did not invite me to go, especially in the snow. He thought women weren't cut out for hunting and brought bad luck to anyone foolish enough to take one along. I moped in silence.

Nellie was my constant companion. Through the window she and I watched chickens eating dishwater scraps. Then she sat next to me as I read my book. Using a thumbpaper with her name on it, I moved her tiny fingers along the printed words like Nellie Sue had guided mine at school. Still, with France not around, even this got boring.

At dusk he and Uncle John returned, crusted with snow and red-faced from the wind. They brought six rabbits already skinned and gutted, ready for cooking. But something was worrying Uncle John—something unrelated to the hunt. He frowned, talking in low tones to Granny as she lifted her iron skillet from a hook and placed it on hot coals.

"Case Muckle's crazy as a dang bat," Granny spat out suddenly. "A dad-blamed fool if I ever knowed one." John drew back at her words.

Startled, Mama got up, putting Noble to her shoulder. "What is it?" she asked Granny. John shook his head at Granny like the cat was out of the bag for sure. Mama turned and faced John squarely.

"Tell 'er. Go on; tell 'er," Granny said. "It's a dang fool what'd believe sich a thing."

John told Mama he'd met Willie Muckle while he and France were out chasing rabbits. Willie said his father had left, and they didn't know where to. Case claimed to have a "lead" on the man who got Nellie Sue pregnant and was "headin' out to git 'im." He'd taken his gun and stuffed a knapsack with plenty of ammunition.

"Case left 'round the same time Jim did," John said. "Willie talked funny, like telling it was liable to git 'im in heap of trouble. Fact is—I'm a-feared Case thinks it was *Jim* what ruint Nellie Sue."

Mama paled like she'd seen a ghost. I looked from Mama to John to Granny, hoping someone would say something I could figure out. My papa wouldn't hurt beautiful Nellie Sue Muckle. I knew that. I slipped my hand into Mama's. It was icy cold.

"'Tweren't Jim," Granny said in clipped tones. "You know dang well 'tweren't Jim." She spat into the flames with a loud *per-tooey*.

John grimaced. "I know it, Maw, and you know it. But Case Muckle is a dad-blamed fool, always has been. You know that, too. They's no tellin' what he's liable to believe."

"Shorely he hain't after Jim," Granny insisted. "What could a-happened since they was here?"

"Accordin' to Willie, his paw went down to Aunt Callie Dock's to get 'er to conjure up the way Nellie Sue's feller looked. Case paid 'er to do it. Aunt Callie Dock told 'im the feller was twenty-five, twenty-six years old, a good looker, and married to a *black-haired woman*."

Granny sputtered, sending spittle in all directions. "May Gawd have mercy! What air we a-goin' to do?" Hands shaking, she reached for her tongs and placed a lid on the sizzling skillet of rabbit.

"I know what I'm a-goin' to do," John said. "I'm a-goin' to find Case and follow 'im. If'n he bothers Jim, I'll kill the son of a gun."

Mama sat down and commenced rocking the baby. She rocked harder and harder as tears streamed down her face. Outside the hounds were yelping loudly. France was feeding them, and I always helped. But Mama needed me, and I had to stay by her. Sitting at her feet, I rocked my doll back and forth. "Everything's goin' to be all right," I whispered in Nellie's ear, and I started to hum "Fly around My Pretty Little Miss."

That night John went to bed before anyone else. His plan was to rise early and go searching for Jim and Case, whoever he found first. Mama knew she would not sleep, so she fetched from the loft an old Graded Classic Second Reader, the one Papa and Harve used at the Settlement school. She patted her swollen eyes with a wet cloth.

"Come on, Sippy, you'ns gather 'round whilst I read," she said. I knew the pretense of cheerfulness was mostly for me. "This here's the story about a little boy who weren't no bigger than your papa's thumb." Noble was on the bed asleep, so she took Met into her lap while I leaned against her legs. Raymond sprawled on the floor, his chin on his crossed arms while France, with big-boy aloofness, listened on the sly. At the end of the tiny hero's tale, Met was sound asleep, and I could hardly hold my head up.

"Let's git on to bed, now," Mama said. "Tomorr'y night I'll read about a feller what slept twenty years."

John was already gone when we got up the next morning. Granny was strangely silent and made no reference to the events of the day before. "I think the grippe's a-comin' back on me," she said. Mama brewed her a pot of herb tea and warned us to stay away from Granny's chair.

"'At snow's a-meltin' fast," Mama said. "Maybe Jim'll be home soon with a job, and we can buy some new things we been a-needin'."

Granny slurped the hot tea. "Gawd knows I want to see Jim with a good job. What'll take me a while gittin' used to is you'ns a-leavin'."

"We'll be a-comin' back to see you, Maw, same as Alex and Loulie comes back to see my maw." Neither mentioned Willie or Case Muckle or why John had left so early, until late in the evening when Uncle John got back.

Granny was sniffling and piecing quilt squares, stopping occasionally to blow her nose, when we heard John at the door. She jumped to her feet, nearly falling over Raymond, who was sprawled on the floor with paper cutouts. "How'd you git along,

Son?" She helped John doff his cloak and draped it over a chair.

John's shoes sloshed with melted snow. He sat down, took them off, and stretched out his legs, his bare feet close to the hearth. Mama quit nursing Noble and laid him on the bed, hastily re-buttoning her blouse. She went and stood next to Granny as they both stared down at John.

"Well, I see'd Case Muckle all right," he said. "That old rascal'd done been all the way to Hazelwood and saw old Aunt Mollie. He come back through Waynesville just in time to see Jim board the morning train fer Asheville."

"What in Jupiter was Case doin' at Aunt Mollie's without lettin' his folks know he's a-goin'?" Granny's voice choked with relief.

"Well, from what he told, he just went out a-huntin' and kept goin'. Ended up nigh Hazelwood and dee-cided to go to Aunt Mollie's, see if she had saved any of them Big Dutch cabbage seed. Said they's the best eatin' cabbages they is in this whole country."

"Oh, they air, they air," Granny agreed. "If'n he's got plenty, I'd like to git me some." Grippe symptoms gone, she was the old Granny again.

John put his wet brogans close to the hearth. "Huh!" He grunted and scratched his head. "At's a mighty long way to go fer a few cabbage seed."

Mama smiled for the fist time in days and I knew the crisis was over. "Jim done gone to Asheville?" she asked John.

"Shore did, honey." John looked happy to share this news. "Alex telegraphed him a ticket. I knowed Alex weren't a-lettin' Jim go bummin' his way in this snow."

"Jim'll pay him back soon's he gits his job," Mama said. "He'll be makin' good afore long."

John pursed his lips in thought. "I think I'll just pay old Aunt Callie Dock a visit. See if she cain't conjure up somethin' fer me, like what she *really* told Case, what she expects he might do now."

Early next morning John left for a day's work sorting and loading lumber. Granny packed his dinner pail well with meat, bread, beans, and stewed apples. He and Granny talked in low tones about dwindling food supplies and having to feed extra mouths but shushed when Mama came within range.

The hills above the cabin soon emerged brown and soggy as January's third blanket of snow began to thaw. Melting slush filled vein-like gullies and trickled into a swollen Jonathan's Creek. We children, tired of being indoors, streaked in and out the cabin door, trailing mud. Granny and Mama mopped and grumbled.

"Ef I've told you onct, I've told you a hun'ert times to wipe them feet!" Granny yelled at France. "First thing you know I'm a-goin' to chain that door shut, and you'll stay in or out fer shore."

With the melting snow, Mama's spirits lifted. She was of a mind that Papa would be home soon with his job news. She decided to settle us down with a never-fail treat. "Bein' as Noble's a-sleepin' so good," she said, "I'll try my hand at molasses stickies. These here young'ns like 'em so much." She placed a thick slab of wood into the fireplace flames.

"Stickies, stickies," Met hollered. "Stickies, stickies!" She clapped her hands.

Quickly I put Nellie to bed beside the sleeping Noble and begged Mama to let me help. Raymond slammed the door hard and stood grinning.

"Quit slammin' that dad-blasted door!" Granny yelled. "Wake that baby, and they'll be no stickies fer you." France began cleaning mud from his shoes. No one dared venture back out until the stickies were reality.

"Maw, reckon it'll take me long to git used to real cook-stove?" Mama let me take a turn stirring the dark mixture. "Loulie said it's a heap easier than this here sort of cookin', 'specially fer fancy vittles." She wiped her hands on her faded blue apron.

"I don't rightly know, Rachel. I hain't never had no cookin' stove myself. I did help Miz Kingsley cook on her'n onct. It weren't easy fer me. I druther have my vittles cooked the old-fashioned way."

With her wooden spoon, Mama pressed the dough into an oblong pan. She shoved the pan into the narrow fireplace oven then banked hot coals beneath. Soon warm sweetness filled the cabin, whetting our senses. I could hardly wait.

Mama peeked inside the oven. "Umm! Umm! These stickies is a-smellin' and a-lookin' mighty good." She motioned for me to take a look. "I'll be a-savin' some of 'em for John. "Tain't a young'n nowhere what likes'em ary bit better'n him."

Granny nodded. "John's always been foolish over sweet vittles. I reckon stickies is his pick of 'em all."

John got home late. He'd stopped to see Aunt Callie Dock on his way and made an appointment with her for the following day. The clairvoyant was a distant cousin of Granny's and lived on the macadamized road near the Settlement. "Got Indian blood in 'er," Granny claimed, adding more mystery to my image of her.

Granny appeared in deep thought as she served up John's supper. She placed a saucer of leftover stickies near his plate, and we children watched, hoping he would not eat them all. When he picked up the last two, he caught Raymond's look of disappointment and laid them back down. He placed a hand on Raymond's shoulder. "Son, don't ever play poker." He laughed at Raymond's confused look and handed the stickies to Mama to divide four ways.

When John got up from the table, Granny broke her silent spell. "I'm a-goin' with you to Aunt Callie Dock's," she announced like the decision had come down from God. "We'll take Sippy with us."

France looked shocked. "I want to go, too."

Granny huffed. "Hain't no place fer the likes of you." He scowled as she shook her finger at him. "Sippy may have a 'gift' herself. She 'feels' things. Me and her maw's both noticed it."

I didn't know what to think. I wanted to go. Aunt Callie Dock intrigued me. I wondered why Nellie Sue had gone to her when she ran away from her father and why Callie Dock couldn't keep Nellie Sue from killing herself. Maybe I'd find some answers to questions I wondered about on nights when bad dreams woke me, and I lay frightened and confused. According to Granny, Aunt Callie Dock used the Tarot, cards with pictures, to tell the future. *Were they like my story cards of Jesus?* I wondered.

I knew Mama was leery of my going. She and Granny got out their tin boxes of snuff to pleasure themselves as soon as we children were in bed. Granny placed a generous dip inside her lower lip, while Mama swabbed hers with a black-gum twig she'd softened by chewing one end. Coating the pliable wet "toothbrush" with snuff, she worked it around her teeth and gums. The two of them talked and spat while John propped his bare feet on the hearth, spreading his toes wide.

Early the following morning, Mama took great pains to get me ready. From the bottom of the quilt box, she pulled my best calico dress and smoothed out the folds with a flatiron. She plaited my hair into a single braid with a scarlet ribbon intertwined.

I looked into Papa's shaving mirror but did not like my image. I wished my hair was like Mama's, dark and thick, and my eyes large and brown. Instead my hair was no-color light brown. My eyes weren't blue like Papa's nor brown like Mama's, but sometimes blue, sometimes green, depending on what I wore. Today they appeared lime-colored above my calico dress. *My eyes look like Kitty-cat's,* I thought.

We usually walked to the Settlement, but for this occasion, John hitched the mule to the wagon and wiped the seat clean for Granny to sit next to him. An old quilt was folded in back for me to sit on. Along the way Granny hummed, finally breaking into "Amazing Grace." Like snuff-dipping, I recognized it as one of her nerve-calming rituals. Before we reached Aunt Callie Dock's, she fell silent, and as we pulled into the drive, she mumbled, "Gawd help us." I stayed well back of Granny as we walked to the door. Just as Uncle John raised his fist to knock, Aunt Callie Dock opened the door.

"Come in, Kate," she said to Granny, who led the way. She nodded at John and stared down at me. The tall woman led us into a room where a square table was centered, covered with tassled green velvet. Upholstered chairs were pulled up, one on either side. "Which of you is the seeker?" she wanted to know.

No one answered. Granny peered around, blinking hard in the dim light. Aunt Callie Dock gestured toward a chair, and Granny sat down. I grabbed the chair's arm with both hands, holding tightly. Aunt Callie Dock's black faille dress swished as she swept into the seat facing Granny.

"You will be the seeker then," she stated. "John and Selena must leave." Her metallic-gray hair, pulled back severely from a prominent forehead, had an inch-wide streak of white through the middle. In the shadowy light, her round eyes and high cheekbones gave a haunting, owlish look. Bright strands of Indian beads dangled from her neck, clicking softly as she leaned toward us. I could not take my eyes from her face.

John was happy to leave the room, muttering something about making sure his mule and wagon were all right. Desperately wishing to both hide and watch too, I clung to Granny's chair.

"Sippy stays," Granny said, patting my hand. "She 'feels things' and has warning dreams. I want her to see the Tarot."

"Very well," Aunt Callie Dock replied. "But she must not utter a word. Concentration is important." She smoothed the plush table covering with her hands and placed on it a tiny silver tray containing several coins.

Granny reached inside her bodice and pulled out a pouch, dropping two nickels into the tray. Without a word, Callie Dock whisked away the tray and laid a thin stack of oversized cards in the center. The back of the cards were gold-colored and depicted a large key. Callie Dock rested her right hand on top of the deck. A silver ring with a blood-red setting adorned her index finger, and circling her thumb was a wide gold filigree band. Like an eagle's talon, the thumbnail curled curiously.

"These are the Major Arcana." She gave Granny a condescending look. "There are twenty-two of them. They reveal important signs and events."

Granny leaned forward, staring at the cards.

"Now, tell me, what is it that you seek?" The clairvoyant's deep eyes probed, and Granny stiffened.

"Case Muckle came to see you," Granny stated slowly and deliberately. "You told him a handsome man with a black-haired wife was the one what got his daughter in the fam'ly way. My son, Jim, is a handsome man with a black-haired wife. I want yer cards to say it weren't Jim Wright what did that to Nellie Sue Muckle." She straightened and crossed her arms over her bosom.

Aunt Callie Dock was plainly taken aback. "I never reveal a person's reading to another. I will ask the cards for a sign, using the Prediction Spread. If you wish for more detail, that can be done, but it may require another session using the rest of the Tarot, or Minor Arcana." She pushed the deck slightly toward Granny. "The seeker will cut the cards three ways."

Granny cut the cards into three thin stacks, placed one atop the other, and looked at the clairvoyant.

Aunt Callie Dock picked up the top card and placed it in front of Granny face down. A succession of fifteen cards were laid out in rows resembling a small hopscotch grid. Some of the keys faced Granny, some the medium. When all were in place, Callie Dock paused. Slowly she began to turn them, one card at a time.

The first depicted a large star with the Roman numeral XVII. A beautiful girl, completely nude, was pouring water from a pitcher into a pond with one hand, and with the other she emptied a second pitcher onto the earth. Callie Dock turned the next card and hissed. "The Fool," she said, speaking of the joker image.

Granny drew back, putting a hand to her mouth. I leaned against her shoulder.

Aunt Callie Dock placed The Fool next to The Star and continued turning cards. The Moon. The Lovers. The Sun. "The Moon is illusion," she said. "Things are not always what they seem. Ah, The World." She uncovered another. "Ah, yes, yes." Judgment followed. She hesitated a long time before revealing the next card, closing her eyes as if in prayer. Slowly she lifted it and Granny gasped. I clutched Granny's arm tightly.

The card portrayed a tall tower in a violent storm being struck by a bolt of lightning. "The Tower of Destruction," Aunt Callie Dock said in a staccato voice. Beside the fateful card, she turned up Justice, laying it gingerly beside Destruction, then pressed her hands together as if now everything were apparent.

Granny was plainly awed by the striking display. "What's it all mean?"

"The Star is Nellie Sue Muckle," Aunt Callie Dock stated matter-of-factly. "A bright heavenly light that was suddenly snuffed out. The Fool was out of order. He is the only card without a number and most unpredictable. But he didn't fool me. Followed as he was by The Moon, I can give you a good *general* reading."

"All I'm asking is fer the Tarot to tell me Jim

Wright is not the man. I know he hain't, but I want the Tarot to say he hain't."

"I can tell you only what the cards tell me. Make of it what you will." The clairvoyant touched the cards in turn as she spoke. "The man who got Nellie Sue Muckle pregnant has gone away. The World tells me he will never come back."

"Jim Wright is gone away," Granny said suspiciously.

"If he returns, then he is not the man. Nellie Sue's lover will never come back. And Case Muckle will never find him. Justice will find another way. The Tower of Destruction tells me the guilty will not escape retribution."

"Does the guilty man have a black-haired wife like Jim's wife?" Granny stared at the cards.

The medium placed her index finger on card No. XIX, The Sun. Beneath the kindly-faced sun depicted on the card, a small child rode a white horse, his arms outstretched. "The Sun is the dark-haired wife." Her words were measured, ominous. "Life revolves around her."

"What happens to 'er?"

Aunt Callie Dock turned the last card over and drew her breath in sharply.

Granny flinched. It was card No. XIII, Death.

CHAPTER 11
Papa's Job

On the way home, Granny asked John for a bite off his tobacco plug then grumbled, spat, and grumbled some more about "wastin' good money on that witch, Callie Dock."

"Them cards was a-stacked just the way she wanted," she said. "'Tain't helped us nary bit." She spat again, leaning from the wagon as a stiff wind whistled out of the gorge, throwing the dark spittle against a weathered flank. Facing the wind, she pulled her fascinator tightly about her shoulders and head. After that day, I never once heard Granny mention my gift for sensing things.

"If'n he's-mind to, old Case done had him a good chance to kill Jim," Uncle John reasoned aloud. "But I'm still aimin' to watch that booger close when Jim gits home." The old mule slowed to a creep. "Git up, Buck," John shouted. That wagon lurched as Buck smarted from a flick of John's whip.

The next day John returned to the Settlement for a day's work at the coffin factory and in the evening surprised us with a letter from Papa. Papa had found a job and was back in Waynesville. Rance Hoaghan, Jacob Kingsley's son-in-law, was getting a crew together to cut timber on Saunook Mountain. Being the first one hired, Papa would be foreman. He'd "explain it all when he got home."

John had stopped by Kingsley's store for coffee after picking up the mail, where he talked to the widow Kingsley about Jim's letter. She told him her daughter, Letty, would be arriving by train at the Waynesville depot next day. Caleb would be fetching his sister home and would be glad to give Jim a lift in his dray. "It'll save Jim a five-mile walk," Mrs. Kingsley pointed out.

"I gave her a mighty big 'thankee,'" John said. "This weather's hard on a body's shoes, and I'm shore Jim's is wore plumb out."

"What the dickens is wrong with Letty?" Granny wondered out loud.

"Fer Gawd's sake, Maw, let me finish telling Rachel about Jim," John snapped. He seemed unusually tired as he worked his boots off and wiped his feet with his socks. "I told Miz Kingsley Jim was a-stayin' at his brother Harve's, accordin' to his letter. Caleb'll pick him up there and bring him as fer as the macadamized road."

"I'm mighty beholden to you fer settin' that up," Mama said. She squeezed little Noble and kissed the top of his head.

"Now Maw, as fer Letty Kingsley, er Letty Hoaghan, a-comin' back home, I've always said a woman's place is with her man no matter if she likes it er not. I hear Rance done built 'er a big house smack in the middle of Asheville. Any other woman'd be happy as a hawg in a peanut stack. Appears Letty's a-leavin' all that behind to come back to 'er maw."

Granny blew her breath out disgustedly. "That Letty *was* always stuck right under her maw's coattail. I reckon she ain't changed." She poured coffee beans into the roasting pan.

"Let me grind this time, Granny," I begged. I got the coffee-mill from its place on the shelf. "France did it last time."

"Well, I suppose hit's yer time," Granny said. "If'n you spill ary a grain, you lose yer turn."

John watched Mama serenely nursing little Noble. "I hate to tell you this, Rachel, but Miz Kingsley told me somethin' else, somethin' she tried to tell Jim afore he left, but he got right riled. It's about yer maw and her fam'ly."

Mama looked up quizzically.

"They's a-goin' to hafta move outta Shingle Cove. Mr. Kingsley done give up sawmillin' afore he died. Now Miz Kingsley's dividin' her property. She don't want no more sharecroppers. Her son, Caleb, aims to raise beef cattle and wants that land fer a cattle range. Her son-in-law, Rance, is a-wantin' to sell his part. I reckon Tom'll have to git hisself a job somewheres."

"My Gawd," Mama said. "Maw hain't never lived nowhere 'cepting this here mountain and that little cove. Hit'll plumb kill 'er to have to leave."

"Miz Kingsley said they's in no hurry, but Tom best find hisself somethin' and git out of The Cove soon's he can."

This news didn't dampen Mama's spirits, however—Papa would be home the following day. Placing the sleeping baby on the bed, she began taking her hair down. As she combed the silken strands, she planned what we'd wear for Papa's arrival. "Sippy, you wear your red calico dress, and Met'll wear her blue one." Suddenly there was a dull thud of hooves.

John peeked out the window. "It's that dad-blamed Case Muckle." He took a red-hot poker from the fire. "He's done heard Jim's a-comin' fer shore." I stopped grinding coffee and waited for Mama's reaction. Holding the poker behind his back, John opened the door to a smiling, toothless Case.

"Ah, howdy-do, Case," John stammered. "Yer folks all right?"

"Howdy, John." Case's beady eyes scanned the room. He looked at Mama, her hair falling around her shoulders like a little girl's. "Where's Jim? I figured he's home by now." Mama stood transfixed, watching John.

"Hain't got no idea when he'll git home," John lied. "He's in Waynesville. Got hisself a job."

"Good news. Mighty good news." Case seemed to be stalling as cold air chilled the cabin and John's poker cooled behind him. "I hope 'twas with somebody else, not that Rance Hoaghan feller." John looked at Granny, and Granny looked at Mama, but no one said anything.

"Well now," Case continued, "I just come over here to fetch Kate some 'termater' seed I got from Aunt Mollie. They's the best termaters I ever put my mouth on."

Granny fairly sprang from her chair. "Come on in. Come on in, Case."

"I cain't stay, Kate." Case stomped mud from his boots, stepped barely inside, and closed the door. "I just come to bring these seed." John quickly replaced the poker by the hearth while Case fumbled through pockets and retrieved a small square of folded newsprint tied with string. He handed it to Granny. "I'm a-sowin' plenty of them Big Dutch cabbage, enough fer us all."

"Mighty obliged to ye," Granny said. She stuck

the package of seeds into an apron packet. "Why don't you'ns stay fer supper? John brung fresh coffee from the Settlement just today. Hit orter be good."

"Hit smells powerful good, but I cain't stay. My old woman's fixin' brined chittlin's fer supper. She's a-holdin' 'em fer me right now."

"Well, do give Surry my regards," Granny said as John let the wiry little figure out the door.

"Good Gawd," Granny sputtered as soon as the door was bolted. "Brined chittlin's!"

John sniggered. "Fittin' vittles fer the likes of Case Muckle." He sighed in relief, got his pipe and filled it. He took a seat by the fire, lit the pipe, and leaned back on two chair legs. "Maw," he said, narrowing his eyes dreamily, "I made the last payment on Roxie's coffin today." Lifting his chin he sent a puff of smoke that circled his head like a halo. "I'm sorta thinking of leavin' here myself, findin' me a *real* job somewhere." He watched for her reaction.

Granny spat a mouthful of tobacco juice into her tin can quickly and wiped her mouth, ready with the words—"Let me tell you something, John Marshall Wright. I's a-born on Shaker's Knob right over yonder and hain't never been nowhere much else in my seventy-odd years. But the day you take France and Raymond away, I'm a-goin' too. Ain't no two ways about that."

John grinned. "That's exactly what I wanted to

hear, Maw." He closed his eyes as puffy clouds of apple-scented smoke hovered in the still cabin air.

∾

All next day we watched for signs of Papa's arrival. The sun was dropping low, casting great dark shadows in the gorge, when we heard his voice ringing loudly from toward the creek. "Hullo! Hullo! I'm home." Without a word Mama handed the baby to Granny and dashed out the door. I raced behind. Soon Met followed, yelling as she went. "Papa's home, Papa's home!"

"You'll ketch yer death," we heard Granny hollering from the open doorway. Noble on one arm and our cloaks on the other, she watched us running bare-armed toward the creek. Papa caught Mama up in his arms, and they embraced. When Met and I reached them, Papa hoisted Met to his shoulders while I clung to his coat, and we trudged the steep trail. Shivering from cold and excitement, we entered the warm cabin to find Granny still wagging her head.

Papa put Met down and grabbed Granny, wrapping her and Noble in a bear hug. I squeezed Mama's arm, and she clung to me as tears streamed down her face.

"Papa's home, Papa's home," Met trilled like a mating bobolink. "Papa's home, Papa's home." Papa picked her up and danced her around while the puncheons creaked beneath his feet. Met was delirious. "Papa's home, Papa's home," rose into high-pitched squeals.

Mama took my hands, and we joined the jig, circling Granny as she cradled Noble in her arms. The frightened baby let out a hefty scream. We all laughed, and Mama took him, kissing and cooing till he settled down.

Out of breath, Papa set Met on her feet and looked at Granny like she might be next. "Maw," he said, puffing, "you got somethin' a feller could eat? I'm hungry as a hound dog."

"Hain't never see'd 'im when he won't," Mama said. "Dancin' done made 'im hungier."

"Hold yer hosses, Jim Wright, just hold yer hosses and set right down," Granny said. "I'll whup up some vittles quicker'n you can say *Jack Sprat*."

Icy sludge had seeped into Papa's shoes, soaking through to his feet. He sat down, took them off, and let Mama peel off his dirty socks. She stretched them across his brogans near the hearth, poured a pan of warm water, and began bathing his feet.

Papa sighed, relaxing. "I stopped by and talked with John whilst I's at the Settlement," he said. "He's drawin' 'is first good pay at the factory after payin' off Roxie's coffin." He looked squarely at Granny. "John talks like he's a-thinkin' of leavin' Utah Mountain."

Granny seemed thoughtful as she hastily set bowls of food on the table.

Papa spoke up louder. "John done saved that mule of his'n, you know. Hit's been nigh onto two years since Roxie died. If he hadn't paid off that debt they'd of come and got old Buck. Said as much on the paper he signed." He flexed his toes in the pan of water. "I'm l'arnin' lots about business, Maw. I asked Caleb Kingsley 'bout sellin' 'im our cows. He offered me twenty-five dollars in trade. Twenty-five dollars! 'At's purty fair. I told 'im I couldn't travel on trade, so he said he'd give me part cash and haul me fer as Waynesville as part of the deal. I reckon I'll take 'im up on it. I'll drive ole Cherry down the mountain and sell 'er soon's I figure what we need." He took his feet from the water, and Mama wiped them with a cloth. She handed him clean socks.

"I shore hate to see Cherry go," Mama said. "I raised her from a little bitty calf. But it's the only thing left to do."

Papa looked at Granny. "I'll leave our chickens here fer you and John. And I'll put part of the trade fer cherry on Caleb Kingsley's books fer John to use as he sees fittin'. Gawd knows I owe 'im more'n I could ever pay."

"Hush sich foolish talk," Granny said. "You cain't pay a body fer love." She sniffed loudly. "And ef you'ns is so hungry, whyn't you git to this table and stop yer mouth with yer vittles. I got browned rabbit meat, stewed pumpkin with 'lasses, sauerkraut, and cornbread."

"Wait just a minute," Mama said, peering out the window. "I see John a comin' up the path. When he gits in, we'll all set down." She poured steaming mugs of coffee. John shed his muddy boots at the door, and we all sat down.

Papa cleaned his plate of second helpings, pushed his chair back, and rubbed his stomach. "I'll swear to you'ns, Granny shore cooks good vittles. I'd heap druther have 'em that fancy mess Harve's wife gorms up and sets on the table."

"Well, sir," Mama said, putting a hand on her hip. "You just better start likin' fancy mess, 'cause that's what I'm a-l'arnin' to cook soon's we git us a shore-nuff cook stove."

"Uh-oh," Papa said. "I done let myself in fer somethin'."

"I think yer a-goin' to swaller yer words right on top of that big meal you just et," John said, grinning at Mama.

"Humph," Granny muttered, unsmiling, "if'n them shoes of yers is worth mendin', Jim, they's cowhide and groundhog skin on the lean-to wall. You can use hit to fix 'em."

"Thankee. Soon's they's good and dried out, I'll patch 'em up. I'm sorta countin' on a new pair, though, soon's I sell old Cherry." He pounded his brogans against the firedogs, knocking off mud, then set them carefully near the hearth. He pulled his chair close to the fire and leaned back comfortably, stretching his long legs. Relaxed, his mood seemed to change. He turned to Mama.

"Honey, soon's you git them young'ns to bed, I need to talk to you, Granny, and John 'bout some things you'ns ought to hear afore we go to Saunook." Puffing his pipe, he stared at the fire while Mama and Granny hastily took care of their nightly chores. John pulled up a chair next to Papa's and bit off a hefty tobacco "chaw." The two seemed quieter than usual.

Soon Mama wiped her hands on her apron and sat down. Only the crackling of the fire could be heard till Papa cleared his throat. "First off, soon's this weather's a-fittin' I got to git on up there to my job. What I have to say is mainly fer you, Rachel—Utah Mountain bein' the only place you ever lived. Saunook hain't *nothin'* like Utah. They hain't a thing up there, honey, 'cept a steep, rough mountain, a deep rocky gorge, and water.

"They hain't a livin' human in miles. Hain't no cow pastures, no cornfields, nothin' but wild animals on a wild mountain—a helluva lonesome place fer a woman. 'Sides that, if you go, you might be the only woman up there."

"Hain't none of t'other fellers married?" John asked.

"I'm the first man Mr. Hoaghan hired, but he said hisself if he hired married fellers, they might not want to fetch their wives up there, 'specially if they had a house somewhere else." Papa puffed hard on his pipe, blowing a series of gray wisps. "Let me tell you'ns about Saunook." A flaming log sent sparks against the stone firewall. He narrowed his eyes. "A long time ago, they was a loggin' camp up there. That company of loggers built shanties on the side of the mountain, nigh the gorge. Further on they dammed up water comin' out of the waterfall and made a floater pond fer logs. Then they built a flume from the pond all the way down that mountain to another pond where the logs ended up. From there a dinkey hauled 'em off to a sawmill."

"Them shanties still standin'?" John asked.

"Nope, they's all tumbled down 'cept one. Some hunters done kept that'n fixed up fer a huntin' lodge. Hit's the one Mr. Hoaghan told me I could live in. But, tell you the truth, John, when I see'd that little bitty shanty a-settin' propped up on long poles, right on the edge of that rocky gorge, I said to myself—I got to tell Rachel the truth."

He faced Mama squarely. "You done got some fancy notions from Loulie 'bout how you want to live. Gawd knows, a loggin' camp hain't fancy."

He rose, knocked ashes from his pipe into the fireplace embers, and got a dipper of cool water from the bucket. "Lordy, that's good water," he said. "Better'n anywhere I've been." He came and sat close to Mama, pulling one small hand into his.

"Honey, what I'll do is work up there a while till I can git you some of them fancy things you want. Hit won't take me long."

Up till now Mama had been silent. She turned and looked into Papa's eyes. "The only thing I want, Jim Wright, is to be with you." Her voice was hoarse with emotion. "I want to go up there with you."

John's chair creaked as he shifted his weight. He adjusted his tobacco cud and spat hard into the flames. He looked at Papa. "Hell's hosses couldn't hold that woman back if you said 'come on.'"

"I hain't aimin' to say 'come on,'" Papa said. "I just want'er to know what sorter place a loggin' camp is, fer Gawd's sake. If she'll stay here, I'll fetch back all the money I can lay my hands on. If she wants to go, shore, I'll take 'er."

"If they's only one shanty on Saunook, where t'other fellers a-goin' to stay?" John asked.

"That's part of my job," Papa said. "Mr. Hoaghan told me to go on up there just as soon as the weather's a-fittin' and start fixin' up one er two of them tumbled-down ones fer the other fellers to stay. I'll meet Mr. Hoaghan in Hazelwood, stay overnight, and he'll take me and a wagonload of supplies up the mountain. He'll git all the stuff we'll need up there inside of two weeks. After that, he told me, we oughta finish gittin' the work done inside six weeks' time."

Papa put his arm around Mama. "Six weeks er so is a long time in a helluva lonesome place, honey. Make up yer own mind on whether you want to go up there er not."

Mama didn't hesitate. "I want to go. As fer lonesome, hit won't be lonesome with all five of us there."

"Well, I reckon that settles it." Papa rapped the wooden chair arm with a fist. "What we got to count on now is the weather."

"The old groundhog'll settle that question fer you," Granny said. "He's due to come out and take a look at his shadder soon."

"Yep," John agreed. "That ole whistle pig—as Paw used to call 'im—will come out and stay out, er crawl back in his hole and go to sleep fer six weeks er longer. We'll see come Tuesday week."

Mama got up yawning and stretching. "Well, I'm a-goin to crawl in *my* hole right now."

"Me, too," Papa said. "I hain't slept a good night's sleep since I left here."

Mama pushed him teasingly. "Why? No *bedsprings* to sleep on?"

"Git to bed, woman." He slapped her on the backside.

CHAPTER 12
Waiting to Leave

Snowflakes swirled from a leaden sky, and brisk winds swept them into soft mounds against cabin windowsills as I lay quietly listening to Granny's fitful snoring and the tick-tock of the mantel clock. Mama, Papa, and little Noble were back at our own cabin. Met and I begged to stay at Granny's so we could play with France and Raymond past usual bedtimes. Quilt tents and pillow fights weren't Granny's cup of tea any more than "sticking our noses in her business." She allowed it because we'd be moving soon. "Them young'ns is a-goin' to miss each other," she told Mama.

John crept from his bed, built a fire, then crawled back in. Shortly Granny arose. Clad in her unbleached shift, she tucked the bedcovers firmly around us children and pulled on a woolen dress. Tiptoeing to the door, she opened it to a white fantasy world. Silhouetted by its dazzle, her hair a halo of silver, she looked like the angel on one of my Jesus cards.

Doleful at first, like a far-off train whistle, Granny's quivery song began: "Tell the good news, wherever you go—Jesus has washed me, whiter than snow." She closed the door and went to the hearth to start breakfast.

Soon Mama and Papa were there, and I crawled from warm covers to hold my baby brother. He looked like a little elf in his red-striped kimono, smiling and cooing at his big sister. It made me feel grown-up.

Granny's song rose above a din of activity: "*Whiter than snow, that beautiful snow. Jesus has washed me, whiter than snow.*" She was mixing a batch of flour dough in a wooden bowl.

"Maw, hain't that wheatbread you're a-makin'?" Mama asked, glad for a break while I entertained Noble.

"Shore is, honey. Today's my France's birthday. I had a smidgen of flour left over from that pokefull John brung fer Christmas. Hain't nothin' France likes better'n sopping wheatbread in sorghum 'lasses and flour gravy."

"Did you take a look at that snow?" Papa asked.

"I always look outdoors first thing ever mornin'," Granny said. She formed the dough into a large loaf.

"Hit's one of them softie snows; hit'll melt real fast." She patted the mound into a greased skillet.

"I shore hope it does. I got that job a-waitin'." Papa took a kettle of boiling water to pour on the frozen cabin steps.

When her bread was done, Granny placed a bowl of flour gravy in the center of the table alongside a Mason jar of molasses. She reminded everyone at the table it was France's birthday.

"Look at 'im," she said proudly. "I recollect when he weren't one whit bigger'n little Noble there—when I's puttin' hippin's on him just the same."

"You mean 'didies,' Maw?" Mama said, proud she knew the latest term for diapers.

"Naw, I mean 'hippin's,'" Granny shot back.

Everyone laughed except France, who smirked without looking up. Brawnier than most eleven-year-olds, he hated tales from his babyhood. With a rare blush, he sopped a hunk of bread in his plate of gravy and molasses.

Granny passed the bread to the rest of us. Pieces were broken off for dipping till all was gone.

"I reckon I'll go up yonder to Piney Ridge today and snake out a pine log fer Caleb Kingsley," John said, rising from the table. "I promised to split one into kindlin' fer' 'im."

"Hit's good weather fer sich," Papa said. "I'll go help you."

"I need to git old Buck out, limber 'im up," John said. "That mule's been shut up and doctored up ever since last fall. Ef he hain't able to pull a log downhill in the snow, he hain't worth a plug nickel."

"He's looking purty good yesterday," Papa commented. "Et everything in his trough." With France and me in tow, the two headed for the stable. Papa got the harness ready and the log-chain. John rubbed Buck down a bit, patted him on the haunches lovingly, and fastened the log-chain to him.

"Giddup, Buck! Come on now, old boy, let's go. Giddup." John pulled on Buck's reins. Tucking his tail, the old mule stood firm.

John jerked the reins hard. "Come out of there, you blasted devil!" he pulled harder, and Buck ambled forward. "Dad-blamed stubborn rascal." John shook his head and spat hard onto the crusted snow. "Has to be cussed afore he'll budge ary step." John and Papa prodded the mule all along the way toward Piney Ridge, Ole Blue and Bossdog stalking behind.

Watching them, Granny yelled from the doorway, "You'ns fetch me a rabbit fer supper!" If they heard her at all, Papa and John ignored it. She slammed the door. "John's madder'n a wet hen over that mule."

"Don't worry, Granny," France piped up. "Sippy and me'll fetch you some birds fer supper. I'm a-makin' deadfall triggers fer us." France knew how to get Granny in a good mood. With the meat larder nearly empty, she'd be happy to get our birds. They made tasty soup bases and the best of pot pies.

I wanted to make my own deadfall trigger. I knew how. But the only pocketknife belonged to France, and he would not let me use it. It made no difference that I was always willing to let him hold my doll, Nellie, when we played house, something I'd never allow Met or Raymond to do. Raymond bit the doll once and sawdust spilled out till Mama sewed the hole up. Raymond would bite anything. Another time we heard Ole Blue yelping in pain. "Raymond bit the dog," Granny explained. No one was surprised.

Met could not be trusted with Nellie either. One day when I was outside, she got Nellie and tried to undress her the way she always did her own doll. Nellie's lace collar was torn. Granny fixed the blouse by pinning it with a brooch Grandpa had given her when they were newlyweds. Nellie wore the brooch from then on. I began stashing Nellie inside Granny's quilting basket when I went outside. Met dared not touch that.

France made his own rules, however, about who could use his pocketknife. He made the triggers for our hunt.

Raymond woke up with the croup as he did so often on winter mornings. When he saw France and me wrapping our feet to go out in the snow, he wanted to go, too. His voice was raspy as a bullfrog's croak as he nagged and pulled on Granny's apron. When we put on our cloaks, he howled even louder, gasping for every breath.

"Gawd bless that pore little chap," Granny said. "I'll praise the day he outgrows that notch in the corner." Mama tried to soothe him with promises of special treats while Granny brewed a dose of poppy-seed tea. They coaxed him to take a few sips.

"Granny'll sing ye a funny song whilst ye rest yer sweet bones," she told him. She hummed a few bars in her throaty fashion then broke into Raymond's favorite English ditty:

> "There was a little boy,
> And he lived by hisself, and
> All the bread and cheese he had,
> He laid upon the shelf.
> Oh, the rats and the mice—
> They led him such a life!
> He had to go to London
> To find a tidy wife.
> Go, wing, wing-waddle, go,
> Jack straw-straddle, go,
> Johnny-fie-faddle,
> From the sun to the broom."

As she sang, Granny patted Raymond on the back to loosen the phlegm. A fit of coughing ensued, and his wheezing seemed to ease.

> "The roads were so rough,
> And the streets were so narrow,
> He had to fetch her home
> In an old wheelbarrow.
> Oh, the wheelbarrow broke,
> And the wife had a fall, and
> Down went wheelbarrow,
> Wife and all!
> Go, wing, wing-waddle, go,
> Jack straw-straddle, go,
> Johnny-fie-faddle,
> From the sun to the broom."

With Raymond settled down, France and I were about to leave when a heavy pounding on the door fairly shook the cabin. "Great jumpin' Jupiter!" Granny blustered, sending Raymond into another coughing spell. "What the devil?"

Mama hastened to open the door. Case Muckle's son, Willie, stumbled in. Below a knitted stocking-cap, his eyebrows were crusted with snow, his cheeks and lips chafed and red-splotched.

"Oh, Lordy, Lordy, Miss Granny!" he cried. "Please let me hide in yer house. Paw's a-goin' to beat me to death!"

"Hush that derned bawlin', Willie," Granny well-nigh shouted, "and tell me what the devil's wrong."

Mama dragged a chair close to the fire. "Set down, Willie-boy."

He dropped into the chair and began peeling off clothes. When he took off his shirt, he leaned forward. "Lookee thar. That's where Paw done lashed me with his hoss-whip. He'd a-kilt me if'n I hadn't run."

"What fer?" Granny was incredulous.

"He's a-fussin' with Maw, drunker'n a fish. Then he lit in on me. Claimed I stole his pocketknife and swapped it fer this here harp." From his coat draped on the chair arm he pulled out a small mouth organ. "I swear to Gawd I swapped a poke-full of chinkie-pins fer it—I swear to Gawd!"

Granny examined the bloody streaks on Willie's back. "Rachel, git my arnicy salve," she said. "I'll wash the blood offen these welts. You kin smear'em careful-like with a bit of salve."

The treatment made Willie open up, and words gushed like a broken dam. "Maw begged Paw to quit beatin' me, then she motioned fer me to run. Maw knows it's all downhill to Aunt Callie Dock's. I reckon she thinks that's where I went. But I figure hit's the first place Paw'd look."

Salve and soothing words appeared to have eased Willie's pain. France and I took off our coats. Bird-trapping would have to wait. For all we knew Case could be on Willie's trail that very instant.

Granny helped Willie get his shirt back on. "I recollect how Case used to git plumb foolish when he got likkered up," she said. "I shore never thought he'd git this mean. I lay it all on 'im troublin' over Nellie Sue. Somehow that done throwed 'im off."

"I cain't go back home," Willie said. "I druther stay here with you'ns from now on." He quickly drank the dipper of water Granny handed him.

"Well, you just cain't up and stay here," she said. "Ef yer paw don't come and find you, I'll git John to take you on back home. He'll speak to Case about how he's a-treatin' you."

"Oh, Lordy! Lookee yonder." Mama was pointing out the window. It was Papa and John, back already. They'd hardly had time to go to the Settlement and back. "It's Buck," she said. She ran to the door and threw it open. "I swear. He's down and they cain't git 'im back up."

Willie pulled his coat on hurriedly and ran out the open door, France and me right behind.

John was beside himself. "Damned infernal mule. Hain't worth the powder and lead hit'd take to blow his brains out." He glanced at Willie in surprise. "Me and Jim done as much pullin' on that log as Buck did, Willie-boy. Now look at 'im—give plumb out and fell over."

Papa was puffing clouds of breath in the cold air. He blew hard on his hands. "I'm glad he helt out till we got 'im back," he said.

Willie grabbed hold of Buck's harness and helped lift the fallen beast. The three badgered and pulled till Buck was on all fours again and inside the stable.

John poured corn nubbins into a trough, spread Uncle Zeb's old army blanket across the mule's back, and closed the door. "One thing's fer shore." He gave a snort. "That damned rascal can still eat." With that, he turned toward the cabin. The rest of us followed.

"You'ns was a big help," Papa told Willie as he stomped his feet in front of the fire and pulled off his coat. "What you doin' 'round these parts, huntin' rabbit?"

Before Willie could answer, Granny piped up. "I'll tell you what happened—I don't want Willie to have to go through it ag'in. Case done had a drunken tantrum and threatened 'im. Case hain't never been a real mean feller. You know that, John. He'll be all right soon's he sobers up."

"Stay on here tonight, Willie," John offered. "You can sleep on a pallet in front of Maw's bed. I'll take you home t'morrow and talk to yer Paw. You'll be all right. I'll see to it." Willie didn't say anything. He appeared to trust Uncle John.

"I'll git some dinner goin'," Granny said. "You'ns split me some wood. I'm a-gittin' low." Papa headed for the woodpile.

France had been watching Willie's every move. "Today's my birthday," he told the older boy. "Granny made me wheatbread fer breakfast."

"How old are you?" Willie asked.

"Eleven." France stretched his husky frame.

Willie was almost six feet tall. "I'm fourteen," he bragged. "Fourteen *and a half.*"

"You like bird-trapping?"

"Shore."

"After dinner you can go with me and Sippy to check bird traps." France reached into his pocket and pulled out his pocketknife. "Here, take a look at my knife. You can use it if you want."

Hurt by the slight, I didn't say a word. I was glad just to be included.

According to Granny, the groundhog rose at noon on his day and came out of his burrow to take a peek at the weather. By her calculations, the sky was dark and a shower of rain descending precisely as the clock on the fireboard struck twelve. But when John returned from Shakers Knob after taking Willie Muckle home, he vowed the sun was shining there at noon.

"Surry Muckle's clock is bound to be wrong," Granny insisted. "This'n here is right and *stays* right!"

"Shore, shore, Surry's clock is wrong." John would rather concede than get Granny riled. Her predictions were like sacred pronouncements.

"Well, now, the sun did come out just after that shower," she admitted, "but it weren't out at *twelve.*"

"One thing fer shore, Maw, I brung good news." The news was that Case Muckle had been so worried about Willie's overnight disappearance in freezing weather, he wasn't just penitent. He told John he'd sworn off liquor-drinking and mistreating his family. And he'd given Willie a pearl-handled pocketknife as a peace offering.

"Hallelujah!" Granny shouted.

"Now, Maw, Case hain't exactly sanctified yet. He's still hellbent on killin' the feller that bigged Nellie Sue."

"And he's still a danged fool," she said. "He hain't got no more idee who the feller was than a jaybird. He just talks big."

"Well, at least he hain't fancyin' it was Jim what did it. Fact is, he spoke mighty friendly 'bout Jim. Wants to come over and see 'em afore they leave, specially that baby. I told 'im to come Sunday and stay fer dinner. You got vittles fer a big dinner, Maw?"

"We got a string 'er two of leatherbritches left. We got kraut. I recollect how kraut's Surry's favorite. We got some salt pork neckbones and a jar er two of blackberries. 'Course we can kill us a chicken-hen. I reckon that'll suit ever'body."

"Shore suits me. I'll git a poke of wheat flour from the Settlement, and you can put some slick dumplin's in the pot with the chicken-hen."

"Jim's down there right now a-talkin' to Caleb

Kingsley," Granny said. "He's seein' about sellin' Cherry and about takin' the family to Waynesville."

"Where's Rachel?"

"She's over yonder trying to rest. That baby done kept her awake all night long, bawlin' with a bellyache."

"Minds me of Raymond, Maw. 'Member how you used to set up at night and rock 'im? His own maw, my sweet Roxie, dead and in her grave, weren't here to tend to 'im." John sighed loudly, and we watched him head for the lean-to. He seldom mentioned Roxie, but when loneliness crept into his busy routine, he'd find a stick of wood just right for whittling and spend an hour or two alone out there.

Mama came from our cabin to help Granny with supper. Noble had slept off his colicky spell. Chubby and bright-eyed, he kicked and gurgled at the foot of Granny's bed. To Mama's joy, his hair had tinged with red and was beginning to curl.

"See, Maw." She twisted a strand over her finger. "Just like his paw fer all the world." The women were setting the table when Papa came in.

"I talked to Caleb Kingsley," he said. "I'm takin' Cherry down to 'im first thing in the mornin'. Rachel, you'ns make a list of what you and these young'ns need. I done picked out some overalls fer myself, a shirt, some drawers, and a pair of shoes. He'll gimme a pair of socks free."

Granny placed a bowl of sauerkraut and a corn pone near Papa's plate. "This hain't no supper to brag on," she said, "but, come Sunday, we'll have us a good dinner."

"I hain't makin' no complaint over these vittles." Papa sopped his bread in kraut juice. "I wouldn't ask fer nothin' better."

"The Muckles are a-comin' Sunday," Mama explained. "They want to see this baby again afore we leave. They's right foolish over boy babies."

"'Specially that Surry," Papa said. He finished his supper, wiped his mouth, and licked his fingers. Mama handed him little Noble to hold. "Well, now, who wouldn't be foolish over this'n." Papa beamed at his little son. Noble gurgled and smiled. When I held him, he seemed to be getting so big, but in Papa's lap, he still looked tiny.

"'At's as purty a baby as I ever see'd," Granny stated, "and I've see'd lots."

John came in from the lean-to. "I'm tired," he said. "Got to git to the factory early tomorrow, so I'm a-turnin' in."

"Me, too," Papa told him. "I'll drive that cow down as you go. Now, honey, git me that list ready," he told Mama. "I'll fetch back the things we're a-needin'."

Early next morning, not an eye was dry when Papa unhitched Cherry to take her to the Settlement. But when he got back in late afternoon, arms loaded with bundles, Cherry was forgotten. We ran to meet him.

"Papa, Papa, let me have my new shoes." I tore off the lid when he handed me my box.

"Wookee, Mama," Met said, holding her box. Mama took Met onto her lap, slipped long black stockings on her skinny legs, and put her new shoes on.

"I got 'em a mite big," Papa said. "She'll grow into 'em soon enough."

"Hit's just what I'd a-got if I'd been pickin' 'im out," Mama said. "You always know just what we want." Papa had bought blue and yellow calico for dresses and cotton flannel for underclothes. Mama and Granny worked into the night sewing garments. By Saturday their fingers were sore, but everything was finished except buttonholes.

"Let me finish them buttonholes, Maw," Mama said. "You best start that dinner."

"I reckon I orter," Granny agreed. "I want it to be ready when Surry Muckle gits here. I can't abide that woman fiddlin' 'round in my kitchen."

Granny's dinner pleased everyone. The chicken dumplings were tender, slick, and succulent. The shucky beans, which she'd mixed with shelly beans to make sure there'd be enough, proved a tasty combination, seasoned well with salt pork. Surry's favorite—steamed kraut—was served with crisp salt pork, chipped and sprinkled atop. Granny's specialty, big round cakes of wheatbread, were flakey and golden brown. For dessert she'd made molasses pudding with sweetmilk sauce, blackberry pie, and ginger-spiced pumpkin. Granny served her fare with a choice of cold sweet milk, coffee with cream, or spicewood tea sweetened with molasses.

As guests and family pushed away from the table, Case patted his belly. "I do declare, Kate, if'n you ain't an expert vittle-cooker."

"Now that's the truth," Surry agreed.

"Shucks," Granny admitted. "Now I do recollect how my Monte called me the 'champeen vittle-cooker of Utah Mountain.' But that was a long time ago. I hain't nothin' like as good as I was then."

"Come on now, Maw. I believe you still git the prize," John said. Papa agreed.

After dinner, chestnuts were roasted for us children while games were played, which also included little Noble. Over and over his toes were counted in "Old William Trimble-Toe." He laughed and gurgled till he became sleepy. Surry held him all during the toe-counting, squeezing him, kissing his toes, and saying how sweet he was.

Mama was clearly uneasy. "I'll take the baby, now," she told Surry. "He's ready for his nap."

"Let me just rock him on to sleep, Rachel, whilst you and t'others sing yer songs."

Reluctantly Mama went along. "We'll sing 'The House Carpenter' then."

"Fiddle-faddle," Granny spluttered about the woman in the song who ran off with another man. "She orter been at home 'stead of galavantin' off with that tricky polecat." Granny grabbed her hearth broom and began sweeping up nutshells.

"Let's sing this'n Harve always liked," John spoke up. "It's about that 'Ole East-Bound Train.' Come on, ever'body join in:

> The east-bound train was crowded
> One cold December day,
> The conductor shouted, "Tickets,"
> in his old-fashioned way,
> In a corner sat a little girl,
> Her hair was bright as gold.
> She said, "I have no ticket,"
> And then her story told.
> "My father is in prison.
> He's lost his sight they say.
> I'm going for his pardon,
> This cold December day.
> My mother's daily sewing,
> To try and earn our bread,
> While my dear old blind father

Is in prison, almost dead.
My mother's very lonely,
And she will be so glad,
If I can only bring back
My poor dear old blind dad."
The conductor could not answer.
He could not make reply.
He could not help from wiping
A teardrop from his eye.
He said, "God bless you, little one,
Just stay right where you are.
You'll never need a ticket
While I am on this car."

Surry was crying, and I didn't know if it was for the girl in the song, for Nellie Sue, or because she wanted to keep my baby brother. But I was glad when Mama took the sleeping Noble away from her and laid him on the bed.

"That's the purtiest baby I ever did see," Surry said as Mama eased him from her arms. Surry kissed Noble's soft pink cheek.

That night in a dream, I was on a train bearing the casket of Nellie Sue Muckle. The casket lay open and someone was bending over it, someone in a conductor's uniform. He was kissing the still cold lips of Nellie Sue. He turned and looked me in the eye. It was Mr. Price, my schoolteacher. "Tickets," he said in the same way he used to call "books" after recess. I threw my ticket on the floor, when I saw it wasn't really a ticket at all. It was the flower-decked thumb-paper I'd made for Nellie Sue's grave. I picked it up and tried to run, but my legs were like lead. A scream froze in my throat.

CHAPTER 13
Hard Lessons

As usual on Monday morning, John arose at daybreak and got a fire going before heading out to the stable. Soon Granny was up, too, making breakfast preparations. She'd hardly begun to stretch thick slabs of bacon into her widest skillet when John flung the door open and yelled to France, still in the bed. "Son! Son! Git up and go fetch Jim fer me."

"What is it?" Granny asked, hands on hips, her still unbraided hair kinked around her shoulders like a tousled child's.

"Aw, Lordy, Maw. It's old Buck—he's done for. I shoulda knowed it was a-coming. 'At pore old critter's stiffer'n a board on the floor out there." He shook his head and started back out as France quickly pulled trousers on over his long johns and went to get Papa.

By the time Papa came on the run, I was dressed and standing next to Uncle John. We gazed down at the beast sprawled on the stable floor, looking larger in death than he had in life.

"Pore old Buck," John lamented. "Couldn't tell nobody how he felt."

"Well," Papa said, panting, "at least he hung on till you got the mortgage paid off." He squatted beside Buck, feeling cold mule flesh. "Deader'n a door nail." He sighed.

"Yep." John pushed the mule gently with his foot, like any minute Buck might start kicking. "Hain't been worth a tinker's damn in a long time." He pulled a bandanna from his hip pocket and blew his nose loudly. "Help me bury 'im if you're a-mind to, Jim. Hit'll take a right big hole." He blew his nose again.

"Shore, shore, least I kin do, all you've did fer me."

John exhaled loudly, folded the bandanna, and stuck it back in his pocket. "I'll git shovels and spades fer us." He mumbled as he walked to the lean-to, France on his heels.

Mama had planned for us all to walk down to Shingle Cove to pay her folks a visit before our move, but Papa told her he'd be along later—after he and John took care of their gruesome task. Granny, too, would hang around to get some mending done before our clothes were packed for the trip. "'Sides," she explained, "my Raymond's still a-coughin', got no business gittin' out."

"My maw's a-wantin' to see these young'ns onct more," Mama said, "'specially this little'n." She wrapped our necks with flannel strips, and we donned cloaks. She bundled Noble tightly in a quilt with a flap hiding his face.

"See 'Ran-ma see 'Ran-ma," Met chanted. In her leggings and heavy cloak, she looked like Tomiko, the Eskimo girl in my picture story book.

Papa and John insisted that France go with us. They wouldn't need his help. All the way to the cove, he ran ahead of me. Since turning eleven and making friends with Willie Muckle, he treated me as rudely as he did most girls. I was no longer his best friend.

At Grandma's, Mama sat rocking Noble while the two women caught up on family news. Mama's brother, Tom, was in Waynesville, having left several days earlier to look for a job. He was staying with his sister, my aunt Mary. France and I found Effie and George, my young aunt and uncle, down in the cellar—out of biting cold weather and away from boring hen talk. The cellar had always been our best place in the winter, though it made Grandma nervous. There, stored neatly on shelves, were precious Mason jars filled with her garden's bounty.

Effie and I staked out a corner where a make-believe house took shape. We pressed sticks into the earthen floor, marking walls and furniture. Effie's rag dolls were our babies, and Met was our child. Met was docile enough, always doing our bidding, but France and George refused to play fatherly roles. "Silly old girl stuff," France jeered, so we pretended they were husbands, off working or hunting. Effie and I busily prepared a meal that awaited their return.

France found a broomstick and was riding bareback. He was "an Indian brave," yelping and shooting at bears when, without warning, a large crock tumbled from its perch on the top step. "What's that?" His make-believe horse reared from the collision and fell to the ground. Something resembling dark red blood spurted from the crock and trickled down the stone steps.

"Hit's Maw's blackberry wine!" George's hand flew to his mouth.

Effie stared in disbelief. "Hit's what she uses fer bowel sickness."

Met started to bawl, and I jerked her backwards. "Hush!" I said. Mama's sensitive ears could pick up Met's cries from a hundred other sounds.

"Don't worry." France lowered his voice but seemed cocky as ever. "All we gotta do is hide the pieces." By now the wine was completely drained from the broken vessel. He picked it up and stuck it behind the corn crib, gingerly covering it with dried shucks. George took two large remaining shards and did the same. Effie and I scooped dirt to cover the small slivers.

"I gotta go wash my dirty hands," I said.

"No, wait." George took fresh clay from the floor and began spreading it over the spots. "We ain't finished. Them steps is the first thing Maw'll see." He rubbed them hard with balls of it till the stains were nearly gone. "France, you and Sippy git clean dirt fer the floor." Like worker ants, to and fro, we brought handfuls of fresh soil from the outer door, sprinkling and patting it over telltale splotches.

"See there," France said. "You cain't even tell." Proud of our teamwork, we moved outside, rinsed our hands in a rain barrel, and played hide-and-go-seek without the usual squabbles, till Grandma called us to dinner.

Furtive glances were exchanged as we filed inside. I was afraid Met would blurt something out, but at only four years of age, she instinctively knew we were all in this together. Papa arrived while we were eating, and Grandma hastily set him a place.

"Well, Jim," she said, piling his plate high with hog jowls and black-eyed peas, "so you got yerself a job." She graced him with a rare smile and sat back down. "Rachel, much as I hate to see you'ns take this here baby away, wouldn't you say this calls fer a celebration?" She patted Noble on his bottom as he nestled in Mama's lap. "Soon's we's done eatin' we'll drink us a little toast to Jim's good luck. Mind you, my blackberry wine is mainly fer medicinal use, but this is a special day."

I looked at France, and he swallowed hard. George and Effie began picking at their food, not looking up. Met kept eating, obviously unaware of what was taking place. But Mama knew me like the back of her hand. She knew something was wrong. "You'ns is mighty quiet," she said, feeling my brow.

"Children orter be seen and not heard," Grandma proclaimed like it was the eleventh commandment. Taking a piece of pone, she mopped her plate clean and popped the soaked ort into her mouth. She licked her lips, sucking them over toothless gums in a final smack. With that, she pushed her chair back, rose, and poured Papa another cup of chicory. Then she headed for the cellar.

We waited for the inevitable. Eons seemed to pass in silence till the door of the cellar finally banged closed and Grandma approached the table. The bristly stuff of her temper seethed, vented only in short, hard breaths.

Papa noticed the change. "What's the matter, Maw?"

I glanced up quickly. Her dark eyes bulged, scanning our hunkered group. They caught mine momentarily, and I ducked my head. She walked to George's chair and stood, hands on her hips.

"Well, Jim, seems my wine's all gone." She waited for a reaction. "Appears we won't be a-toastin'." George sat frozen, gazing at his half-eaten food.

"Well, now, what happened?" Papa grinned and winked at Mama. "Lots of sickness? Er you just fergit?"

"'Tain't neither." She placed a hand firmly on the shoulder of her youngest son and squeezed. "There's some right tall explainin' George here needs to do. But I'm a-waitin' till you and Rachel is gone."

Mama kept eyeing us like the mystery would unravel before she left, but with Grandma in charge, she didn't pursue it. Her suspicions seemed to grow when France and I asked to go back with her and Papa. Any other time we'd be begging to stay till dark. She frowned at me disapprovingly. "You'ns stay on, Sippy, so's yer papa and me can git some packing done. You'ns can keep Met here outta our way. This baby's trouble enough."

We fidgeted while Grandma packed dried apples, a Mason jar of pears, dried tansy root, and a baking powder can of her wintergreen salve for Mama to take on our trip to Saunook. "This here can's my special salve," she said. "Hit's fer sores, bites, achin' joints, and all sich ailments." She placed a bunch of mint with the tansy root. "Now this here mint'll make tea fer settling nervous er sick stomachs."

"Lawsey me," Mama said, "I shore thankee,

Maw. Hit'll be a big help. A body never knows when they're liable to need sich."

"Well, I'm just glad the Good Lord gimme sense enough to know how to use what he put here fer us. Now, honey, what about feverfew and poppyseed?"

Mama insisted Granny'd loaded her up with plenty of both. "I swear to Gawd, I cain't take ever'thing up there."

"Cain't be too careful, Rachel. I cain't abide the thought of them babies gittin' sick and you so fer away."

I started to think Grandma had forgotten about the wine crock. Maybe concern about our moving had mellowed her, or the anxious waiting had been punishment enough. But as soon as the door slammed behind Mama, Papa, and Noble, hugs and goodbye kisses vanished like snuffed candlelight. She turned on her heel and faced the five of us. "All right," she said, black eyes snapping, "I'm ready fer the truth. Which one broke my wine crock?"

No one said a word. Then Met started squalling like someone had taken a hickory switch to her legs.

"Hush up, Met. You'ns is too little to've broke it, but if'n you know who did, tell me now." Met dried her eyes and glared at the rest of us. She didn't know who it was.

If only I could get off as easy, I thought, but I dared not say anything. George and Effie kept staring at the floor.

"I'm a-wait'n," Grandma said. I sneaked a peek at France. His eyebrows were raised, innocent as a newborn, his eyes a blank. I tried to do the same.

"Well, I got me a sure way to find out who did it. Works ever'time." Grandma went to the fireplace and picked up her largest poker. "I'm a-goin' to stick this here poker into the fire." She punched the fire-poker into the middle of a brightly burning log. "By the time that poker gits red-hot, if the one who broke the wine crock hain't confessed, I'll toss it in the air!" She thrust her arm upward.

Startled, I jerked backward.

She paused, eyeing me suspiciously, then continued: "The red-hot poker will fall down on the head of the guilty one." She walked past each of us, studying out faces. Her cross look gone, she seemed to relish the tension.

"Huh!" France scoffed. "How can an old poker tell who's guilty?"

Grandma's eyes fairly danced. "You'll see, you'll see."

We watched the poker getting fiery red in the burning log. Soon it would be too hot to handle. I'd seen Grandma play-act many times, and she was good at it. But this time was different. I was sure she believed the poker had power to do her bidding.

She picked up one of Tom's leather gloves and slowly pulled it over her right hand. "Yes." Her voice was low, her words deliberate. "The Bible says, 'Be sure your sins will find you out.'" Carefully she retrieved the red-glowing poker from the flames and pointed it, sword-like, toward the ceiling. She mumbled gibberish, like speaking in tongues, and her body commenced shaking. Her right arm, holding the poker, began to twitch.

"Stop!" France screamed. "Stop, Grandma!" He was trembling, his face white as ashes. "I did it. I did it. I didn't mean to." He broke down sobbing, bawling like a baby.

"Why didn't you say so afore now?" Grandma gave him a stern look and quickly placed her smoking rod back on the stone hearth. "I don't punish fer somethin' you done accidentally."

"I don't know," France said, rubbing his eyes and trying to recover. "First, I didn't think you'd throw that poker. Then I's a-feared you would."

"Well, the poker done all I expected it to do. Now your paw can bring me some blackberry wine to pay back what you destroyed."

"Yes'm." France wiped his face on his flannel shirt sleeves and was quiet the rest of the day.

On the way home he walked beside me, like old times—before turning eleven. We talked about how high the creek had risen and about our leaving for Saunook, but neither of us mentioned the poker lesson.

When we got home, France told his papa he had to pay Grandma back for spilled blackberry wine, but Uncle John was in no mood to ask for explanations. Old Buck had been buried in a special spot behind the stable, and John had spent the rest of the day helping Papa make wooden boxes for our household goods.

CHAPTER 14

Saunook Mountain

Mama was in a tizzy trying to decide what to pack. With Papa it didn't seem to be a problem. "Tain't like we're movin' permanent," he said. "'Tain't a bit of use takin' nothing up there 'ceptin' dishes, pots, quilts, and warm clothes. Mr. Hoaghan done showed me how small that shanty is. Hit's got bunks, tables, chairs, a stove. When we git us a proper house, we'll come back and git what we leave."

Papa had a wallet full of greenback dollars from the sale of our cow. I'd never seen folding money before. He pulled out two bills and let me hold them. "Now George Washington and Abraham Lincoln were important men in the history of our country," he said. "That's why their pictures are on these greenbacks."

"Maybe someday Noble will git to be president, and they'll put his picture on one," I said.

"'T'won't surprise me ary bit."

After the packing was done, we stayed the night in our cabin and at sunrise headed for Granny's to await the wagon. On the path, we caught sound of a cowbell ringing. It was Cherry. She was running down the lane as fast as her legs would take her. In pursuit were two big boys.

One, lariat in hand, hollered, "She done broke away from Mr. Kingsley's pasture."

"We see'd 'er hiding 'twixt a clump of bushes in Mr. Wright's cabbage patch," the other followed up. "But afore we could catch her she done headed straight here." Red-faced, he was breathing hard.

Papa laid down his bundle and went to help round her up. Dallying now, the cow seemed confused. "Come on, Cherry-gal," Papa coaxed. "You don't b'long to us no more." He walked to her slowly. This time she didn't run. Taking the rope from the boy's hands, he placed it around Cherry's neck. She stood like a pet dog while he patted her side.

To Cherry, this was home; she wanted to be with us. I began crying, and Mama put her arm around me. Kitty-cat rubbed against my legs, trying to cheer me up. He purred when I stooped to stroke his mottled coat. "What about Kitty-cat," I asked, "and Ole Blue?" Kitty-cat didn't like France or Raymond.

When they came around, he slinked away. If cornered he hissed and spat, fur standing on end.

"Your granny'll take care of 'em," Mama promised. I wondered. Granny believed cats carried evil spirits. She tolerated them only because they were mousers. I had my doll, however; Nellie would go with me to Saunook Mountain.

Papa said nothing as Granny loaded up Mama with food and potions. Telling her goodbye was the hardest part. When the wagon finally rounded the trail's bend, we watched her waving till the cabin with its oak-scented curls of smoke disappeared from view.

When we arrived at Aunt Mary's in Waynesville, Mama's brother, Tom, was still there. He'd spent his days checking job notices in newspapers and the post office, with no luck. Aunt Mary's house on Water Street was too small to get all our stuff inside, so we piled much of it on the porch, hoping it would not rain. I slipped Nellie from her bed amongst our quilts, and we all prepared to spend the night. The following day Rance Hoaghan's wagon was to pick us up for the rest of our journey—Hazelwood and finally Saunook.

I warmed quickly to Aunt Mary, Mama's sister, mainly because she looked so much like Mama. Her hair was not as dark as her younger sister's, she was an inch or so taller, but the doe eyes were the same.

She was a widow and had a daughter named Burzilla (my middle name). "Burr" was younger than I, but older than Met. In a generous mood, I let Burr play with Nellie. I planned to listen to the grownups' conversation. Aunt Mary was mesmerizing, running on and on. She had plans to remarry and move to a farm on Richland Creek. There she'd have a larger house with an apple orchard out back. Met and I could come and visit, she said. We'd help harvest apples. It sounded exciting. Her voice droned pleasantly till Met fell asleep on our pallet bed.

Next day we made a hasty stop at Aunt Ruanna's in Hazelwood, ate a meal, said goodbyes, and were off again up the trail to Saunook. Mama greased Noble up good with ointment Aunt Ruanna provided, placed disposable rags beneath his bottom, and swaddled him tightly. He had a case of diarrhea and a rash and was fretful in Mama's arms. Mama and I rode side by side in the back of the wagon, covered with blankets. Nellie was cradled in my arms as we tossed and pitched over rocky roads and up steep inclines. At times the trail vanished completely, only to take up again past a shallow creek or beyond a pile of brush. Mr. Hoaghan's driver said little as he coaxed the horse with whip and commands. Papa hunched soberly beside him, Met wedged between his legs to steady her and keep her calm. "I want to go back home," she whined repeatedly.

When the wagon lurched to an abrupt halt on top of the mountain, we sat frozen. Before us lay a ghost town of tumbled-down huts. Weather-whitened boards protruded among the remains like dinosaur bones. Leaning lopsided against a tree was, according to Papa, a former commissary. Twisted vines now bound it to the tree in a strange fusion and were all that kept it from falling into a ravine. The only house in repair was the one we would occupy. It stood with one side wedged against the mountain, the other supported by long poles driven into the ground.

Papa jumped down from the wagon and began unloading. "We got just enough food fer two weeks," he reminded the driver. "Be sure and git back up here afore it runs out. I got my fam'ly here to worry about."

"I'll be back in two weeks with two more timber cutters," the wagoner said. "I'll bring supplies fer you then." He motioned toward the row of shanties in stages of disrepair next to ours. "Mr. Hoaghan wants you to git one of them other shacks fixed up fer the men to stay in."

Mama and I jumped down. We stomped and stretched our legs. Near the house we'd occupy was a deep ravine over which a flume was built. Water gushed through the structure like a noisy freight train. Papa led Mama over for a look, explaining how lumberjacks used the flume to send logs down the mountain. Mama listened attentively but said nothing. Papa had warned us what the campsite would be like. Still I knew Mama expected something different.

Papa appeared not to notice Mama's disappointment. He spoke cheerily. "Let's git these things on into the house."

The wagon jerked when the driver turned to head back down the trail. I felt strange, as if we'd been left at the end of the world. Mama was wanting to nurse Noble in a comfortable place, and we hurried inside.

The shanty was a single large room with no windows. Bunks were built into a wall. In the middle of the floor stood a large iron stove for both cooking and heating. Papa found some wood and got a fire going, lit a lantern, and closed the cabin door. Mama spread a quilt on one of the bunks and put the baby down to change him. I laid Nellie on another and covered her against the cold. As the room warmed, we began to make ourselves at home, brushing away cobwebs, dusting shelves, stashing dishes, unpacking clothes.

With darkness the noise of the flume's waters seemed to increase. On my bunk built into a wall, the sound was as close as the floor beneath me. I clasped Nellie and thought of Granny, France, and Raymond, Kitty-cat and Ole Blue. France would not let Ole Blue go hungry, but I worried that Granny might forget Kitty-cat.

After that first night, the flume's steady roar proved harmless enough. It no longer kept me awake. There were plenty of real dangers, according to Papa. He told us Saunook was a timbered wilderness, merging with the Balsam Mountain range of the Appalachians. Bears, panthers, and wild boars roamed these wilds. Lest we meet one of them, Met and I dared not venture out except when Papa was working nearby.

One crisp morning, I heard Papa tell Mama, "If that wagonload of groceries don't come today, we'll be a-leavin' this mountain tomorrow." Over two weeks had passed, and we could wait no longer. Our food had dwindled to a handful of dried beans, molasses, and a parcel of cornmeal. I hugged Nellie and whispered in her ear, "I hope that wagon don't come."

Before noon an ominous cloud appeared, hovering over the northeast side of the mountain. By nightfall the wind blew cold and raw. Papa built a crackling hot fire in the heater, and we went to bed early. All night long the wind whistled and roared around the shanty and sleet lashed its tin roof. In my mind I could see the little house wrenched from its shaky moorings, crashing into the cavernous ravine. Pulling the covers over my head, I thought of Granny. She would not be afraid. "Think of somethin' pleasant," she would say. "Granny," I whispered like a prayer. "Granny." On one of my Bible story cards Jesus was not afraid. "Peace, be still," he said on a storm-tossed ship, and immediately the sea became calm. I hugged Nellie tightly and pretended my bunk was a ship. Soon we'd be safely into harbor.

After what seemed hours, the howling winds subsided, the pelting sleet ceased. Even the flume's waters were muffled in an eerie stillness.

When I awoke, I watched signs of morning break through a knothole above my bunk. From tiny cracks in the mud-daubed walls, thin slats of brightness filtered down, dotting my bedcovers. Papa was up. He pulled trousers on over his long underwear, walked to the door, and turned the handle. The door would not budge. Placing his full weight against it, he rammed several times till it crunched ajar over a crusted snowdrift.

"Come 'ere, Sip," he called when he saw I was awake.

Blinding rays of sun poured through the open door, and I shielded my eyes for a look. Before us stood an ice-glazed mountain. The ground was a million sparkling diamonds. Icicles, big as church spires, surrounded the flume, and its mighty gush had slowed to a trickle. Below the falling water, evergreens bowed low, weighted by brilliant ice clusters. Above them, mighty spruces sagged with their garlands of snowballs. I shivered as Papa closed the door.

He took the remaining firewood and added it to the heater's smoldering logs. Mixing cornmeal in a pan of water on the stovetop, he heated it to a thin mush then poured on a heavy dollop of molasses. By now Mama was breast-feeding Noble, and Met was stirring beneath a heavy quilt.

Papa divided his meager meal into four portions. "Eat all you can," he said. "We gotta git down this mountain somehow, and we'll need all the strength we can git." I wasn't hungry but forced down several spoonfuls of the mush. Met refused the sticky pap, so Papa ate what was left on our plates.

"Put all the clothes on your back you can git," Papa said. I pulled on three pairs of stockings, several petticoats and dresses. Over these I donned a wool sweater Granny had knitted for cool days at school. Mama helped Met with the layers of clothing. Papa cut strips of quilt with his knife and wound them around Met's feet and legs. I snickered at how fat she looked. It made her mad, and she kicked me hard.

"You won't be a-laughin' when you're in that freezin' snow," Papa said, cutting more strips to wrap my feet and legs, then Mama's. Mama swathed Noble in yards of blanket, and placed him inside a small, heavy quilt. She strapped a leather belt around the center of the bunting. We put on our cloaks, wrapped our heads with our fascinators, and pulled on double-knitted mittens. Ready for the trek, I picked up Nellie.

"You cain't take that doll," Papa said. "When this weather lets up, we'll come back and git our things. It'll be all we can do to git ourselves down the side of this mountain."

I started to cry. Papa knew how much I loved Nellie.

"Watch out now!" he said. "Them tears is liable to freeze on yer face."

Sniffing loudly, I laughed through sobs at the thought of icicles hanging from my face. I wiped away tears with my mitten and laid Nellie gently on a bunk. As her eyes closed, I pulled the covers over her and kissed the top of her green bonnet. "I'll come back and git you," I promised.

Papa latched the door behind us, and we searched out the creek. Following its icy flow, he led the way as we slipped and slid down the crusted mountainside, grabbing frozen bushes and snow-laden trees along our descent. Papa carried Met most of the way, setting her down only when Mama's arms gave way carrying Noble or her legs buckled beneath her. Then he took the baby, and Met clung to Mama. I stayed close behind, stepping in Mama's footprints, teeth chattering, trying not to cry.

After a while my feet became numb. I felt tired and very sleepy. Beside an ice-caked tree I stopped and lay down. Papa looked back and saw me. He sat Met on a tree stump, came and picked me up. "I'm so tired, Papa. Just let me sleep a little while."

He carried me to a rocky ledge and set me on my feet. "Stamp them feet," he told me. "Clap them hands." I clapped and stamped till my hands and feet were prickly, and he said we were ready to move on. He tied Noble to his back and took Met in his arms.

Miles later, we reached a valley. The sun was setting, casting long, dark shadows over the gorge's brilliant incline. Ahead was a cluster of farmhouses, snow-laden fences zigzagging. Here the snow was softer, etched with scatterings of sleigh tracks.

"We'll be all right, now, honey," Papa told Mama.

Her face was splotchy, and her nose was running. She nodded but didn't reply.

As we approached the first house, we smelled bread baking. I thought of Grandma's wheatbread she made for special days. I was hungry, but my legs were like logs, and I could hardly move one in front of the other. Attached to the house was a blacksmith shop, and Papa said we'd stop there. He knocked at the door. A grizzled man opened up, peering at us curiously.

"Can we git ourselves warm by yer fire?" Papa asked.

The smith scratched his head. "Shore, shore." He let us in. We stamped our feet and began taking off layers of wet leggings.

With a crusty hand he brushed grit from a bench and motioned for Mama to sit down. "Mighty bad weather to be out with yer family." He looked at Papa.

"Had to er go hungry," Papa replied. "We been on top of that there mountain, a-waitin' fer a man name of Hoaghan, Rance Hoaghan. Know'im?"

The man raised his brows. "Well now, you'd a-fiddled out waitin' fer that feller. He's done gone 'way from these parts. Law's after him." He pointed a grimy finger toward a crumpled newspaper by his coal bin. "Just read 'bout him in the *Asheville Citizen*. Been accused of fraud, 'bezzlement, and the like."

"Is that so?" Papa rubbed his palms together before the open fire. "I reckon sometimes a man learns the hard way who 'e can trust." He shook his head disgustedly. "I expect I done learned a good deal on top of that mountain."

The smith gave us a snack of cheese and freshly baked bread. He arranged for a wagon to take us to Waynesville. Mama was feeling bad, and a bed of quilts was made for her in the back of the wagon. She fainted dead away when we got to Aunt Mary's house, and her sister took charge like I'd seen Grandma do so many times.

"Don't worry none about this baby," she told Papa. "He'll be just fine." She bought Noble a bottle and gave him cow's milk to drink. At first he spit the nipple out, crying and heaving, but soon began to drink every drop, "like a good little boy."

Aunt Mary was so attentive to Mama and Noble that Papa began to leave and be gone all day looking for work. If I were ready and begged hard enough, he would take me along. We'd head out in early morning and go to his brother's house to borrow Harve's horse and wagon. I endured the boredom of job-hunting because we always ended up at the railroad station.

Located in the heart of Waynesville, the depot was a splendid place, a crossroads where modern locomotives brought travel and trade into mountain wilderness. Passenger trains chugged in and out of the bustling station, rumbling, hissing, spewing like steel dragons. For an eight-year-old like me, this was where fantasies played out—in the parade of those who rode the silver tracks. Most were tourists. Easy to spot in their finery, they came from points north and south to revel in the beauty and experience the mountain climate. Women in billowy skirts, clutching large hats, and men in pinstriped suits with pistol-legged trousers descended to the wooden platform from plush coaches, preening, stretching, breathing deeply of the crisp mountain air.

Even Papa stopped to gawk. "That's how rich folks look," he said, not in envy but matter-of-factly. Sometimes children were in tow, with white middy blouses and curls, long stockings, and shiny patent shoes. Nannies and servants and redcaps rushed to accommodate, grasping small hands, pushing carriages, lugging carpet bags, or hoisting belted trunks onto dollies.

Papa had told me about black people, but I had never seen one and could not imagine such. He said to be patient and keep watching. I might be lucky enough to spot one among the liveried servants. "Now, don't stare," he warned. "'Tain't polite to stare. Just kinda look out the corner of yer eye." Their skin was black, he explained, their hair kinky, and their lips "thick and poking out." They had flat heads, so heavy objects could be carried on top. "Most curious of all," he said, "is inside their hands and bottoms of their feet—*pinker'n mine!*" It seemed incredible that God made them black but gave them white palms.

When I spotted one—tall, stately, her head bound with a colorful scarf, I edged toward the small entourage of family and servants. She looked ten feet tall, balancing a white bundle on her head. Steadying the load with one hand, she followed a matronly woman into the station house. I tagged a safe distance behind, trying, without success, to glimpse the palms of her hands.

Papa said there were scouters among the passengers, hiring workers. They stayed at local hotels while filling job quotas from among those, like him, who checked the listings daily on the depot bulletin board. He talked to one of them a long time, only to learn the best jobs were for cotton mill work "way south, more'n a hundred miles away." Some of the men signed up, but Papa walked away, shaking his head. He figured Mama would never be willing to move that far away.

"That's where the jobs are," I heard him tell her later, back at Aunt Mary's. "Ain't nothing at all 'round here." Mama had been sick for a week and was feeling better. But not Papa. He seemed more depressed with each passing day. His greenbacks from the sale of our cow were almost gone. Our household goods, along with my doll, Nellie, were still atop Saunook Mountain with chances of going back for them growing slimmer. Papa was so blue that I did not mention his promise to go back for my doll. My cousin, Burzilla, had two dolls, and she let Met and me play with them. Neither were pretty like Nellie. I cried for her, but only at night when no one else knew.

Aunt Mary bought cow's liver and cooked it rare, braising it lightly on both sides. "Rachel, honey, eat this liver," she told Mama. "A nurse told me it'll build up your blood."

Watching Mama drink blood that trickled from the meat made me queasy, and I had to leave the table. At hog-killing time, Granny served pork liver and I ate it, but Granny cooked it well-done with lots of brown gravy and onions.

Aunt Mary made squaw vine tea for Mama to drink at bedtime, a sedative learned from her mother. "It'll soothe them insides," she said, using Grandma's very words. As Mama sipped the potent brew, her sister rocked Noble to sleep. "I do hate to see you take this'n away," she said, kissing the baby's cheek. "Sweetest little feller God ever made."

Like Papa, Tom, Mama's brother, had about given up finding a job. Caleb Kingsley wanted Tom out of Shingle Cove and time was running out. Yet, going far south or east meant uprooting Grandma from the cove where she'd lived for forty years, ever since Grandpa brought her there as his bride. It would not be easy. Loading the wagon for our return trip to Utah Mountain, Tom spat tobacco juice hard onto the red clay soil, looking disgusted and saying little.

On our way, as mile after mile stretched between them and job prospects, Papa and John rumbled along on the wagon seat, chewing and spitting. They spoke hardly at all. But nothing could dampen Mama's eagerness to get back to our little cabin next to Granny's. That's where our good times had always been, where she felt secure.

"You'ns will find work soon," Mama said, trying to brighten the mood. It was more balm than reality. But I basked in her high spirits, leaning against her shoulder as we jostled along. She hugged Noble tightly in his warm bunting.

"Let me see 'im." I peeked under the blanket flap. Noble was sleeping soundly, his cherubic face serene. *Babies don't worry,* I thought. I did, though, especially now. Since our stay at Aunt Mary's, fear nagged in my breast. *My Mama could get sick.* What would Papa and I do if she got *very* sick? The best thing to do was keep her well, but I wondered how.

With each bend of the road, I pictured France and Raymond and Granny not far beyond. Ole Blue and Kitty-cat, too. More loyal than the truest friend, Ole Blue would be there barking a hearty welcome when we rounded the creek's bend. I wasn't so sure about Kitty-cat. Sensing Granny's dislike for cats, he may have left for friendlier quarters.

At the Settlement we passed the two-story farmhouse where France and I had rested during the storm. The buxom woman, in a yellow apron, was sweeping the steps. She paused to wave and Mama waved back. A sweet incense of oak-scented smoke rose in gentle puffs above the stone chimney. In my mind, I visualized a table with real china plates, waiting for the ladling of piping-hot food from her kitchen. My empty stomach growled.

"Someday I'll have me a house like that," I told Mama. France had made fun when I said that to him, but Mama patted my hand.

"Shore you will, Sippy honey. Someday when you're a big girl."

"I'm going to marry a bossman. You and Papa can come to visit and stay as long as you want."

We were approaching Jonathan's Creek Crossing on the macadamized road. The wagon lurched as Tom's mule clomped over the wooden bridge. Mama could contain herself no longer. She broke into song:

> "Mid pleasures and palaces though
> We may roam
> Be it ever so humble, there's no
> place like home.
> Home, home, home, sweet, sweet home.
> Be it ever so humble, there's no
> place like home."

After Papa told Granny about our Saunook Mountain experience and what the blacksmith had said about Rance Hoaghan's trouble with the law, he confessed something else, something he'd been afraid to mention at the time. "It's about Letty Kingsley, er Letty *Hoaghan*," he said. "'Member how she came home to 'er maw, and we said it weren't natural, a woman oughta be with her man? Well, on that wagon ride back from the train station, I saw lots—a black eye, Letty's wrist in a sling. Her brother, Caleb, said Rance near 'bout beat 'er to death. I's afraid to tell Rachel."

"Well, maybe you orter have," Granny said. "Maybe Rachel would of stayed home."

CHAPTER 15

Greenville Bound

One March morning when the weather warmed spring-like, Papa sat gazing out the doorway where he could see the trail leading to the Settlement. Though we seldom had visitors, he seemed to expect something or someone. A man was coming up the hill, almost at a gallop. It was Uncle Tom, holding a white paper high, waving it like a flag. There was no doubt it was something important. It was a letter from Alex, Tom and Mama's brother, who worked at the depot in Asheville.

There Alex had noticed a flood of job postings for mill hands to work in Gastonia and Greenville, South Carolina. He'd talked with an agent who was hiring for Greenville. The news was good. Mills there provided houses for those hired. Employees could draw an advance to purchase furniture and other necessities. "Mill workers eat wheat bread every day if they want it," the letter stated, "and fresh meat on weekends. All employees can get credit at the company store."

The "super" of the mill emphasized a hiring limit—only the first to come would be assured of a job. Alex underlined the words, "Let me know right away," and enclosed greenback dollars as a loan. "Pay me back when you start earning wages," he wrote.

Tom was breathless with excitement. "I'm a-goin'. Praise Gawd, I'm a-goin'—me and Maw, George, and Effie. Go on, take these here greenbacks, Jim. I don't need 'em. Caleb Kingsley's done said he'd buy my stock and help me git moved. Said I could use the mule right up till the day I leave."

Papa wasn't "rarin' to go" like Tom. He had Mama and Noble to worry about, he explained, and Met and me. Still this was the best opportunity he'd been offered. I'd watched my papa worry about making a living on the mountain, and though I hated to leave, I knew we had little choice. So did Mama. Papa didn't like owing money, not even to his own brother-in-law, but he took it anyway, folding it slowly into his wallet.

Papa made wooden crates for the few items we'd accumulated since leaving everything on Saunook. Granny'd given us heavy quilts and two of her prized iron skillets. She'd passed on coats and sweaters France and Raymond had outgrown. The things I loved most would not be making the trip—my doll, Nellie, who was still on Saunook, and Kitty-cat and Ole Blue. They would again be left in the charge of Granny, and I didn't feel as bad about it this time. One day I caught Granny, the cat-hater, reaching down to stroke Kitty-cat's warm coat as he purred and rubbed against her black calico skirt. Noticing my surprised look, she pushed him aside with her foot.

"Git outten my way, Kitty-cat, afore ye git stepped on," she said. But I was not fooled. While denying any love for "critters," Granny had betrayed a soft spot for my pet.

We spent the night before our departure at Granny's. Firmly convinced that only *her* knowledge of herbal cures had brought us through our illnesses, she worried about Mama's health. "You'ns is going where I cain't be nigh to help," she told Mama, wagging her head resignedly, "so I've bundled up tea makin's fer ye." On her sideboard, bunches of mountain herbs were stacked in neat rows.

"This here tied with red string is bloodroot," she stated. "Hit's what you've took ever since Noble was born. Keep on takin' it fer a while. Now, this here with yellow string is Joe-Pye weed." She sniffed it as if checking the strength. "You know what it's fer."

Mama looked puzzled.

"You done tuck it all yer life, honey—hit's fer fever." She picked up a cluster of dried leaves with small white flowers. "This boneset, tied with blue, is fer grippe, colds, and the like. Now this here big snuff box is full of poppyseed." She opened it, peered inside, and closed it tightly. "'Spite of how you feel 'bout giving young'ns poppy-seed tea, when that pore baby's belly aches and he cain't sleep, hit's the best thing in the world." With a masterful air she placed it beside the dried herbs. "This here *little* snuff box has Jerusalem-oak seed. They's fer belly worms in young'ns." She glanced at me. "Ef one gits worms in their bowels, cook these seeds in a bit of water and some sorta sweetener—I use molasses. Give ever which one a spoonful er two, and they'll pass the worms. Hit may make'em sick on their stomachs. Ef it does, give 'em a sip er two of cold mint tea." She placed a packet of dried mint tied with green ribbon with the other items.

"Now this bakin' powder can is full of my special salve. Hit's fer sores of any kind, and hit's fer sore joints and aching joints. Hit's also fer headache er toothache, if it's rubbed on the head er jaw at bedtime."

Mama looked overwhelmed. "Lawsey, Maw, I shore thankee fer all this medicine."

"Well, just don't fergit how I told you to use 'em."

Next morning Granny was up like a jack-in-the-box when her clock struck four. She made a quick breakfast of cornmeal mush and milk. Papa and John were soon out loading our stuff on a big sled with heavy split-log runners, used mostly for hauling firewood. When fully packed, they hitched Tom's mule to the rig, and Uncle John stood with a foot on each runner as it slowly descended the steep hill. Mama followed, Noble in her arms. Met and I walked behind, sheep-fashioned. I carried a small bucket of butter Granny insisted on sending for breakfast at Grandma's.

When the trail became rough or gully-filled, Papa grabbed hold of one side of the sled to balance the load. As we approached Shingle Cove, we saw Caleb Kingsley's large dray with its team of two already partially filled with Grandma's possessions. Papa and Uncle John began transferring our boxes and bundles from the sled to the wagon till everything was secured for the next day's departure. Only a few quilts were kept out to use for pallets that night. John bade goodbyes all around then headed back to Granny's. He'd take care of delivering Tom's mule to Caleb Kingsley.

It was black as midnight outside when Mama got me up the next morning. Tom had a hot fire blazing in the fireplace and a steaming tub of soapy water stood in the middle of the floor. In a matter of minutes, Mama had Met and me in and out of the tub, scrubbed clean as whistles. We ate a breakfast of ash cake (cornpone cooked in hot ashes). The warm crust was peeled away, and it was spread generously with Granny's butter.

Met and I donned our red-striped galatea dresses and pulled on new black stockings. I knotted mine above the knee with string like Mama wore hers and laced up my shiny high-top shoes. Papa tied the laces in a bow. Mama combed tangles from my curly hair and plaited it into two braids. She tied the ends with strips of galatea. Then she did the same with Met's.

Papa beamed at us. "I swear by the saints above if these ain't the purtiest gals I ever did see." Full of excitement, we ran outside to be the first ones on the wagon.

Chilling gusts of March winds ballooned our dresses as, giggling, we climbed aboard only to have Mama shout from the cabin door: "Git outten that wagon." Papa and Tom needed to adjust the load and strap everything down before we could board. Quilts were placed at strategic points for bolstering and draped over boxes for sitting. Papa and Tom jumped onto the seat with Caleb Kingsley's driver, and the rest of us climbed in back. Met and I encased ourselves in quilts against the frosty morning's bite. We swayed as the yoked horses struggled over rocks, gullies, and tree roots, till we reached the familiar creek at the foot of the mountain. There the driver paused to let the animals take a long draft of clear water.

I peeked over my cover at the two-story farmhouse. Smoke was rising from the chimney, but the woman was nowhere in sight. I wondered if she were baking wheat-bread for her family's breakfast. They'd be gathered around a large table set with fine white linen and real china plates.

The sun was up and bright by the time we passed the Settlement on the macadamized road leading to town. The gravelly rhythm of the wagon wheels and the steady beat of hooves lulled me. I fell asleep, waking only when we reached the outskirts of Waynesville.

At Aunt Mary's we piled out, and she came running to greet us. She took Noble from Mama's arms and kissed him from head to toe. Papa and Tom and the driver rode on to the depot with our baggage. It was hours till the train time, so Mary insisted we rest and have something to eat.

Effie, Met, and I went out to play in the backyard with our cousin, Burr. The tiny yard, identical in size to others stretching one after another behind the row of small unpainted houses, made me think of ones Effie and I drew on the cellar floor when we played house at Grandma's. Toilets, one for every two houses, hugged a creek bank, and clotheslines filled with white linens stretched from house to privy.

Aunt Mary told us the clothing, fluttering in the wind like mischievous ghosts, belonged to wealthy townspeople who hired women here on Water Street to do their washing and ironing.

Past the creek, above the trees, I could see the smoky outline of Utah Mountain. I pictured Granny as she'd looked waving from her cabin door and hoped she remembered to feed Kitty-cat.

It was late afternoon when Papa announced it was time to leave. Grandma gave Aunt Mary the quilts we'd brought. They were too bulky to take aboard the train, and the ride to the railroad station was a short one. We found places to sit in the wagon.

"Let me take one more look at this precious feller," Aunt Mary said. She took Noble from Mama and kissed his face. He was wearing a petticoat of flannel outing and a long dress of red dotted calico. The red and white wool cap Granny had knitted for him was tied with a bow beneath his chubby chin. "He won't never look the same when I see him again." Aunt Mary's voice broke. She sniffed hard and handed him back to her sister when Mama was seated in the wagon.

As we pulled away, Mary took from her apron pocket a large handkerchief and wiped away tears. Waving it high like a farewell banner, she trailed our wagon till we turned the corner into the street that led to the depot.

"Chestnuts, chinquapins, five cents a string; chestnuts, chinquapins, five cents a string." The familiar chant caught my ears, and I turned to see a ragamuffin, my age, garlands of the tasty nuts draped over his arms. We were the objects of his pitch. Once my fantasy world, now the station house buzzed with reality. *We* would mount the steel dragon. *We* would travel the magic tracks. The thought of it made me giddy.

"*Asheville Citizen, Asheville Citizen!* Git yer paper right here. *Asheville Citizen!*"

Papa stopped to buy a copy. And today's chronicle was not day-old or discarded as in times past. My papa kept up with the news. He had an air about him that made me proud. Were it not for ill-fitting clothing and makeshift luggage, he could've been an aristocrat like those he and I had observed on our job-hunting trips. Papa'd studied their habits and had their mannerisms "down pat." Some he'd adopted as his own—clearing his throat to command attention, conversing easily with strangers, walking ramrod straight, head held high.

"Shine, mister? Only a nickel." The boy snapped his polishing cloth to let Papa know he was a pro.

Papa glanced at his dusty new shoes. "No, son, not today." Barely missing a step, he wiped the toes of his shoes on the backs of his trouser legs.

Stale chewing tobacco curdled with discarded orange peel in shiny brass spittoons. Boot black and shoe wax blended with cigarette and pipe smoke that swirled above clustered businessmen, the mingled odors stinging my nostrils. Papa herded us toward the ticket office. He knew this station like the back of his hand, so Tom let him lead the way. The rest followed single file, lugging our bundles. Mama found a bench and settled down with Noble on her lap. She draped a light blanket over his head and her bosom as he nursed. Panting, Grandma dropped beside her and pulled Met up, while Effie hovered, afraid to venture far. Not so, George.

Restless, he wanted to explore, and I tagged behind. He strolled the aisles checking out everything in sight—bulletin board messages, railway maps, racks of penny postcards and souvenirs. "Lookee here, Sip," he said, rubbing a lucky rabbit's foot across his cheek. "'Twern't so lucky fer the rabbit." He laughed and hung it back with the others. I caught Papa glaring our way with his special frown, the one he used when children were getting out of line. I went and stood with him until departure time.

Soon the Asheville-bound chugged into the station, and people spilled out to the wooden platform. Some looked to be seasoned travelers. Others, like us, came from nearby coves and mountainsides, marked as greenhorns by our dress, conversation, and baggage.

"All aboard!" the conductor yelled, and the great locomotive groaned and spat as if in dread of the rugged journey. Steam belched from her belly while we cautiously mounted steel steps and entered passenger coaches.

Grandma hied to the nearest seat and jerked me down beside her. She placed her homespun bag between her feet. "Just lookee here, Selena," she said, rubbing leathery fingers over plush red velvet. "Softer'n biddy down." Heaving a sigh, she settled back comfortably.

I sat on the edge of my seat, unable to relax, as the train's engine released steam with a loud *whoosh!* And we lurched forward, nearly toppling me to the floor.

"Better sit back, gal," Grandma warned. "We got a fer piece to go." I slid back, pressing my face to the window as "Waynesville," in block letters, passed from view. Houses inched by, curtains parted. Wisps of smoke circled above stone chimneys. People paused to wave. A factory clattered past, then trees, faster and faster. The train's whistle shrieked a startling clarion and I clutched Grandma.

She sniggered excitedly and wiped away snuff juice that trickled from a corner of her mouth.

"I ain't never heard it up close before," I said.

"That's the train a-talkin', Sippy. It's a-sayin', 'Git outta my way, git outta my way, git outta my way, ever'thing.' Them cows and pigs better skedaddle else they'll throwed from the tracks, *ka-plamm*." She sliced the air like a cowcatcher.

We sped past a row of shacks and on through Holcomb's Cut. Here and there russet hills were splotched with stretches of unmelted snow. I caught sight of a snow-capped peak. "Ain't that Saunook?" I asked.

Grandma squinted dark eyes for a better view. "I expect it is."

"My Nellie's still up there. I wish she was here." I fought back tears that burned behind my eyes. Grandma would think I was too big to cry over a lost doll. Papa'd told Aunt Mary we'd come back someday. Maybe then he'd buy a wagon and team, and we'd all drive up to Saunook, get Nellie and our things. He might even buy me a pony and cart, like the children's who lived in the two-story house. I'd drive, while Met rode beside me with Nellie and Kitty-cat. Ole Blue'd tag along, yelping like a brand-new puppy.

We picked up speed, and the clickety-clack whirred into rhythmic beat like pelting rain on a tin roof. Smoke billowed past, filtering through windows, sharp and offensive. I settled on the padded seat, my eyes fixed on the mountainous skyline, and wondered what Greenville would be like. It was big, Papa'd said, with cotton mills and stores and lots of houses. I pictured Met and me on the porch of a two-story dwelling like the one at the Settlement. We'd look so pretty in dresses of ruffled lace.

Darkness engulfed us. We were passing through a tunnel, and only the coach's dim lamps flickered assurance we hadn't gone blind. I blinked my eyes, searching for objects. As suddenly, we plunged back to brilliant sunlight.

"The light hurts my eyes," I complained, rubbing them hard.

"Close 'em," Grandma said. As she spoke, something surged in the pit of my stomach, souring my jaws like the bite of a briny pickle. My tongue grew thick and cottony. I clutched my stomach with both hands and looked across at Papa. Unlike Mama, Papa never got upset over illness.

"I'm sick, Papa," I said. I felt I'd die if the train kept moving. I wanted it to stop and let me off.

"Are ye goin' to vomit?" he asked.

I could only moan.

"Just put your head down in yer grandma's lap and don't look out that window no more," Papa said. "Lookee here at Noble. He likes the train, but then he ain't a-lookin out the window."

Grandma reached beneath the seat and pulled out her carpetbag then rummaged till she found a tiny cloth pouch and placed it beneath my nose. The sharpness stung my nostrils and eyes. Gasping for breath, I pushed it away.

"At'll fix ye fer now," Grandma said. She took a dried leaf from an old snuff box. "Now put this on yer tongue, but don't swaller it." I did as she said, laying my head in her lap. Soon the clickety-clack trailed to hazy numbness.

I woke to a din of people milling about, preparing for the train's arrival. Papa stood in the aisle with his hat on, pulling baggage from an overhead rack. Dazed, but not wanting to be left behind, I jumped up just as the train lurched, throwing me into Grandma's lap. "Fer heaven's sake, sit back down, Sippy," she said. "The train ain't stopped yet. I'll see you and me git off all right." We kept our seats till the train chugged to a halt beneath a vestibule.

Leaving Grandma behind, I followed close on Papa's heels to a large dome-shaped building. "Is this the cotton mill?" I asked.

"This is Asheville depot, honey," he replied. "We still got us a long ways to go. Here we'll catch a train that'll take us right to Greenville, South Carolina. That's where the cotton mill is." He glanced back at Mama alighting to the platform, little Noble in her arms. The baby'd slept through most of the train ride. Mama looked haggard, and I thought of my pledge to keep her well. I waited till she caught up to me.

We passed through revolving doors to a vast rotunda. Like *Alice in Wonderland* in my picture storybook, I felt as if I'd stepped into another world, one where everyone was hurrying to be someplace else. Passengers rushed to and fro, up massive staircases to elevated platforms and down them to canyon-like corridors. Trains huffed and clanged just beyond, restless giants of steel, impatient to be on their way. Above the din, loudspeakers reverberated in fearsome cacophony, and porters shouted through megaphones. Met became frightened and started to cry. I pulled her to me, and we clung to Mama's skirts.

"Mr. James Wright, come to baggage check; Mr. James Wright, to baggage check." Startled, Papa looked above the crowd at the loudspeaker as his name echoed through the enormous hall. Then he grinned broadly and nudged Tom.

"That dang Alex," he said, speaking of Tom and Mama's brother, who worked at the station, "having me paged." He and Tom started toward the baggage hub, but Alex had spotted us and was heading our way. He grabbed their extended hands then embraced Grandma and Mama in a bear hug.

Loulie was sorry she couldn't come, he told us. She was home expecting their firstborn any day. "Else she'd sure be here," he vowed. "She wouldn't miss these young'ns." Mama pulled off Noble's cap, so Alex could take a look at his crop of reddish hair. Alex wagged his head approvingly. "Well, he might have Jim's hair all right, but he looks like a Robinson to me." He winked at Grandma. "And just looka here." He examined us children one at at time, placing a hand on our heads. "I can't believe how they've grown."

Papa asked Alex when the next train was due going south to Greenville.

"Not till noon tomorrow," he said. "Wish you could all stay the night with us."

"Too dang many," Papa said. "We'll just git rooms close by." Papa found a row of seats where we could all sit together, then he, Tom, and Alex left to find us lodgings for the night. Soon they were back bearing mesh bags of fruit. Papa held some out we'd never seen before—yellow with black spots, on a stalk. He said there were enough *bananas* for each of us to have one. He peeled one partially and held it out for me.

"Take a big bite, Sippy. This fruit come all the way up from South America. It's like God hisself wrapped it up fer yer lunch, and all you have to do is unwrap it and eat it."

It smelled a little like Granny's corn liquor, sweet and fermenty. I took a bite, heaved, and ran to the nearest spittoon to spit it out. Papa laughed.

Mama ate hers slowly, breaking off a section for Met. "'Tain't so bad, Sippy," she said. Met seemed to like it, but Papa produced a big fat orange for me.

Alex returned to his work, and we headed for a small inn near the depot where we'd spend the night. When we got there, a family-style supper was being served. It was late and most of the guests had eaten, except for a few, like us, who were spending the night.

Mama was concerned about our lack of table manners and warned Met and me to watch her example. She unfolded her napkin and placed it neatly in her lap. We did the same. Having eaten the fruit, most of us weren't hungry and picked at the food. But George was fifteen, growing by leaps and bounds, and his appetite was insatiable. Leaving his napkin by his plate, he launched into the food like a bear in a honey tree. He kept asking for the biscuits to be passed while Mama glared at him across the table. He appeared not to get the message. After his sixth biscuit, Papa and Tom were amused and started keeping count.

George felt justified. "They's the smallest biscuits I ever et," he said. "One bite each, but I made 'em two just fer manners." He grinned at Mama like a cat caught with a bird in its mouth. Other guests were snickering, but Mama and Grandma did not think it funny.

Baby Noble had slept through the meal but awoke as Mama and Papa went upstairs for the night. Their room had a double bed, and Noble would sleep with them as he always did. Met and I sat on the edge of their bed while Papa took Noble in his arms.

"Just look at my purty boy," he said. "First thing

you know, he'll be a-holdin' out them little hands fer me to take 'im." He placed Noble on his knee and bounced him while the baby gurgled and cooed then laughed out loud. Mama smiled as she took the pins from her hair and brushed long tresses that fell across her laced bodice.

Tom and George shared a room next to Mama and Papa's, and the rest of us were several doors down the hall in a room with double beds. Grandma sent Effie, Met, and me to bed early, but we couldn't sleep. Beds with springs were a novelty, and all we wanted to do was bounce and giggle. On hands and knees we bobbed like apples in a water barrel. Met laughed so hard she fell on the floor. With that, Grandma'd had enough and threatened us with a hairbrush thrashing if we didn't settle down. When the others got quiet, I still could not sleep. The creaking bedsprings made me feel as if I were still on the train.

Hazily I saw myself seated in a coach. Hovering in a conductor's uniform, a man stood peering into an open casket holding the body of Nellie Sue Muckle. In her long tapered fingers a white lily rested, and I wanted to place my prettiest thumbpaper there, but the conductor would not let me. He turned, scowling. It was Mr. Price, my schoolteacher. Someone was screaming, someone very familiar.

"It's Nellie Sue! Nellie Sue's dead. She's gone!" The cry broke into sobs that tore through my senses.

"Sweet Nellie Sue! Oh, she's gone." Someone else was moaning, too. A male voice. "My God. My God! He's dead!" The nightmare gave way to consciousness. Someone really *was* sobbing loudly. It was my mama!

Grandma lit a lamp quickly. Dawn was breaking, pink light filtering through white ruffled curtains as she slid into her slippers. I got up and followed as she ran down the hall to Mama's room. Papa was rocking Mama back and forth on the side of their bed, and she was crying inconsolably.

Noble was dead.

I ran to Mama, too full to hold all the anguish, and it poured out in torrents. We cried till there were no tears left. Finally, drained of emotion, Mama sat like a statue, staring at the baby—refusing to dress or eat.

The innkeeper called the coroner. Soon Alex was there, too, making arrangements for burial. Other good people, guests at the inn, offered condolences, wanting to help any way possible. They passed a hat and gave Papa the money.

Papa blamed himself that Noble had smothered as they slept. He was distraught, saying again and again how Mama noticed Noble was not breathing, how he tried to breathe life back into the tiny form to no avail. "His name was Noble Garrett Wright," he said to no one in particular. "We expected someday he'd be president." Papa dropped his head, his shoulders shaking. The tears flowed, dropping to the floor in pools. I'd never before seen my papa like that.

Mama had to be restrained when they took the baby away, but he had to be buried that morning. It took all the money Papa and Tom could scrape together to pay for a tiny coffin and plot in a strange cemetery, one we never expected to visit again.

"Don't worry about anything," Alex told Papa. "Loulie and me—we'll tend the grave, just like he was our own." Uncle Alex hugged Mama, but she stiffened. Speaking only in monosyllables, she refused to talk about the baby at all.

Our fare was paid on the train leaving at noon for Greenville, and Papa insisted we needed to be on it. "Rachel, honey, we got no choice," he said. Grandma dressed Mama and combed her hair while Mama stared fixedly at the floor. Rain was forecast when we boarded the southbound train under bleak March skies.

CHAPTER 16
Mill Town

It was late afternoon when we arrived in Greenville, South Carolina. The cotton mill scout was waiting at the depot. He told Papa and Tom their jobs would be in different mills and, while each had its own "village" of houses, they were close enough in proximity that Mama and Grandma would be able to visit. Tom awaited his instructions, and the agent took us to the office of the mill where Papa would work. There Papa received a set of house keys and a paper authorizing credit at the company store. The man then led us to a yellow four-room bungalow located behind the mill on Pelham Street. It stood bright and newly painted like a giant daffodil in a row with others. The man said the house was sturdily built, tightly sealed, and easily heated. Out back was our own privy with septic tank.

I could tell Papa was impressed. When the agent left, we went inside. Papa ran a hand over the smoothly plastered walls. "Best house we ever lived in, honey," he said to Mama. He grabbed her and hugged her tightly. While we were examining the unheated rooms, a mill company wagon pulled up to the door with loads of coal and wood. "Dang," Papa said, "if this don't beat all." Later that day, he bought furniture on credit and had it delivered.

Papa was in a good mood. He whistled as he hung framed prints of "The Blue Boy" and "Pinky" in the front room just where Mama wanted them. "Next thing on my list is dresses fer my purty little gals," he said, catching Met's eye. She clapped her hands then skipped through the four rooms and back to where he stood. Papa grabbed her, and they waltzed across the parlor's red linoleum. Met squealed, doing pirouettes and giggling till she fell dizzily to the floor. I laughed at their antics till I noticed Mama. She sat staring wistfully out the window at blackbirds sitting in a leafless tree.

That night I lay awake in the strange darkness and heard Mama's quiet sobs. Papa was telling her not to cry, things would be better now. "A new start" were the words he used. To me, new always meant something pretty. Granny had said to think of something pleasant when I couldn't sleep. I lay thinking of the new dresses Papa had promised Met and me.

Early next morning Papa went with Tom to see the superintendant of the mill about the jobs assigned to them. He learned Tom was unhappy with his place to live. There was a vast difference in the conditions of the houses in the two villages, as well as the overall appearance of the neighborhoods. Where Tom and Grandma lived, privies were old-type outhouses that had to be cleaned by a crew who came once a week with wagon, shovels, sand, and disinfectant. After the gruesome task was completed, a foul odor hung heavily in the air till it was time for it to be repeated. Paint on the outside of their dull gray house was peeling badly, and the grooved walls and ceilings inside were infested with well-entrenched bedbugs. As soon as Mama got word, she went to Grandma's to help clean.

They began by scalding walls with a mixture of kerosene and boiling water. "It's a filthy fam'ly what'd sleep here with these," Grandma said as they scoured everything in sight. "Gimme roaches over bedbugs any day. Now this treatment orter git'em both."

Papa, Tom, and George raked the yard with brooms made of dogwood branches and burned the piles. They scattered lime and sulphur beneath the house. Mama was very tired when we got home and went to bed early. By day she seemed better, but when night came, the melancholy returned. I listened as she cried herself to sleep and knew it was not just for

Noble. She was homesick, and so was I. I missed my baby brother, but I also missed Granny and France, Kitty-cat and Ole Blue. Papa heard my whimpers and came to my bed. He smoothed the covers like when I was Met's age.

"Go on to sleep now, Sippy," he said. "Think about purty things." I knew who he'd heard say that. I knew he missed Granny, too.

I pressed the pillow to my face and pictured a dress with ruffles and lace and a big sash tied in a bow. If Papa bought me one like that, I'd wear it to school. There I'd find a new friend, someone my age, someone to play hop-scotch with and giant step, someone with whom I could share secrets. Effie didn't play games anymore and had given Met her rag doll. She was twelve now and working in the mill, helping Tom and Grandma pay their debt at the company store. Effie frizzed her hair and rouged her lips and cheeks. She liked boys and had a sweetheart. The only boy I cared about was France, and he was far away.

School in Greenville was not at all like our one-room mountain school. There were rooms here for each grade and a teacher for each room. I was placed in the third grade, though in arithmetic I tested below average. My spelling was excellent, and I was a good reader.

Miss Harris was my teacher's name. She was

older than Mama, not pretty at all, and no one ever talked back to her except to say, "Yes, ma'am" or "Yes, Miss Harris." Still I liked her a lot. She made each day an adventure with stories and pictures and wonderful bulletin boards that changed with the seasons. As days warmed and grew longer, her bulletin board blossomed with flowers and birds and a pond with frogs poised on lily pads. On our windowsill, exotic plants in bright ceramic pots climbed trellises toward the sun, alongside shells she'd brought back from a vacation at Myrtle Beach. Glass jars with holes in the lids held captive insects, and we poured through our encyclopedia to find out what to feed them.

One day Miss Harris asked me to stay in during recess and handed me a box of colored chalk. "You have a talent for seeing beauty in God's creation, Selena. Will you draw us a pretty bouquet in a corner of the blackboard?"

I was nearly stunned by such a request. I was afraid to say I didn't know how to draw. Miss Harris was not someone you said "no" to. "What should I draw?" I asked timidly.

"How about pretty wildflowers, like the daisies you drew on the front of your writing tablet?" Miss Harris had noticed my clumsy flower garlands!

Erasing and starting over many times, I finally did the best I could, with black-eyed Susans and red lilies beside a yellow two-story house. Ivy trailed on an open gate, and behind it all a giant sun shone through cottony clouds. Miss Harris was pleased with my attempt. She kept the drawing on her board through arithmetic problems and sentence parsings, till school was out for summer.

Located in the last row of mill houses near a pine thicket, our house was directly in front of a slaughter pen. On certain days (and we never knew when), beef cattle and porkers were slaughtered and drawn there. All day long we'd hear bellowing and smell the blood of dying animals. One day a pig got away after being pierced through the neck. Squealing and bleeding profusely, the beast took refuge beneath our house. Met stood transfixed in our yard till Mama ran out and pulled her inside. I ran into the house screaming and hid in a wardrobe, sticking fingers in my ears to shut out the porcine shrieks.

After what seemed an eternity, Mama knocked on the wardrobe's door. "Come on out, Sippy-gal, honey. They done come and caught that pig." I came out slowly, my hands over my ears. "It's okay, gal, they done took it away." In the kitchen Met was still crying and had thrown up all over the floor.

On pretty days when the slaughterhouse was quiet, Mama liked getting outside, working in the yard. She planted marigolds, touch-me-nots, and dahlias next to the house with rose-moss in front. She and neighbor women on Pelham Street exchanged plants as seedlings were thinned, and Mama made flower beds in every available space. "You and Met stay outta my flowers," she warned. We were glad to comply. Summertime enticed us to roam red dirt paths and jump weed-snarled ditches, discovering places she knew nothing about.

Mud Creek was a splendid place, meandering close to the mill, not far past the last privy on Pelham Street. By tucking our skirts into waistbands, Met and I could ford the shallow stream. Once after a hard rain, the water was deeper than usual as I waded in. Met was fastening her skirt to follow when my feet began sinking into the creek's soft bottom.

"Wait, Met," I hollered. "Don't come in." Soon I was up to my knees and couldn't pull my foot up for another step. In my mind flashed the story I'd heard of a girl who stepped into quicksand and disappeared forever without a trace. I panicked. "Help, I need help. Go get somebody!"

It seemed hours till Met returned with some older children. Frantically I waved my arms. "Help! Help me, I'm going down fast!" They formed a line and joined hands, like in tug-of-war, reaching and pulling me from the murky water.

As we wiped our feet in tall grass before trudging home, I cautioned Met, "Don't dare tell Mama and

Papa, else they'll make us stay close to home." She didn't tell. We spent happy hours catching tadpoles and crawdads along Mud Creek's banks that summer, but never again went wading.

In Grandma's family there were three who worked in the mill—Tom, George, and Effie. Grandma kept house. Tom worked in the card room where cotton was carded into soft white rolls. "Dang noise," he complained as he sat in our parlor on a Sunday afternoon. "It's enough to wake up the dead. Ain't no kind of work fer mountain people. I done breathed so much lint I'm pure fleece-lined down to my shoe tops. Come winter, I won't need no long drawers."

George's job was simpler. He pushed boxes of full bobbins to replace empty ones as needed on the spinning frames. Soon he and Tom became accustomed to the noise, as well as the danger that lurked amid rows of whirring machinery.

But Effie was only twelve, and it was harder for her to adjust. On Sundays at Grandma's house, she and I talked about what was taking place in her life. I was a sympathetic ear. Sometimes we combed one another's hair, sometimes we quoted tongue twisters or harmonized in an old mountain ballad, like on those snowy nights in front of a fire at Shingle Cove. It was a brief respite from her daily grind.

Effie worked in the spinning room where rolls of cotton were spun into warp (or filling thread) for making cloth. Any child tall enough to reach the top of a spinning frame was considered ready to be put to work there, and some were as young as I. Prone to play or stand looking out windows and doors, they were kept in line by sharp words or curses from overseers. Bad work was often the result, or accidents, and occasionally firings. Some children became hardened to the life and mastered tending the machines. A few learned their bosses' foibles, dared calling them by first names, and discovered tricks for evading the tougher jobs.

Effie's background had not prepared her for such a system. Often she rebelled against eleven-hour stretches behind brick walls, running home crying, vowing never to return. Grandma would bring her back and make excuses to her supervisor. Hardest for her to take were the taunts of other children, those in her own circumstances, who called her a "know-nothing greenhorn" and a "mountain-hooger." While bosses looked the other way, they found sport wherever they could, and greenhorns were prime targets for fun and games. Effie related to me what happened her very first day on the job:

"You gotta clean under this spinning frame," one of her young co-workers explained. "Ain't but one way—you gotta *lift it up*." Several lent their backs, huffing and straining hard to no avail. Soon laughter commenced with back-slapping and finger pointing in derision as Effie kept pushing and pulling the stubborn machine. Only they knew it was bolted to the floor!

Another time, someone hid her jacket, fascinator, and lunch pail. She got home late, mad as a wet hen, vowing to take revenge. Next day she confronted a suspect and started a fight. The others took sides, egging them on in a face-slapping, hair-pulling exchange till the bossman came along. The incident only made matters worse. She soon learned it was best to take these things in stride, and her tormentors began backing off. Before long, Effie was playing the same pranks on others who showed up "green" to the job. My young aunt had become a different person, and I missed the innocent girl with rag dolls who used to play house with me.

In our family, Papa was the only one who worked in the mill. His job was to oil machinery, sweep floors, and sift through the debris before it was discarded. Examining the trash was the part he disliked. "Derned snuffdippers and tobacco-chewers," he complained, "ain't learned what a spittoon's fer. I swear if it ain't enough to make a feller give up the habit."

Work hours at the mill were from six o'clock in the morning until six in the evening Monday through Friday with an hour each day for "dinner." Saturday's hours were from six until eleven in the morning. Operation was then shut down till Monday.

Sundays were sweet relief for workers, a day for fresh air and recreation. Children whose weekdays were spent tending machines and breathing lint were glad to be outside regardless of the weather—playing ball, jumping rope with us more fortunate ones. Met and I had warm feelings for the gang who "rescued" me from Mud Creek. We joined them to build fabulous tree houses in a pine thicket known only to us keepers of wild imaginings. The cool woodiness could have been a Utah Mountain cove, and in a game I pretended to be back there—with Granny and France only a stone's throw away.

I remembered France and I swinging on a grapevine rope over a make-believe snake nest, flailing and screaming like we were goners for sure. Then we'd run with the wind through hay-strewn pastures on a quest for black and gold butterflies, an eye out lest a bull came from nowhere, making us hightail it to safety. Perhaps, as my rocks skimmed the mottled surface of Mud Creek, France was on Utah tossing big ones into Jonathan's frothy waters. Or might he be setting deadfall traps to catch Granny a rabbit? She'd be happy to get one, to brown and serve it with gravy. Or—could he be alone in the lean-to, sad—because he missed his very best friend?

On Sundays our family got together at Grandma's or sometimes our place, sharing the expense and preparation of a big dinner, till a friend of Tom's invited us to dine at her place. Mag was a widow who worked with Tom at the mill, and she was sweet on him. According to Mama, Mag wanted to impress us with her cooking and was fixing a fine dish called "Mulligan's stew."

"I ain't never heard of 'Mulligan's stew,'" Mama admitted, pointing out that mountain people never put vegetables and meat together in one pot. Met and I did not want to try it all, because if our mama didn't like something, we knew we wouldn't either. But Papa insisted we had to go for Tom's sake, whether or not we ate anything. Mama sent potatoes ahead of time to go in the stew, but what else it contained, we didn't know and speculated about.

"Mag's got goats in a pen," I said to Mama. "Some people eat goat meat."

"I won't eat goat meat or rat meat or snake meat," Met vowed.

"Hush up," Mama told her. "Mag's stew ain't a-goin' to hurt you none."

At Mag's we sat gazing at plates of gravy-covered lumps, taking occasional tiny bites so she wouldn't be offended. George wolfed down biscuit after biscuit, sopping them in the gravy but carefully avoiding unidentified chunks sitting exposed on his plate like greasy cockroaches. All the while Grandma apologized to Mag for George's love of a "good biscuit." Tom, however, ate his stew and asked for a second helping. When Mag offered more to Mama and Grandma, they changed the subject quickly from food to the pretty tableware it was served on.

"I didn't pay one red cent for this dinnerware," Mag boasted, making sure Tom caught the remark. "I earned every piece by getting up orders for King's Catalogue Products."

"Well, I must say you got yourself some right purty stuff," Grandma allowed.

Mama sipped her coffee from a flower-decked cup, her little finger poking out daintily, and had nothing further to say. The boring business of etiquette soon had Met nodding, and Mag insisted she lie down in her bedroom. Afterwards the women began clearing the table, and the men went into the parlor to smoke. When Met woke from the nap, her eyes were puffy and pink, her cheeks purple-splotched. Mama was stacking dishes in a cupboard. When she saw Met, she let out a scream that brought Papa from the front room. Calmly placing his pipe on Mag's metal smoke-stand, he took Met on his lap and rubbed her cheek hard with a moistened finger.

"Better git a rag and wash this young'n's face." He laughed at Met's dazed, unearthly look. What appeared to be a horrible disease was only dye from Mag's brand-new comforter. Mama was ready to leave.

Later, at Grandma's, Papa said he was "hungrier'n

a dang bear" as he hurriedly built a fire in her cook stove. Mama fixed fried fatback with milk gravy while Grandma made a batch of man-sized biscuits. They heated a pot of navy beans, and we all sat down to eat.

"I declare," Tom said when he came in and found us all eating, "you can take people out of the mountain, but you shore cain't take the mountain out of the people." So saying, he got himself a platter and took hefty portions of everything on the stove.

George poked him in the ribs when he sat down. "Well, brother, Mag must've been goin' out to slop the pigs when she learnt how to make Mulligan's stew." He laughed and took half a molasses-filled biscuit in one bite. "Still and all, I expect you better learn to like the dern stuff, if'n it kills you."

Tom glowered while George heaped his plate with more beans and another of Grandma's buttermilk biscuits.

Papa made between five and six dollars for a full week's work. From these wages, he had to pay house rent of thirty cents a week, buy groceries, which he did every Saturday afternoon, make installments at the company store for furniture and supplies bought initially, and buy wood for cooking and coal for heating. Wood was $2.25 a cord, and coal, $4.25 a ton.

The millhouses had no electricity; lamp oil was used for lighting. Water was free, and we shared a water well with three other families. There was no milk delivery service. A neighbor owned a cow, but we did not buy their milk.

"I'd rather do without than drink anything that come from *that* house," Mama said about the people whose children went unbathed and whose dogs were mangy and flea-bitten. Except for special times, Papa drank his coffee black.

We missed the fresh milk and churned butter we'd enjoyed on the mountain. There milk, butter, and other perishables were kept in a "spring box" (heavy wooden chest set over the outflow of a cool spring). Most mill town people had no way of keeping food cool in hot weather. Some with highly-paid positions owned ice boxes—too few, however, to warrant delivery service, so they traveled a good distance for their ice. Buttermilk could be kept without a cooler. Occasionally Mama bought some from a farmer peddling his wares from a wagon. It was a real treat. I thought it tasted best poured over crumbled cornbread in a bowl, like eating cereal with milk.

In Greenville we developed tastes for what, to us, were gourmet foods—bologna, potted meats, rice—as well as imported fruits—oranges, bananas (which I'd learned to like). These were expensive, and we did not have them often. Papa tried to limit our grocery bill to three dollars a week, so bread, salt pork, potatoes, beans, and cabbage were the staples of our diet. Breakfast seldom varied from fried side meat with flour gravy and boiled coffee. If biscuits were left over from Sunday dinner, which George seldom let happen, Mama split them to serve with gravy. For a sweet treat, Met and I added a smidgen of sugar to our gravy or sprinkled it inside the split biscuit to eat like a sweet roll. Candy, jelly, and preserves were foods we had only at special times such as Christmas or Easter.

Papa carried his lunch with him to work in order to have part of his meal break for resting. One day Mama decided to take him a jar of fresh buttermilk she'd just purchased from a street vendor. Met and I had never seen the inside of a cotton mill and were excited about going. Like everyone in the village, we were used to the mill's constant noises that hummed, roared, and clattered from sunup to sundown. They were as comforting as a cricket's chirp or the sing-songing of frogs in a pond. And they were the sound of security—a pay envelope on Saturday and groceries on the table.

But we were not prepared for what lay behind the brick-walled barrier. When Mama tugged open the mill's steel door, we were overwhelmed with the deafening cacophony. Met bolted and ran toward the street.

"Stop!" Mama yelled, her voice barely audible above the roar. She handed me the jar of buttermilk to hold. "Stop, Met!" She ran and grabbed her arm. A man was leaning out the window, amused at the scene. He cupped his hands and hollered something, but we couldn't make out a word. He laughed, turning away.

Mama struggled again with the heavy door and pushed Met inside where we stood frozen by the grinding roar, afraid to venture farther. A man approached, smiling, his shirt drenched with brown circles of sweat, his hair a cottony halo of dirty lint.

"Who are you looking for?" He put his ear close for Mama's response.

Goggle-eyed, Met was no longer crying.

"Mr. James Wright." Mama was yelling as loudly as she could.

"Oh, yeah—Jim," the man shouted back and turned to hunt for Papa. But Papa'd gotten the message somehow and was on his way. He threw up his hand, signaling.

Papa didn't try to talk above the noise. He got his lunch pail and herded us back outside, pointing to a spreading oak tree where we could all sit while he ate. Afterwards he wanted to take us back in the mill for a look at his workplace. This time Met was not as frightened, though she held Mama's hand tightly while Papa showed us the big looms on which wide cotton sheeting was woven. Above each machine thick leather belts circled large wheels and extended onto smaller ones. As the belt-driven wheels spun the looms to action, the floor vibrated beneath our feet.

"Watch out, Sippy-gal," Papa hollered as, getting bolder, I eased to where a worker stood tending his massive machine. "Now don't git too close. You'ns stay right here in this spot. I'll be back."

Papa walked to a cubicle that looked like a closet, went inside, and the whole little room began rising from its moorings.

Met looked at Mama. "Where's Papa?" her lips formed.

I could only watch dizzily as the floor lifted with Papa on it. Soon he was completely out of sight, the cubicle merged with the floor above us. Minutes passed. The ceiling re-opened. Papa was descending, still planted firmly on the platform. When the floors were even, Papa stepped out grinning like a mischievous boy. He came where we stood.

"What you just seen was an elevator." Papa raked a lock of linty red hair from his brow.

I was too awestruck to say much about it till that night when Papa got home. "I was a-feared that elevator would fall and kill you. What holds it up?" I asked.

"Steel cables." He explained how strong they

were. "Ten men er a ton of iron can ride one up three stories. Now that shore beats a-luggin' things up steps, don't it? One day you'll ride one, Sip—mark my words. They's a-puttin' the dang things ever'where."

"Can I ride that'n at the mill sometime?"

"You mean you ain't afraid?"

"Naw, not if you ride with me."

Tom was getting more and more unhappy with his mill job. He was also sick of Mag and the way she "chased" him. His plans were to go back to Utah Mountain and marry Florie, a girl he claimed was waiting for him. Mama was glad. She'd never like Mag, thought she was a "hussy." Mama said Florie was the "purtiest gal in the whole country," and Tom agreed. He made five dollars a week at the mill and was putting a little away each payday. The day he'd saved enough for a suit of clothes, all of us went with him to town.

A trolley line ran from near the village into the heart of Greenville, with a fare of only pennies. Riding it was a rare thrill for us. The trolley cars were covered inside, end to end, with advertisements, and part of our fun came from listening to Papa read them.

Do you have a little fairy in your home? one of them posed. A pretty little girl was pictured in a sea of soapsuds. Another said, *Please DO NOT spit on the floor. Remember the Johnstown flood.* We thought of that one later on our way home from the trolley stop when rain pelted us and red clay soil gummed our shoes like a walk through wet paint.

On our way, George claimed he, too, needed new clothes. "I'd like to get me a John B. Stetson hat and a pair of them peg-top britches," he told Grandma.

She hadn't the slightest intention of spending good money for such impractical togs. "You're old enough fer yer wants not to hurt you," she retorted.

At a mercantile store in Greenville, she pulled a pair of overalls from a stack and held them up to George for sizing. "We'll take these," she told the clerk and drew a small purse by a string from inside her bodice.

The following Monday, Tom informed his overseer it would be his last week to work. The overseer reported it, and Tom was called to the superintendent's office. There he was reminded of the hiring agreement to make them a good hand so the company would profit from his employment. They had trained him for the job, and he was still in their debt. Without a ready answer, Tom went back to his job and said nothing till later that month. On a hot Sunday afternoon in August, he left Greenville to go back to the mountains. All of us went to the depot to see him off. Effie had a bag packed and wanted to go with him.

"You cain't go, little sis. I'm sorry," Tom told her. "They ain't enough money for another ticket. Besides, you and George gotta work if'n Maw's to stay in that mill company house."

Effie bawled like a two-year-old and said she'd be coming to live with him and Florie as soon as they set up housekeeping. "I'll hitch me a ride like a hobo," she vowed. She ran from the station, heading for home, leaving George to carry her bag back. No one took her seriously, Grandma least of all.

When the rest of us got to Grandma's, Effie had locked herself in a room. She stayed there for hours, crying and threatening to kill herself.

The following morning she was having chills and fever and was unable to go to work. George told Effie's spinning room boss she was sick, and at ten o'clock the same morning, a man knocked on Grandma's door. He had a message for her to come to the mill office. Grandma sent for Mama to stay with Effie and asked me to go with her to the mill company office.

CHAPTER 17
Doomsday Warning

Grandma's head was high as we trod the dirt road on the way to the mill office. Her gray hair, intermingled with still-black strands, was combed into a tight bun at the nape of her neck, and angel-fine curls, wet with perspiration, pulled from the sides. She pursed her mouth smugly. I'd learned it was best not to talk to her when her mouth was tight like that.

She wore her black taffeta dress trimmed with white at the throat for this occasion, her Sunday dress, the one she told Mama she wanted to be buried in when the Lord saw fit to take her. I knew the taffeta dress meant the mill superintendent was close to God in importance. The ankle-length skirt swished in time with our footsteps and red dust swirled, collecting at her hemline and on tops of our shoes. She gazed straight ahead.

By the time we reached the mill, Grandma's mouth was agape, stretched tautly over her gums, and she was huffing so loudly it frightened me. "Wait here a minute, Sip." She dropped onto a bench shaded by a large willow. "I gotta git my breath." She brushed grit from her skirts and leaned back, breathing hard. All at once the mill whistle blew, shrill and startling. Workers poured from open doors. A few gathered nearby, opening lunch pails, talking loudly above the mill's clamor. They eyed us curiously. I was too small and Grandma too old to be part of their crowd.

Grandma smoothed away folds in her skirt and took me by the arm. "I'm a-ready," she said. I felt her stiffening as we made for a low brick building. Though it was well-known the neat hedge-bordered structure housed the offices of mill executives, neither Grandma nor I had been there before. I'd guessed she brought me along in case something needed to be read. Sure enough, inside, we paused in a hallway where names were engraved on brass plates above each office door.

"Read me them names, Sip," Grandma instructed. Just then a tall blonde woman in a white high-buttoned blouse emerged from one of the doors. She saw us and smiled.

"Can I help?"

"I'm looking fer Mr. Reid Kirkland," Grandma said in her most polite voice.

"His office is on your right at the end of the hall. I'm Eva Letchworth, Mr. Kirkland's secretary. May I ask who you are?"

Grandma stretched her full five feet. "I'm Nancy Robards Robinson, and this here is Selena Wright, my grandchild."

Miss Letchworth nodded. "Come with me, please, and I'll take you to Mr. Kirkland." The scent of lavender trailed her, enticingly fragrant, and I vowed one day I'd smell like that. We followed to an office at the end of the hallway where she swung wide the brass-handled door to a room opulent with leather chairs and heavily-draped windows. Our feet sank into plush carpet, like a barefoot walk in a mossy glen.

The balding man, dwarfed by a massive desk, looked benign—fluffy white sideburns above waxed mustache, his eyes, through thick glasses, small as peas. Mr. Kirkland rose slowly, gripping the mahogany desktop.

"Mr. Kirkland, this is Mrs. Nancy Robinson and her granddaughter, Selena." Miss Letchworth motioned toward us.

"Please have a seat, ladies." Mr. Kirkland dropped to his winged-back chair. He removed a tobacco pipe from a bowl and filled it slowly and precisely from a wooden humidor. Settling back comfortably, he lit the pipe. Bluish smoke spurted in quick puffs and piqued our nostrils with the scent of apples. "Now, what brings you to my office?"

Grandma jerked at the question and leaned suspiciously from her perch on the edge of a leather-bound chair. "You *told* me to come." Her voice was sharp like when she caught one of us children in a lie.

Mr. Kirkland grimaced at her belligerence. "Ah, yes." He picked up a sheet of paper and perused it. "Mrs. Robinson—Tom, George, and Effie. A four-room house at No. 128, Second Street." He squinted at something on the paper scrawled in red. "I have a report here that you son, Tom, has quit his job in the card room and no longer lives with you.

"Yes, sir." Grandma narrowed her eyes, studying his face. Above us a ceiling fan clicked softly with each revolution.

Mr. Kirkland rattled the papers and cleared his throat. "It's this way, Mrs. *ah-h* Robinson. You and I had an agreement. The agreement was that in return for occupying that four-room house, and in order to pay for furniture bought on credit at our store, *three* of your family must work in the mill."

"George is still working. Effie's out sick, but she'll be back. I'll see to it."

"I'm sorry, Mrs. Robinson. George's job does not pay enough to meet your obligation. I'm afraid I must ask you to vacate the house. There's a waiting list for our houses, you know."

Grandma sniffed loudly. "Mr. Kirkland, when we moved into that house, it was swarmin' with bedbugs, fleas, and every kinda critter. I scrubbed it with kerosene, ammonia, and lots of elbow grease. We painted. We dug up all the grass. We raked, we burned, and made that house so's a human being could live there."

"I'm really sorry." He voiced was gruff now. "I'm not here to bargain, Mrs. Robinson. You have two weeks to vacate. That's a generous amount of time." He stood up. We knew that meant we had to leave.

Grandma walked to the door then paused a moment. She looked back at Mr. Kirkland, who was already seated behind his desk. "I'm a widow woman." Her voice was shaking. "But I'm proud. You can have yer house *tomorrow*."

Mr. Kirkland did not even look up.

Outside, Grandma grabbed a handful of black skirt and hiked it for a fast getaway. "Grandma," I said, wanting desperately to ease her humiliation.

She didn't respond, just peered straight ahead, mouth open, almost at a trot.

"Grandma," I tried again, panting, "when I git married and live in my big two-story house, you can come and live with me." I'd never shared these plans with Grandma, so hastily added, "When I grow up, I'm going to marry a bossman. That's why I'll be living in a two-story house."

Only then did Grandma seem to hear. She stopped abruptly and took my arm, staring me in the eye. "Listen to me, Selena Burzilla Wright, don't *never* marry no Mr. Kirkland, else you'll not be *my* granddaughter!"

When we got to Grandma's, she headed straight to her bedside table and picked up her snuffbox. With three fingers she drew out an enormous dip, placed it inside her lower lip, and plopped into her rocker. "Huh!" she kept muttering. "Huh!" It was all she could say while rocking and spitting into an empty snuff can. "Huh!"

George completed his workday at the mill and was paid wages due. When he got home, he and Papa carried Effie on Grandma's quilt-draped rocker to a bed at our house. Mama and Grandma made hasty plans to get her out and into our house till George could find another job. They packed everything Grandma had brought from the mountains, leaving behind only the furniture she still owed for. By nightfall, Grandma, George, and Effie were living with us on Pelham Street.

The first place George looked for another job was the mill where Papa worked, but word had gotten out and they refused to hire him. While job-hunting, he made friends with a young man his age who'd heard of a cotton mill in need of workers thirty miles away. Days later the two left on foot for the mill at Spartanburg, South Carolina. Effie was recovered but still a little shaky when, in three weeks, a letter arrived from George saying he'd gotten a job and a house in Spartanburg. He was sending a wagon to fetch Grandma and Effie.

The news seemed to unsettle Mama, and she didn't want to talk about it. Still, when time came for Grandma and Effie to leave, she pitched right in to help load their belongings. Grandma sat with the driver, and Effie in back. They waved till the turn was made at the end of Pelham Street, Grandma's maple rocker, tied upside down amid stacks of bedding and bundles of clothing, arching its legs in an ominous farewell. Mama raced inside and threw herself across the bed. She was still sniffling when Papa got home. The next day her face was sallow and puffy like after Noble died. I wanted to stay home with her. "Don't you miss no school on account of me," she said. "I'll be all right."

On Sunday afternoon, Met and I begged her to hike dirt paths with us where we'd spent entrancing summer hours. I knew they'd remind her of Utah Mountain trails, the ones that zigzagged alongside Jonathan's Creek and through pastures of grazing sheep and cows. She decided to go and found it all we'd claimed.

Soon these Sunday excursions became a thing we looked forward to. Each time we roamed farther, pretending we were back where just beyond the crest of a hill Granny's cabin might appear. Kitty-cat would be perched on the top step snoozing in the sun, and Ole Blue, from her haven just beyond, would spot us and yelp a doggie "welcome home." We walked till we were bone-tired, past pokeberry bushes heavy with purple berries and past poison sumac, its leaves crimson-splashed as if painted by a mad artist. We gathered Queen Anne's lace and goldenrod to take home and arrange in green bottles.

Papa stayed home from these outings, preferring to read story-magazines, shoes doffed, feet propped up. "Young Wild West" and his sweetheart, Aretta Murdock, and their friends, "Cheyenne" Charlie and Anne, his wife, were his favorites. The tales took the four through hair-raising adventures—busting broncos and taming the west. Papa could hardly wait to finish one so he could tell it to us, play-acting the parts, a different voice for each character. He barked like a prairie dog and wailed like a coyote. When he thumped his knuckles on the wooden table, we could see horses galloping through purple sagebrush.

One Sunday, just before my ninth birthday—November 10, 1909—Mama, Marietta, and I walked through the pine thicket, past the creek, and all the way to town. The air was brisk, invigorating. Oak and sweetgum leaves were falling, spreading our path with red and gold. Ahead we heard voices and people were gathered. Some were singing, shouting, and clapping hands. Others were on their knees, praying, begging for mercy. We edged forward. High on a wooden platform stood a preacher, somber in black suit and string tie. His gravelly voice rose above the din. In his left hand he held a Bible, and with his right hand he pointed first to the open book, then to the crowd.

"Repent ye," he shouted. "The Scripture says, 'Repent ye, for the Kingdom of God is at hand! Prepare ye the way of the Lord.'" He raised the Bible high. "Judgment is come to this generation. Behold, a great star with a tail of fire will appear. That star will come from heaven and all the wicked of the earth shall perish."

"Hallelujah!" A woman's voice was piercing. "Come quickly, Lord Jesus!" The crowd joined her chant, some shouting, "Hallelujah!" some, "Amen!" Others moaned and wailed.

The preacher pointed a finger toward the sky. "Yes, that star will come with its fiery tail and sweep the entire earth." Everyone looked up as if it were happening that very instant. The voice of the prophet crescendoed. "Everything in its path will be purged with white heat. People will cry out for rocks and mountains to cover them. Oh yes, and for a cave in which to hide." He paused, now plaintive—"But there will be no hiding place.

"Get your house in order, brothers and sisters. Get it in order *right now,* for that great and certain day of judgment is upon us."

I took Mama's hand. It was icy cold and limp. Her face was ashen. "Let's go home," I begged. Met grabbed my other arm, pulling me toward the speaker. She appeared driven, trance-like. Pulling free, I jerked her by the coat.

"Stop!" I said, my teeth clenched.

Turning, she kicked me in the shin. "I don't want to die in that fire, Sippy." She spat the words like a snake spitting venom.

I winced in pain. "You won't die."

The exchange seemed to shake Mama's senses. "That's right, Met, honey. God's a *good* God. He won't let you die." Mama seemed buoyed by her own voiced assurance. Turning, she guided us through the crowd. Soon we were back at the red dirt road. A catbird's call and the soft plodding of our footsteps muffled the distant harangues of the preacher. Somewhere someone was burning leaves and the pungency piqued our nostrils with a familiar earthiness.

When we got home, Papa was fast asleep in his favorite chair, an open Wild West magazine draped across his face. "Sh-hh!" Mama whispered, and we tiptoed through the kitchen. Everything was fine again. The world was not coming to an end, not yet anyway.

"Go on out and play awhile," Mama told us, "till I git supper fixed."

I dashed ahead of Met to the full hickory tree near the pine thicket. A playful west wind teased us, ruffling our skirts as we tucked them to free our legs. I scrambled to a low branch, chattering like a squirrel, and shook it hard as I could. Brown nuts rained onto Met's head. She squealed and gathered them into her skirt.

November's early sunset sent a golden spotlight through a clump of long-leafed pines while we counted to see who had picked up the most. Then home we trudged, loads sagging against our legs.

CHAPTER 18

Nelse

Papa got his hammer to help us crack the hard nuts. We dug out the stubborn meat with hairpins, and Mama made a hickory nut cake for my birthday. But the party mood, livened by Papa's latest Pat and Mike joke, a song to the tune of "In the Shade of the Old Apple Tree," did little to boost Mama's spirits. She was still pondering the words of the preacher.

"I want us to go to vesper services in the village square," she told Papa.

Papa never went to church and was critical of those who did. "Hypocrites," he called most of them. "Holier than thou" and "self-righteous" were choice words for those who wanted to "reform" Jim Wright. But, with Mama, he was gentler, afraid her fragile feelings would be hurt.

"Why don't the three of you go, honey? I ain't one to walk no aisle and git religion."

"You don't have to walk no aisle, and you won't be out of place. They's a heap of folks goin' that ain't never darkened the church doors afore."

"And why might that be?" Papa's blue eyes twinkled. He knew why. Out of Mama's vision, he winked at me.

"It's the prophecy, plain and clear. It's what that preacher said and what ever'body's a-talkin' about. That comet's a-comin' soon, and it could be the end of the world."

"Rachel, honey, I read the newspaper. That's *Halley's Comet* they're a-talkin' about. It comes ever seventy-five years, and it's time fer it to come again. They's a scientist in Germany trackin' the thing. He says it'll come 'bout May next year."

"Whatever time it comes, the thing's fiery tail'll sweep across the world. Only God can save us from it."

Papa knew it was no use arguing with her. The ramblings of a few astronomers had made front-page news. Some claimed the comet's tail contained poisonous gas that could ignite and explode on the earth. Others speculated "the head" would hit the earth somewhere between Boston and Boise, knocking the earth from its axis and into outer darkness, far from the sun. Mama knew for a fact there were people in Greenville "comet-proofing" their homes with strips around windows and doors. More than ever she talked about how much she missed the mountains, how much safer she'd feel "back home" with Granny nearby. In her mind, the comet's imminence was a fearsome thing, and she wanted us to attend vesper services on Sundays and Wednesdays to pray with others.

She so seldom made demands on Papa that he decided to appease her and go to church. "One time cain't hurt me none," he said, though not in her presence.

Mama was right about the number of folks going to vespers. It wasn't long till every pew in the small chapel was filled and a large tent had to be put up. Bibles and hymnbooks slid from dusty hiding places and moved to prominence amid beaded purses and bright parasols. A strange mood surfaced, permeating like a benevolent disease through the village and into town. Feuding neighbors patched up grievances, mill bosses waxed a tad kinder and cleaned up their language, borrowers paid back long overdue items. The village quartet, who sang "Sweet Adeline" and "Lonesome Road" on Saturday nights, led the burgeoning congregation in "Heavenly Sunlight" and "Rock of Ages." Young people, ever-present, were caught up in a festive spirit, swaying, clapping hands, jazzing up favorite old hymns with a new beat. Papa's "one time" stretched to two, then three, and soon he looked forward to the meetings more than any of us, his old "hypocrite" and "holier that thou" pronouncements laid to rest along with choice cuss-words. In an off-guard moment, we might hear him breaking into a few bars of "The Rugged Cross" before he caught himself.

It was at a Wednesday night tent service that we met "Nelse." He was sitting closeby, grimy hat in calloused hands, head bent low like he was studying sawdust patterns that covered the red clay. No one spoke to him or seemed to know who he was, but when the preacher's voice got low-like at the end of the sermon, the shabby young man looked up. The preacher was asking all present who were unsaved to raise their hands. Nelse lifted his high.

"Come on down, brothers and sisters, all who raised your hands," the preacher implored urgently. "Come on, get right with Jesus before it's everlastingly too late."

Nelse was the first on his feet, bounding down the aisle like somebody was chasing him. He mumbled words in the preacher's ear, and they dropped to their knees, taking turns praying—so loud you could hear them above the quartet's "On Jordan's stormy banks I stand and cast a wishful eye."

When they got up, the preacher raised his hand, the music stopped, and a hush fell over the crowd.

"This sinner is Nelson Little," the preacher said, and he placed an arm around Nelse's shoulders. "He's asking God to save him tonight. Praise God and hallelujah, he's now a sinner saved by grace!"

"Hallelujah," "praise God," "amen" rose from the congregation in ripples of acceptance.

"Nelson wants to give his testimony," the preacher continued and stepped to one side. Heads craned for a better angle, and everything got quiet as a funeral.

Nelse looked first to one side, then the other. Finally he spoke. "Y'all don't know me." He twisted his greasy hat between his hands. "I'm a drifter, up from Georgia. I'm alone, ain't got no family, no money, not even a place to stay tonight." His voice broke. "But I stand in the need of your prayers. I'm asking everybody here right now to pray for me." He dropped his head low, his shoulders shook.

Here and there people were crying openly. I heard Mama sniffing. She pulled a handkerchief from her crocheted purse and dabbed her eyes. When the reverend pronounced the benediction, she spoke quietly in Papa's ear, and he got up and went to where Nelse stood near the altar. Papa shook Nelse's hand and invited him to come home with us.

"We ain't got much," Papa said, "but such as we got—a place to sleep, food on the table, you're welcome to share till you find yourself a job and a place of your own."

The following Monday Nelse went with Papa to the mill and got a job. He started paying two dollars a week board and was soon like a member of our family. With a new set of clothes and a haircut, Nelse's personality came out, sunny as May and full of humor—and catching. There was a noticeable change in Mama. Talk of Halley's Comet seemed not to bother her at all. She sang the old mountain songs while she cleaned, and laughed a lot. Nelse and Papa were "like two peas in a pod," she claimed. Both were avid readers of Wild West stories. Both loved politics almost as much as they did Mama's cooking, which got better and better with the extra money Nelse contributed. She clipped recipes, tried fancy dishes, even Mulligan's stew (now that she knew what was in it).

"Just don't fix no chit'lin's," Papa cautioned. Both he and Nelse hated chitterlings, "dressed-up dudes" who spent their hard-earned cash on clothes, and howling dogs. "One night, Nelse and me's going gunning fer them dang dogs what robs a body of sleep ever' night." Nelse laughed at all of Papa's brash remarks. Papa was so flattered, he dredged up every story he could think of about Pat and Mike, the dumb Irishmen. No matter how many times he heard them, Nelse laughed just as hard.

Nelse became a big brother to Met and me, bringing us chocolate candy or peppermint sticks every payday, or some goody we'd never heard of. We fought over who'd fetch his shoes, his magazine, or get him a dipper of cool water. "Watch out now, pretty sisters. I'm a-mind to marry one of you someday when you're all growed up, but I cain't make up my mind which." The teasing made us work even harder to please him. I was nine now and Marietta not yet five, but we knew Nelse was handsome. His wavy blonde hair and blue eyes had caught the attention of all the girls at the mill, according to Papa.

"Papa, when I git big, I'm goin' to marry a man just like Nelse," I declared one day.

Papa chuckled, crinkling freckles that covered his nose. "Well, now, what about that 'bossman' you're supposed to marry and that 'two-story house' you'll live in?"

"My bossman husband'll be like Nelse."

Papa wagged his head. "I expect there'll be lots o'water over the dam 'twixt now and then."

On Sundays, Mama took Met and me to Sunday school. Nine- and ten-year-olds sat in a circle, and the teacher asked us to raise our hands if we had a prayer request. A girl raised her hand and said her mother was sick. The somber mood made me think of Nellie, my doll we'd left on Saunook Mountain in the snow and ice, the doll I'd cried about many times. My hand crept up.

"What's your request, Selena?" the teacher asked.

"It's for Nellie. I want God to send someone to get her and look after her."

"Is Nellie your sister?"

"No, ma'am. Nellie's my doll I had to leave in North Carolina."

Two boys beside me started snickering, and I wished I could take back my words.

The teacher did not think it funny. She stared at the boys very hard till they finally dropped their heads. Then she said, "I'm glad you reminded us that God cares about everything, Selena. He who notes the sparrow's fall loves each of us. He wants us to be happy." She prayed, naming all the things we'd talked about. She asked God to send someone to find Nellie, someone who would love her as I had.

Papa had not played his fiddle for months, but with Nelse around, the period following supper became fun time with games or riddles or singing songs. He got out his fiddle, blew the dust off, and plucked out some of his favorites.

Mama wanted to sing. "The good Lord's blessed us so much," she said. "We got ever'thing a body could ask for and more. This here song's about a little girl who had no home or food."

> "No home, no home," said a little girl.
> At the door of a rich man's hall.

> As she, trembling, stood on the marble step,
> And leaned on the polished wall.
> "My father, alas, I never knew,"
> And her tears did fall so bright,
> "My mother sleeps in a new-made grave,
> 'Tis an orphan that begs tonight."

I blinked back tears as Mama sang in a quivering voice. Met didn't like the song. She had climbed into Mama's lap and kept trying to put her hand over her mouth.

> The night was dark, and the snow did fall,
> But the rich man closed his door,
> His proud lip curled as he scornfully said,
> "No room, no bread, for the poor."
> The morning dawned and the little girl,
> Still lay at the rich man's door,
> But her soul had fled to that home above,
> Where there's room and bread for the poor.

"We got bread, we got a house," Met announced when the song was over.

Mama hugged her. "Shore we have. And you got a mama and papa, too."

Papa reached over and poked Met in the ribs. "Come on, gal, let's see you dance." He struck up the tune of an Irish jig. Nelse grabbed her, and they cavorted across the kitchen floor while Mama and I clapped our hands.

Christmas Eve fell on a Friday, and the cotton mills closed till the following Monday, giving mill hands a long holiday. Papa and Nelse came home, arms loaded with bags of food and gifts. Met jumped up and down in excitement, and I could hardly be still. There were oranges, tangerines, bananas, and a huge tin of assorted hard candies.

Mama cooked corned beef and cabbage, since Papa and Nelse both liked it so well, and Grandma's famous stacked applesauce cake. The combined aromas tantalized Papa.

"I swear if I ain't goin' to have a hard time waitin' fer dinnertime Christmas Day," he said. Mama let him sample everything she had on the cookstove.

The next day Met and I were up at dawn. Our stockings were fat with candy, an orange, and Brazil nuts. Beneath my stocking was a music box that played "Skater's Waltz" and a book about Robinson Crusoe. Next to Met's was a music box that played "Blue Danube" and a pop-up storybook, *Who Killed Cock Robin?*

Nelse watched us, shifting from foot to foot, like waiting for something. "You know," he said finally, "I happen to know that 'jolly old elf,' Santa Claus. In fact, he's a good friend of mine. Now would you believe that old fellow done slipped something under my bed that was too big for your stockings?" He tugged at two boxes, pulling them from beneath his bed, and handed one to me and one to Met.

Parting layers of tissue paper, I lifted out a beautiful brunette doll and cradled it in the crook of my arm. Nelse was grinning real big, and I went and hugged him tightly.

"Mind you, the doll's from Santa," he pointed out.

I gave him a sly smile. "I know." Carefully I placed the doll back inside her box.

Met squealed with surprise at sight of her blonde doll. It was her very first one with a china-head. She grasped it in her arms, crumpling pink tissue into puffy piles around her. Both dolls had curls of real human hair, eyes that closed when you laid them down, and pearly teeth inside pouty red lips.

Mama came in from the kitchen and took my open box in her lap. "Your doll looks a lot like Nellie," she said. "Maybe you could name her 'Nellie.'"

"There ain't no other Nellie," I said. "This'n will be her sister, like Met's *my* sister." I took her from the box and looked into her sky-blue eyes. "This'n is named 'Georgia,' 'cause that's where Nelse is from." Nelse seemed to like the name.

On New Year's Eve, sleet fell like a chilling pall. It flicked the windows and tin roof with scratching sounds. Supper was over, and Papa and Nelse lingered at the table, sipping the last of their coffee, buried in Wild West books. Mama was humming a mountain tune, clearing off one end of the table for a game of Chinese checkers. I waited to set up the marbles.

Suddenly the door shook with a loud pounding. Before Papa could get up, there it was again, urgent, demanding. He opened to find two policemen, burly in overcoats, shiny gold badges reflecting from billed caps. They blinked in the light of the door.

"We're looking for Mr. Nelson Arrington," one of them spoke up forcefully.

Papa seemed stunned by the sight of them and the strange name they repeated. He cleared his throat and stammered, "Nelson, Nelson who?"

They shuffled feet impatiently as if Papa were trying to thwart their purpose. One of them consulted a paper in the dim light. "Nelson *Arrington*, alias Nelson *Little*." His voice was gruff.

Mama stopped clearing the table and wiped her hands on her apron while Met and I grasped her skirt. By now Nelse was by Papa's side.

"It's me they want," he said. One of the policemen unfastened a pair of handcuffs from his belt. Nelse asked if he could get his coat, and Mama helped him find it. She walked with him to the door and stood shivering in the icy blast.

"Wait here," Papa told her and went outside with Nelse to the porch, closing the door behind them. Mama paced, wringing her hands. They stayed on the porch for what seemed an hour till Papa came back in, cold and shaking.

Mama poured him a cup of hot coffee, and they sat down at the table. "Nelse is a wanted man," Papa said. "He saw his best friend kill a man over cheatin' at a gamblin' table. Both of 'em was fightin', but then his friend pulled a knife. They both ran, different directions, been dodgin' police ever since."

"Nelse ain't no criminal." Mama's tears spilled onto the open magazine Nelse had been reading. "I won't never believe he did anything bad." She put her head down on her folded arms. I went to her and put my arms around her.

Papa pulled his chair up to Mama and kissed the nape of her neck where dark wisps of hair pulled free. "Nelse was *relieved,* honey. Said as much, said he's glad to be facin' up to it, said at last he could be at peace with himself." Papa looked at me. "And he said somethin' else."

Mama raised her head, eyes blurred with tears.

"He said to tell you and the gals he loves you and hopes we all have a happy 1910."

CHAPTER 19
The Return

Papa found out Nelse had been sentenced to two years in prison for aiding and abetting felony manslaughter. "Nelse'll be out afore long," he told Mama. "You can bank on that. Model prisoner, Nelse'll be. Son-of-gun'll charm the socks right off'n the warden."

His words did little to cheer Mama. She lapsed into periods of silence like after Noble died. She began getting sick mornings, and I remembered she was the same way before Noble was born. I wondered if this meant another baby was on the way. She and Papa didn't talk about it, and I could only guess.

I got Georgia, the doll Nelse gave me, and kept her nearby so Mama could see I was taking good care of her. The pink satin dress was still like new, and her dark hair as neat as when I opened the box on Christmas Day. Each time I put her away, I placed my doll ever-so-gently between folds of tissue.

Met, on the other hand, played with hers all the time, dragging "Susie" around like she was just another rag doll. Susie's blonde tresses became ratty, her lavender dress soiled.

One Saturday Mama was resting after a spell of nausea. I was feather-dusting in the parlor, and Met decided to give her dolls a tea party. She propped up Susie in one chair and her rag doll in another. We could hear clinking of cups and saucers and Met's gentle coaxing of her dolls to mind their manners as they drank their tea. Without warning she let out an ear-piercing scream.

Mama sprang from the bed, and both of us ran to her. Mama grabbed Met by the shoulders. "What's the matter?" She searched Met's face for a clue. Met sucked her breath in and held it like something was gagging her, and Mama probed her mouth with a finger.

Met finally released her breath and pushed Mama's hand away. She pointed to her doll. "S-Susie's eyes are gone." She commenced howling, louder and louder each time she looked at the doll. Mama picked Susie up. Deep holes gaped where the doll's eyes had been.

"I gave her 'creamy coffee,'" Met confessed between sobs. An almost empty cup of milk and coffee sat in front of Susie's place. Her open red lips drooled telltale drops and the front of her satin dress was stained.

Mama folded to a sitting position on the floor, cradling Susie in her arms. She wiped the doll's mouth with the tip of her apron and placed her fingertips on the empty eye sockets. She began rocking back and forth. Inside her coffee-logged head Susie's eyeballs rattled like marbles in a bowl. A tear slipped down Mama's cheek and onto the doll's soiled dress. Soft as distant wind, she hummed the lullaby she used to sing to Met, then little Noble—"Fly around My Pretty Little Miss (Boy)." When Mama cried, I did, too. The three of us sat in a circle on the floor, moaning or bawling, while Mama rocked the disfigured doll. Met began to nod, put her head down, and soon fell asleep.

When Papa came home from work, we were still there. He didn't ask where dinner was. He took the doll from Mama's arms. "I'll just see if I cain't fix this baby doll." With tweezers from his shaving box, he pulled the bulbous eyeballs from the doll's head then drained the coffee out. Using wood glue, he anchored Susie's eyes permanently into the sockets. "She cain't close 'em no more, but she's got eyes." The doll's glazed orbs stared like a bullfrog's. He handed the doll to Met.

"No! She's ugly," she screamed. "I don't want her." She slung the doll across the room where it came to rest face-down against the cookstove. Mama started sniffling again, quiet-like.

"Well and good," Papa said. He went and picked up the doll. "We'll give her away then. Some little gal'll be glad to git 'er." Met didn't care.

A few days later, Papa came home from work earlier than usual. He acted secretive, strange. He wrapped his arms around Mama, and they swayed back and forth slowly like dancing to a tune only they could hear. A tear made its way down Mama's cheek, and he brushed it away with a thumb. "We're goin' back, honey," he said.

Mama pulled away and looked him in the eyes. "Goin' back?"

"I'm taking you back to the mountains. Back where you'll be happy."

Mama slipped from his arms quickly and went to the front window. A flock of crows were prancing around in the gray-bleak yard, scratching and pecking at the ground, searching for seeds. She gazed at the birds as if somewhere out there an answer lay.

Soon Papa was by her side. I went, too, and nestled my head against his linty overalls. He patted my cheek. Met pushed between us, hugging his leg.

The crows puttered around, cocking heads this way and that, when a streak of bright flame swooped suddenly from a tall pine. It was a male cardinal.

I pointed a finger at the bold color that livened the mid-winter setting. "Look at the pretty red bird." As I spoke, the larger birds flapped their wings wildly, chasing him away. "Mean old black birds!" The cardinal's mate descended, joining him in midair, and they flew to a berry-laden holly.

Mama's face lit up. She clasped her hands tightly. "Them cardinals got no call to worry none. The Lord sent lots of berries this year, more'n any bird could ever eat."

Papa took her hand, and they went to the table and sat down. He reached in his pocket and pulled out a letter. It was from Uncle John. "I wrote John two weeks ago, and today I got this." He began reading aloud while Mama gazed at the penciled pages.

John had moved from Utah Mountain and was living in Waynesville where he'd found a job at a tannery. Granny liked Waynesville just fine, he said. So did France and Raymond, who were "getting biggedy as dudes" living in town. Uncle John named places Papa might find work—a lumberyard, a tanbark hauling crew. "Houses ain't hard to come by," he wrote, "but you're welcome to stay with us till you're on your feet."

Papa seemed pleased. "I figure we can afford to move now, honey. I don't owe the mill store another red cent. I ain't aimin' to say nothin' to Mr. Kirkland yet awhile, but come February when this weather lets up, I'll turn in a two-week notice. By then we'll have enough for train tickets and whatever else we might need."

"What about Sippy, and school?"

Papa laid the letter on the table and pulled me into the crook of his arm. "Ain't no reason to worry 'bout this here gal. She's the smartest young'n ever come outta Haywood County. Be even smarter when she gits back." Mama smiled for the first time in weeks.

I liked school in Greenville, and leaving would be hard, but the thing I wanted most was for Mama to be happy. Seeing Granny and my cousins again filled my thoughts as we made preparations to leave.

Late February, we left Greenville to go back to the mountains. This time we did not stop overnight in Asheville, the place Noble had died on our way the year before. Instead our overnight stop was Hendersonville, where Papa's sister lived three miles from the railroad station.

It was getting dark when we got off the train, but the weather was fair, so we set out walking to Aunt Sallie's. When Met got tired, Papa gave Mama our small valise to carry and picked her up. I dropped behind, my feet cold and stiff. Mama handed the bag back to Papa, took Met, and Papa hoisted me to his back. "Sallie's 'three miles' must be 'country miles,'" he said.

I rode the rest of the way, my feet tucked beneath Papa's arms. We groped in the darkness, stopping several times for Mama to rest.

At Sallie's Papa put me down and cupped his hands. "Hullo." He waited then yelled again, "Hullo, Sal." She came to the door, holding her lantern high.

The next day Mama was nauseated and had a very bad headache. Each time she raised her head from the bed, she retched till she was spitting green bile.

"Got the 'blind staggers,'" Aunt Sallie said, and she took charge like Granny always did when someone was ailing. She made tea of white yarrow mixed with honey and held Mama's head up while she drank. "Best thing a body can do for sich a headache."

I stayed close by Mama's bed in case she needed something. She took my hand. "I'm just dizzy, Sippygal. Go on and play with yer sister."

We'd planned to stay one night, but it was three days before Mama could raise her head without getting sick. All four of us stayed in Aunt Sallie's bedroom. She said she'd be just fine sleeping on the sofa in her parlor. One night we heard a loud rapping at the front door. Met was asleep on our floor pallet, but I was still awake. "Don't go in there," Papa told me. I lay in the darkness wondering who the late visitor could be.

"Come 'ere, Sal, sugar," a man's throaty voice drawled.

"Sh-hh!" Aunt Sallie hissed. "I got kinfolk visitin'." The man didn't say anything else.

Aunt Sallie began giggling softly. I heard sighs amid a lot of heavy breathing. Soon someone was grunting like a pig. There were thuds then a loud moan. "Hush!" I heard Aunt Sallie say. The talk became subdued. After a while, the front door slammed shut and all became quiet again.

Papa never mentioned the nighttime visit and neither did Aunt Sallie. I wondered about it but sensed it would not be proper to ask.

While we were there, Aunt Sallie told me a lot about our family's history. She wasn't really my father's sister, she explained. She was his aunt—my great-aunt. Papa's father had been killed in a hunting accident when Papa was a baby. His mother, Anne, found work in town and soon remarried, leaving the baby in her mother's care. Granny raised him to manhood as if he were her own, and he took her name, "Wright," instead of his father's, "Waldrop." I'd heard this story before from Granny but not with the details Aunt Sallie provided. She seemed willing to tell me anything I was ready to hear.

I'd figured out for myself that Mama's tale of

finding me and Met in Mr. Kingsley's field was just a fable, her way of avoiding answers to delicate questions. And from earliest recollections I'd known the scope of Granny's mountain medicine practice. "Was Granny the 'doctor' when I was born?" I asked Sallie.

"Nah, that was your mama's maw. But I'll tell you what your granny did do when you was three days old. You was havin' a smotherin' spell. Your granny took you and blew the breath of life back into you. Your maw was a-screamin' and done give you up for dead, but your granny brought you back. You can thank her, gal, for bein' alive."

I knew Granny had midwifed when Noble was born. Aunt Sallie said she helped when John's wife gave birth to both France and Raymond and was there when Roxie later died in childbirth. Afterwards Granny was like a mother to France and Raymond while their father worked the fields and lumberyards.

"How could Granny do all that? She's so old."

"Honey, your granny ain't always been old. When I was a little girl, my maw was pretty as Rachel is. Only my maw had blonde curly hair and blue eyes. After Paw died she coulda got herself another man, easy. They come a-callin'. But maw was set on raisin' us, and she worked like a man to do it. Your granny's always been smart as a whip—still is."

My granny was once young and pretty. I'd never thought about that. She'd spent a lifetime doing things for others, raising her children alone and raising orphaned grandchildren. Yet she was once young, attractive, with blonde, curly hair. I looked forward to seeing France and Raymond again, but it was Granny I thought about most on our journey back.

In Waynesville, Uncle John met us at the railroad depot and took us in a borrowed wagon to the house where our families would live together till Papa could afford a place of our own. When Mama saw Granny, she grabbed her and they hugged and cried, pulled apart, then hugged cried some more. Papa and John stood around, laughing at "how women-folk are."

France and Raymond talked non-stop, bringing Met and me up-to-date. Ole Blue had died, France said, and they buried her on Utah Mountain. It made me sad to think of her. No dog could ever have been more faithful. They brought Kitty-cat to town with them in a chicken coop, but when they let him out, he ran like crazy and never came back.

"Cats don't like movin'," Granny'd told them. "Tom-cats has got 'territories.'"

"I don't care, I'll find him." I told France. "I'll look this whole town over till I do." Just knowing Kitty-cat was out there somewhere made me feel better. Maybe he was waiting for me to come back, and now I was here.

Granny made room for us and for our furniture, which came by rail a week later. It wasn't easy. Her house had only four rooms, with attic space, which she converted into another bedroom by making pallets on its narrow flooring. France and Raymond slept there, claiming it was real warm, and they liked climbing the disappearing staircase at night.

Granny's rented house was located off Main on East Street, a narrow road near the heart of town where the clatter of horse-drawn traffic on cobblestones could be heard day and night. It was only three blocks from Water Street where Aunt Mary, Mama's sister, lived.

Soon Papa was out looking for a job, the way he had before we went to Greenville. Whenever I could, I made the rounds with him. One place we stopped was the tannery where Uncle John worked.

"What kinda place is this?" I asked Papa.

"It's where they tan animal hides into leather. Them shoes you're a-wearin' was tanned afore they was stitched into a pair of shoes." Outside the tannery men were stacking tan-bark, and Papa asked them if I could stay there and watch while he went inside.

"I want to go in, too."

"It stinks to high heaven inside."

"I don't mind." He took my hand, and in we went. Papa talked to the foreman while I watched Uncle John plunging a grappling hook into a vat of brown, slimy water.

"What's that in the tub?" I asked John.

"It's tannin. 'At's lime and tan-bark seeped together. Now don't git close." He hooked a dripping cowhide and threw it across a long table. Some men began scraping hair from it while another put more raw hides into John's vat.

The horrid smell was nearly overwhelming. I held my nose and clutched my stomach. "Git on back outside," Papa said when he saw me, and he followed me out. I noticed he kept swallowing hard then spitting.

"Are you goin' to work there?" I asked after sucking fresh air into my lungs.

"Nah. They got all the men they can use."

We walked down Depot Street to Water Street where Aunt Mary lived. She had a quilting frame up, covering most of her parlor space, and was busy with her needle.

"I'm makin' this here quilt fer Miz Kingsley," she said. "It'll take me another coupla months. She wants the tiniest stitches I can make." We edged around the frame to her kitchen, and Papa sat down.

He started talking to her about Mama, how worried he was about her health. "She ain't the same

Rachel," he told Mama's sister. "She ain't never got her strength back since Noble died. Now this'n's due afore long."

"Rachel ain't been well in a long time. She's got no call to git another young'n."

Papa nodded agreement and dropped his head.

"Have you talked to Granny about this?"

"I cain't bring myself to tell 'er how worried I am. Maw's gitten' old."

"Don't think she ain't figured out somethin's wrong. You cain't hide nothin' from her. She ain't practicin' like on Utah, but she knows ailments." Aunt Mary poured Papa a cup of freshly brewed coffee. "Waynesville's got some real doctors. You best git one of 'em."

"How? I ain't got no job, no money. And I ain't about to beg."

All this talk worried me. Papa and I were supposed to take care of Mama. Aunt Mary saw me watching Papa drink his coffee.

"You want some, too."

I squirmed. "Yeah." She placed another cup in front of me and looked at Papa.

"She's nine, goin' on twenty-one," he explained.

On a corner near our house was a meat market with pheasant, goose, turkey, and every kind of meat, including sides of beef that dangled just inside the door of a cooler. Granny sent me there often to buy ten-cent soupbones. She used them for soups, stews, and to season vegetables. I hung around as long as I dared, watching the butcher trim and wrap choice cuts for his more affluent customers. Sometimes he'd slip me some scraps with no charge. Granny was tickled pink to get these.

My next favorite places were the livery stable directly across the street from our house and, a little farther down, a blacksmith shop. The men at the livery stable warned France, Raymond, and me to stay out of their way as they currycombed the horses. We ran like crazy when they gave them full rein to our next stop (the blacksmith shop). The noise of the smith's bellow blowing black chunks into red-hot coals drew us like a magnet. "You young'ns wanta find out what hell's like? Then you best git the h—-outta here," he yelled. We'd drop back then edge forward till he yelled again. Papa'd gotten part-time work at a lumberyard only blocks away, but we'd seen plenty of those, and they held no fascination.

Days when Mama felt well enough, we walked to Aunt Mary's. The two would laugh and talk and share things like they did with no one else. Aunt Mary still "took in" laundry, and Mama would help her with it. Burr, Mary's daughter, and I would do our part, piling wood on the fire beneath iron pots of boiling water. With Mama helping, they laundered so many shirts, shirtfronts, and collars that there was extra money to spend. We decided to have "penny pictures" made and got twenty-four for twenty-five cents, posing separately, then two together. Enough was left to buy cloth to make Mama a dress. She was so bloated and heavy that all her clothes were too tight.

"We'll make this'n big enough fer the circus fat lady," Mary said, laughing. With no sewing machine, it took a long while. Burr, Met, and I played on the creek bank out back, building a secret playhouse in a ditch between a privy and a tree, a fun place, one the mean boys on her street could not find to tear down.

Shortly before Met's fifth birthday, May 10, 1910, soft breezes were blowing. The sun was shining above hazy distant ridges. It was the day Mama's dress was to be completed. "Let's go to Aunt Mary's," I said to Mama.

"I don't feel like walkin' today, honey. My head's a-hurtin' somethin' awful. I'm goin' to lay down a while." She asked me to watch Met for her, stay in our own yard, and help Granny with chores.

Later Granny called us to come in. "Your maw's sufferin' from a blind headache," she said. "I gave her a pain potion, and it did no good." She told France and Raymond to go draw water and fill the kettle, both water buckets, and her tin lard tub. She sent Met to bring in more wood and pile it next to the cookstove. "Now, I want you to go fetch your papa," she told me.

I ran all the way to the lumberyard. "I'll go see if I cain't fetch a doctor," Papa said. "You go on back home."

When I got back, I went into Mama's room. Her face was swollen and her head was swathed with a cloth soaked with camphor. "Are your feelin' better?" I asked. She didn't answer, just looked at me like she didn't know who I was. When Papa came in, he pulled a chair up and took her hand. Her eyes opened again, and he kissed her brow.

"Rachel, honey, 'member Halley's Comet, how scared you was?" Her eyes seemed to focus on his face. "Nothin' happened. The thing went right on by and nothin' bad happened."

Her lips parted, closed, and opened again. "I won't scared for myself." Her voice was quivery. "Just for the gals."

"The gals'll be all right." He kissed her brow again. "It's you needs to git well."

CHAPTER 20
Resting Place on Utah

When the doctor got there, Granny made me leave the room. It was late afternoon, and the warmth of the sun felt good as I went outside. France and Raymond were off somewhere, watching the grooming of horses at the livery stable or seeing how close they dared get to the blacksmith's forge. Those places held no appeal for me. In my mind, all I could see was Mama, cheeks pale, eyes closed, hands not much bigger than mine crossed over her bosom. All I wanted was for her to be well again, to be happy, to laugh or sing an old mountain song. I sat down on the top front step. Soon Met was beside me, her skinny arms hugging bony knees. She looked so small today.

"What's wrong with Mama?" she asked.

"She's goin' to have the baby. The doctor's helpin' her."

"Why cain't we see her?"

"The doctor has things to do. He don't want us in the way. If you want her to git well, you just have to wait."

"I want her to git well."

Soon the doctor came out, banging the screen door behind him. We moved over to let him get down the steps. He wore a short gray beard and a dark suit. The black bag he carried was bulky and well-worn.

"I'll be back in about two hours," he told Papa, who'd come to the door and stood there, looking worried. "We'll have something started by then." He paused at the last step and turned. "Your wife's a very sick woman, Mr. Wright. For now all we can do is wait. I'll be at my office."

Papa had emerged to the stoop. "Thankee, doctor."

He watched till the doctor turned the corner onto Main, then grasped his chin, like puzzling what he should do next.

"Can I go see Mama?" I asked.

"Not now. We need to let 'er rest." Met took hold of his leg and clung to it. He picked her up and brushed a matted curl from her eyes. "We might have a special somebody here by tomorrow," he told her.

"Will it be Nelse?"

He shook his head then grinned. "Well now, I expect we could name 'im 'Nelse.' What we're a-gittin' is a little bitty baby."

She made a face. "I don't want no baby. I just want Mama to git well."

Papa set her down and went back to Mama's room. Granny was in and out several times, carrying pans of water, before the doctor arrived. She said little till France and Raymond came in. By then it was getting dark. She stoked the cookstove with firewood, placed the big kettle on, and removed her Dutch oven to the sideboard. "They's beans in this oven," she told France and me. "Git bowls, and the four of ye can eat some supper."

When we went to bed, there was still no news from Mama's room. I'd caught glimpses of her through the door when Granny went in or out. She was lying in the same position, so still. I could not sleep for a long time.

At daybreak I heard unfamiliar voices coming from Mama's bedroom. I got up and opened her partially closed door. Granny was holding a tiny blanket-wrapped bundle. The doctor leaned close over Mama, and a large woman in white clothes stood next to him. Papa sat in a chair holding one of Mama's hands.

"Oh God, Rachel!" His voice cut me to the quick. "Oh, honey!" Blood was gushing from Mama's nose and mouth, and the big woman began sponging it away.

"I'm sorry, there's nothing more I can do." The

doctor's voice was resigned. Papa began kissing Mama's blood-stained face.

I ran through the door to her bed. "Mama! Mama!" I plunged onto the counterpane. "Mama! Mama!" The woman in white snatched me up and clamped a hand over my mouth. She carried me outside the room while I struggled and kicked to get free. Her hand was pressing like a band of steel when everything went black.

I woke up on Granny's bed. The woman was still there, holding a cloth wet with camphor near my face. A cut inside my lip burned. "Where's Papa?" I wanted to get away from this horrid person who snatched me from Mama and let her die. When Mama needed me most, she kept me from her.

"He's gone out. Are you feeling better?"

I nodded yes, and she finally allowed me to get up.

"Just don't go in your mother's room."

"Why?"

"They're fixing her."

I went out the back door and sat on the bottom step. Met was still sleeping, and I didn't know where France and Raymond were. I laid my head on my legs and cried and cried till there were no tears left. Something soft was caressing and tickling my legs. I opened my eyes to a yellow kitten. He purred and snuggled against me, and I picked him up. For a long time we sat there, the kitty nestled in my lap, so cozy. I wanted to never go back inside and face the awful sadness.

Met came out. She began rubbing the kitten's fur the wrong way. He jumped from my lap and ran. "Granny said tell you to come in," she said. Her hair was a tangled halo around a face grimy with dirt and dried flecks of food. Mama wouldn't have liked that.

"Let's go wash your face," I said.

Inside people hovered in a corner of the parlor. They stared down, mumbling in somber tones. Mama had been moved from her bed and placed there in a coffin. I wet a rag, washed Met's face, and smoothed her unruly hair into place. I guided her to a bedroom where Granny sat rocking the new baby. He'd lived and Mama had died, and I harbored resentment for him in my heart. Granny pulled back the blanket for us to take a peek.

"He looks just like Noble," I said. He was wearing the same red-dotted dress Noble used to wear. I couldn't hate him. I kissed his little face, sniffing the moist fragrance. Granny drew Met and me into the circle of her embrace, and we hugged and cried.

Papa came and told us Aunt Mary was there and wanted to take us home till time for the funeral the next day. Neighbors had brought food, the aromas overpowering rank camphor smells from the night before. "Eat somethin' afore you go," Papa told us.

"And I want you'ns to see yer maw afore we close the box." Papa looked gaunt, two day's growth of beard shadowing his cheeks and chin.

Aunt Mary was in the parlor, leaning over the casket, fussing with Mama's hair. She picked Met up so she could see. An elderly woman stood beside me, crying and dabbing her eyes with an embroidered handkerchief. "She was so pretty, so young," she said to no one in particular. "They say she was only twenty-five."

Mama's black hair was sleeked into a pompadour above her creamy white brow. She was wearing a white dress with lace-trimmed jabot at her slender neckline. In her hands was a nosegay of red-throated lilies, placed there, Aunt Mary said, by an elderly couple who grew them in their yard.

"Thankee, thankee, Miz Kingsley," I heard Papa telling the woman who thought Mama was so pretty. She was on her way out the door. When she was gone, Papa told us the woman was Mrs. Jacob Kingsley. She felt Mama should be buried on Utah Mountain where she'd lived most of her life, and had made him that offer. Her son, Caleb, would have his men dig the grave.

"I told 'er Rachel always b'longed on Utah. She weren't never happy nowhere else." He broke into sobbing, and Aunt Mary went to him.

Early the next day we were all dressed in our best.

Aunt Mary had combed and braided my hair and Met's. From across the street, livery stable attendants sent carriages for the family to ride in, and the butcher offered his covered dray for the coffin. The cortege traveled slowly down Main Street to the courthouse corner where we turned onto Depot Street and out toward Utah Mountain on the macadamized road. Near Jonathan's Creek bridge, I turned to look at the yellow two-story house. The woman was on her front porch sweeping. She stopped when she saw us and stood very still, watching our procession.

The trail was gnarled with undergrowth and rockier than I remembered. I hardly recognized it till we got to the clearing.

Ahead was Granny's old cabin, bleak and gray except for creeping vines that hugged the stone chimney and sent fingers of green across the roof. Beyond was the cabin that had been our home when Noble was born. It seemed smaller as it leaned left-ward from its moorings. Almost obscured by tall weeds was the window, broken now, where I used to stand and watch our chickens eating dishwater scraps. Between the two houses, a deep hole had been dug and two boys stood by, shovels in hand. We stopped not far from the open grave, and everyone got out, except for Granny. She stayed in the carriage, the baby in her lap.

Weeds pulled at our stockings, and the sun

was warm on my neck as Met and I walked behind Papa and John toward the freshly dug earth. Tom was there with Florrie, his wife. She was big with child. Around us birds chirped and twittered loudly above the muffled thuds of footsteps. In the distance a mourning dove called dolefully to its mate from a thick piney glen. Stopping a few feet short of the gaping hole, Uncle John put his arm around Papa's shoulder. Two men placed ropes around Mama's coffin and lowered it into place.

"Papa, Papa!" Met's scream was shrill. "Don't let them put my mama in the ground!" She pulled from me and ran toward the grave. Papa lunged and caught her up in his arms. She kept bawling.

"The Lord is my shepherd; I shall not want," someone began reading loudly above Met's sobs. "... Though I walk through the valley of the shadow of death, I shall fear no evil, for Thou are with me ... "

Met had the "snubs" by now, and Papa stood her on the ground next to him where she held on tightly to his leg. We heard wheels behind us and a horse's whinny. Everyone turned to see a black chaise approaching slowly. It pulled beside the dray. A woman stepped out, dressed from head to toe in black. Unhidden by the veil over her head was a bold streak of white hair.

"It's Callie Dock," John whispered to Papa.

She slipped to a place behind Aunt Mary and

Burr and stood with head bowed. Someone led out in *"Amazing grace! How sweet the sound, that saved a wretch like me."*

I thought of my Bible cards Mama used to read out loud to Met and me. "Will you be in heaven someday?" I asked her when she described what heaven would be like.

"Shore, honey," she'd said. "I love Jesus." If Mama were in heaven, I wanted to go there, too. I'd have to wait till then to see her again.

"Ashes to ashes, dust to dust ..." A man was sprinkling a handful of dirt over Mama's casket. Aunt Mary went over to it and dropped a wildflower she'd picked. She handed one to me, and I did the same. Aunt Callie Dock darted like a bird to the head of the grave where a large stone dredged from Jonathan's Creek had been placed. She stuck something into the soft soil.

"What's that?" Papa asked John.

"Looks like a totem."

Before we left, we went near the stick she'd placed in the ground. A wolf's head was carved into the wood.

"At's same as a guardian angel to them Injuns," Granny described the totem on the way home. "Callie Dock's got her ways."

I wondered if she'd placed one on Nellie Sue's grave. As we clattered and swayed on the trail's descent, that event seemed long ago. The thought of it once gripped me with pangs of heartache. Now it merely haunted like the refrain of a sad song.

When we got home, the house was clean and neat, and a woman was in the kitchen preparing a hot meal. She knew Papa and wanted to help in this way. Papa introduced her as "Clemmie Messer, a widow." Granny, who usually ran other women out of her kitchen, seemed relieved to have someone there. Her own time was taken up with "Little Doc."

Papa named the baby "Samuel Joshua" after the doctor who tended Mama, but Granny dubbed him "Little Doctor." The baby didn't want to eat, and all Granny's know-how seemed to no avail. She tried spoon-feeding him a thin mix of oatmeal and cow's milk. He spat it out continually. She fashioned sugar-tits to soothe his incessant crying. He refused them, gagging and turning red. "Dr. Samuel" sent bottles by his nurse with instructions to give the baby goat milk, but Little Doc heaved it up and turned his head away from manmade rubber nipples. He died in early June. Papa put the tiny body in a box made at the lumberyard. He and John made the trip up Utah and buried him there beside Mama.

It was only then that we realized Met's fifth birthday had come and gone, and no one had remembered. May 5, 1910, was the day after Mama was buried. Granny made Met sugar cake when we thought of it, and I let her play all day with Georgia, the doll Nelse had given me. She promised not to undress her or give her milk and coffee.

Papa moved out and went to live with Clemmie Messer. He didn't give a reason, and if Granny knew why, she didn't talk about it. Clemmie lived way across town and "took in" sewing. They came to see us now and then and brought gifts—books, games, snuff for Granny, but Papa wasn't the same. He seemed distant, like an uncle or cousin, not like our papa. Clemmie tried to talk to Met and me when they came over, but I could tell it was faked. She had no children of her own and didn't know what we liked. Clemmie was buxom, with red cheeks and blonde hair. She laughed a lot, even when there was nothing to laugh about, and teased Papa till he'd grab her and kiss her right in front of us. It nearly made me sick that he could forget Mama so soon.

It was in late summer when they came and told us they were getting married. "I loved Rachel," he told Granny, "but she's gone. I know Clemmie ain't nothing like Rachel was, but she says she loves me and wants to make me happy." He laughed. "We'll see about that." They were leaving for the town of Gastonia as soon as they got married, a place east of Asheville. Both had been promised jobs in a cotton mill there. "We'll send fer the gals as soon as we're settled and in a house," he said.

Mama was gone, and Papa was not the same papa he used to be. I did not want to go to Gastonia or anywhere else. I'd stay with my granny.

CHAPTER 21

Life with Granny

The summer of 1910 was humid for a mountain clime, hot, a time when insects bite harder, animals are jumpy, and children yen to follow their noses beyond set boundaries. Granny was nearing eighty years of age, but that fact did not faze France, Raymond, Met, and me. After all, she was spry as women half her age and sharper than a brier.

"When your paw gits home from the tannery, he'll have some more hides to tan," she promised France and Raymond if they stayed out past dark or she found her woodbox empty. Yet when John came in, smelly and tired from a ten-hour stretch, she never burdened him with their trespasses. She tiptoed around verbal threats to Met and me. Our mama was freshly in her grave. And we quickly learned from the boys that Granny's brash words meant little. Her heart was too big, her love for us motherless children too forgiving.

Rather than upset her, an unwritten code emerged, covering all transgressions. It was secrecy. What she didn't know couldn't hurt her. This became our key to thrills, romance, and occasional treasures life in town provided.

Our best route to Depot and Main streets was down an alley overgrown with bee-covered honeysuckle vines and bordered by rows of staked green beans. Before Granny could say, "Now don't go too far," or "I got things fer you'ns to do," we were out of sight. First stop, a garbage dump chock-full of valuables like tin boxes, steel bearings, broken wrenches—pure gold when trading with the "downtown" children or "slummies" (as Granny called them). It might take a bit of wrangling, but the payoff—comics of *Slim Jim, Happy Hooligan,* or *Mutt and Jeff*—were worth the bargaining.

The depot was our very best place. "I'll beat all three of you there," Raymond challenged, his skinny legs freed by rolled-up pants, bare feet hardened to leather. He'd gotten fleet as a dog-chased fox. I never tried to outrun Met. Her threats to tell Granny gave her an edge.

In the station yard, stately carriages stood waiting for the elite to arrive by train. Sleek horses in tasseled harnesses stamped restlessly, held in rein by liveried coachmen. They called out their hotels' names in chants, like a peddler selling his wares: "Eagle's Nest"—my favorite because it was perched on a mountain peak, requiring four horses to pull the red-lacquered carriage to the top. The peak was depicted on a brass-handled door.

"Hotel Branner." France liked this one. It's where Uncle Harve clerked and was near the railroad. Guests could look out their windows at passing trains. Someday when we got rich, we'd ride the coaches, each to his chosen hotel.

"There's Uncle Mortimer," I said, pointing to an elegant gentleman in a black silk hat. The woman beside him carried a parasol to shield her pale complexion from the sun. Met curtsied in mock obeisance.

"Yeah, and there's my aunt Gertrude." France could play this game as well as I. If our pretend relatives saw us at all, they simply turned up their noses.

"Hotel Gordon, finest in town." The coachman's royal blue uniform with gold epaulets confirmed his claim. This was Raymond's choice. A gentleman assisted as silken skirts rustled, gingerly folding into the plush coach's open door. I lifted my tattered dress-tail to mimic the courtly ascent.

"My hotel's Hotel Sueta," Met bragged, and

France broke into gales of laughter. To him, the way she pronounced it sounded like an ugly forbidden word.

"Su-et-a, Su-et-a," he said when he gained control of himself, but Met wouldn't say it again. She stuck her tongue out at him.

"*Asheville Citizen, Asheville Citizen,* git yer paper right here, *Asheville Citizen,*" a newsboy's chant rang out as we filed through the station's open door. Smoke greeted us, smarting our eyes. It blended with spittoon snuff and fruit peels to produce a tantalizing potpourri, exciting our senses. The voices of porters and peddlers, bootblacks, and businessmen intermingled, peaking with each arrival and departure. Above it all, like pronouncements from God, loudspeakers reverberated with times and destinations. A day passed quickly at Waynesville Depot.

On the first of July, the sun beat down, and Granny prayed for rain, "else them termaters'll be dried up afore I put up a single one." France made three trips to the pump, and she poured buckets of water on the plants, but "'tain't goin' do no good," she lamented. Tomatoes didn't worry me none. Nor did they Met nor France nor Raymond. Rain interfered with our plans.

That day we bypassed the depot and headed

straight to Main Street where, beyond the slum area, fashionable shops with sparkling glass windows held goods for the privileged. Consuming with our eyes cost nothing.

"That's my hat with all them feathers." I pointed to a mannequin sporting a brown felt hat with peacock plumes. She stood coyly beside a marble-topped table, a tasseled fan pressed to her bosom. As we gazed, grimy hands and runny noses smeared patterns into the glass.

"Get away from here, you ragamuffins! I just washed that window this morning." The storekeeper stood in his doorway, raising a fist. We skedaddled across the street to a corner jewelry shop and stopped at a display we'd never seen before.

Gold chains with fancy fobs surrounded plush boxes of sparkling diamonds, but my eyes were drawn to an alabaster figurine. It stood centered on a red velvet pedestal. The pale bust, high above pendants of emerald and gold filigree, was chiseled to perfection, a froth of white at the slender throat, blank eyes cold as if closed in death. Clutched in white hands across her breast, opaque lilies were set with rubies. I sucked my breath in and strained to see it better.

France caught my stares. "Looks like yer mama in her burial dress," he said.

Tears welled, and I brushed them away to gaze harder. Met leaned on my arm then clasped my hand.

No one said anything for a long time. Then Met broke the spell.

"If I had a hundred dollars, I'd buy that doll." She sighed with finality.

The ground beneath our feet began to vibrate, and a distant roar emerged. We recognized the sound. Echoing from mountain slopes, a huge freight locomotive was lumbering through Holcomb's Cut. "Last one there's a rotten egg," and we hightailed it toward the depot. I forgot about waiting for Met.

A clarion of blasts rose from the mighty train, and a flurry of activity broke out near the tracks. Thunder and clanging shook the earth, and above it, ominous and shrill, came a shout: "Look out! Look out! A runaway horse!" Women and children ran helter-skelter toward safety, and men-folk raced to catch the beast. Down the line the great steam engine was rolling in. "Clear the tracks, clear the tracks!"

Cabbages, cucumbers, onions, and ears of corn bounced and rolled into the locomotive's path. A peddler's upturned cart was perilously close to the ties. "Get back! Get back!" Two men sprang from the throng, grabbing the cart's wooden handles, and jerked it free just as the train smashed through piles of vegetables. The crowd retreated, some falling to the ground. I turned to get Met out of the way, but she was not there.

Two men kneeled over a child on the cobblestones. She was crying and writhing in pain. It was Met. Her arm was bloody, and she was holding her foot.

"What's wrong?" I pushed through them and dropped to all fours.

"I want Granny," she bawled. "Take me to Granny."

Between sobs we learned she'd stepped on an open goods box and pierced her heel with a nail. Her arm was skinned when she fell. Blood oozed from it, and she wiped it on her clean dress.

"She ain't hurt bad," one of the men said, examining her heel. They helped her up, but she refused to take a step and sat back down. France and Raymond found us and the two men left.

"Granny'll skin us alive," France said, surveying the scene. "We need to wash that blood off." He looked at Met's heel. "Ain't no reason you cain't walk."

That set her off again. "I cain't walk, my foot hurts too bad. I want Granny."

We tried to think of a plan. "Ain't but two blocks to Aunt Mary's," I said. "Let's take 'er there."

She started in again. "I don't want to go to Aunt Mary's. I just want Granny."

We offered to support her while she hobbled on one foot. She refused, so France and I made a pack-saddle seat with hands and arms. We carried her that way to Aunt Mary's house on Water Street, Raymond running ahead to announce the news. From West Knob the afternoon sun cast our freaky shadow across Depot Street's cobblestones—like a long-legged, three-headed monster. By the time we got there, Met had stopped crying, but she saw Aunt Mary waiting and commenced anew.

"Lordy, I reckon your granny's a-goin' to whup the lot of you." Aunt Mary stripped Met to her under-drawers and looked her over. She washed the wounds, applied soot from her fireplace to stop the bleeding, and turpentine to combat soreness. She dabbed Met's heel with more turpentine and padded it so she could stand up. "You'ns is lucky that nail won't rusty. You could git lock-jaw." With strips of old sheeting, she bandaged both areas. After dropping Met's dress into lye-soap water, she gave her one of Burr's to put on. Pleased with her battle casualty appearance, Met was satisfied at last.

While she rinsed Met's dress out, Aunt Mary told us about a letter George had sent from Spartanburg, South Carolina. He still worked in the cotton mill, and Grandma was fine. But Effie had married and moved out. She was only thirteen, and Grandma had given her permission because Effie was expecting a child. George said he felt sorry for Effie. Her husband was a drunkard and gambler and had trouble keeping a job. I remembered how Effie wanted to come back with Tom to the mountains, and wondered how different things might have been.

It was nearly dark when we got home, and Granny was waiting at the door with a sweet gum limb in her hand. All except Met got a flogging. It was the first time Granny had ever switched me, and the fullness in my chest hurt more than the stinging of my legs. I pulled my doll, Georgia, from her frayed box and crawled under my bed. Curls of lint and cobwebs tickled my face, and I wiped them and the tears away. I kissed Georgia's pink cheeks and thought of Nelse and Mama and Nellie Sue Muckle. All gone now. I whispered the song:

> "Fly around my pretty little miss,
> Fly around my daisy,
> Fly around my pretty little miss,
> You almost drive me crazy."

At this point, I used to ask Mama if I were pretty, and she'd always say, "My, yes."

> "Fly around my buttercup,
> Fly around my daisy,
> Fly around my buttercup,
> You almost drive me crazy."

"Is Met pretty, too?" I would ask.

"Both my gals is pretty." And she'd sing the last verse.

"Fly around my pretty little miss,
Fly around my honey,
Fly around my pretty little miss,
You'll be sixteen on Sunday."

I saw two feet, one bare, one bandaged. Met lifted the tail of the countpane. "Granny said, 'Come on out and eat.'" She said it self-righteously, as if she were the older one.

I lay awake for a long time that night while Met was breathing deeply. I tried hard to remember Mama's face. It used to be tanned in summer, and her dark eyes glinted. In her casket the face and hands were too white, like her dress. The alabaster figure in the shop window blended with that image till I could not tell them apart. I saw Nellie Sue Muckle's face, long wavy hair pulled back with a silver comb. In her tapered fingers she clasped my red lilies, sniffing them and smiling. From the shadows, a figure came and snatched them from her. He stomped them on the floor. It was Mr. Price, our schoolteacher. "No, no!" I screamed.

"Wake up, honey. Wake up." It was Granny. She hugged me. "It's all right, now. You had a bad dream."

"I saw Nellie Sue, Granny." It was still fresh in my mind, so clear. "It was *Mr. Price. He* was the one that bigged her and made her take poison."

"Mr. Price?"

"Our teacher at Utah Mountain School. I saw them one day. He was kissing her hard."

She kept smoothing my hair back and didn't say anything for a long time. "Who else did you tell this to?"

"Nobody."

"Then don't never tell nobody else. Case Muckle's got no call to go a-gunnin'. Goin' a-gunnin' ain't never solved nothin'."

"I won't never tell nobody."

"Now think about pleasant things, Sippy honey, and go on back to sleep."

CHAPTER 22
A New Nelse

After the incident at the depot, I hung around the house for a few days, not wanting to get Granny riled. I choked up each time I thought of the switching she had to give me. Sometimes I felt the need to think things over or remember Mama and how it used to be. That's when I'd go and sit on the back steps. The morning sun felt good there, and by afternoon a rock maple provided shade. Squirrels played in the tree, swinging from branch to branch. Today they were excited, chattering, swishing tails downward like small feather dusters. Below on an old stump, I saw the reason why. It was the yellow kitten. There he sat sedately, watching their every move.

"C'mere, kitty. Kitty, kitty, kitty."

He looked at me like, "Why should I? Who are you?"

"Don't you remember me? Kitty, kitty, kitty!" He jumped leisurely from the stump, stretched, and ambled to the steps.

"Meow." *Here I am, now what?*

I picked him up, and he let me rub his fur as he did last time. He settled in my lap and purred till his eyes went closed. We'd been sitting a long while when Granny opened the screen door.

"Watch out, Sip, I got a full dishpan." She threw the contents over her marigolds and dahlias, and the frightened cat jumped from my lap. He looked back to see if he were Granny's target, then sniffed at a dishpan ort and began eating it.

"He's hungry, the poor little thing's hungry."

"Humph," Granny muttered.

"Can I keep 'im and feed 'im?"

"We don't need another mouth to feed."

I ran to pick him up again. "He's little. He won't eat much. Please, Granny."

"Well, he's got no business eatin' dishwater scraps. Git 'im a saucer of milk."

I knew that meant I could keep him. I took him inside to the screened-in porch and fed him. He purred loudly while drinking every drop. Granny watched through the kitchen door. "His name'll be 'Nelse,'" I said.

"Nelse?"

"Yeah, that was somebody I used to know. His hair was the same color, and he was, he was …"

"A feller?"

"Yeah."

"Well, this here 'Nelse' may be a gal."

"I don't care. His name's still Nelse." Nelse curled up and went to sleep on an old rag pile. He knew he'd found a home.

School started in early September. I was put in a fourth grade class, but soon my teacher spoke with the principal and they transferred me to fifth. This put France and me in the same room. I liked sitting up front and asked for a desk there. I didn't want to miss anything. France sat on the very back row, so we saw each other only when school was out for the day and we, with Raymond (now in third), walked home together. Met hadn't started school. With her not tagging along, there was no one to tattle if wanderlust took control.

Ahead Raymond kicked a stone as we trekked the road home. It was Friday, October 7, sunny and unusually warm. I dropped my fascinator to free my shoulders and tied it around my waist. Capricious breezes caught my hair, and I happened to glance upward. Directly above us a giant balloon loomed, striped in rainbow colors.

"Lookee." I'd never seen anything like it except in pictures.

France shielded his eyes. "It's the carnival balloon, the one we saw on the posters." We waited to see which way it was going.

Part of the balloon collapsed. "It's coming down! It's coming down *here!*" France's voice was shrill.

Raymond stopped short, slurping his breath in. "Gawd-dang!"

It was descending rapidly, drifting into our path. The balloonist might be in danger. "Oh no, no!" By now I could see the gondola clearly. "Lookee, it's a *woman!*" I could hardly believe my eyes.

The basket hit the ground, ropes dropped and dragged along. The woman jumped out. She pulled the ropes, trying to steady the now-limp balloon. We ran to where she was.

"Help me, please help me weeth ropes." A light breeze gusted, jerking her gondola.

France grabbed the cords from her. He anchored the basket and began gathering the ropes into coils. Two men came running to her aid. They were dressed in black suits trimmed with gold braid.

"You good boy," she said to France. "You ver' strong, too." We had never heard an accent like that. She was dressed in white knitted tights and a bright pink tutu, her blonde hair piled high on her head. Her lips and cheeks were rouged and her eyes outlined in black.

She smiled at each of us. "Here, I geeve you tickets for show." Taking a packet from her wide sash, she reached in and pulled out three tickets. "Eet will be tomorrow at three, at fairgrounds." She handed them to France.

"Thankee, thankee." We ran the rest of the way home.

Raymond beat France and me there. "Granny, Granny," he was yelling when we went in.

She came running, wiping her hands on her apron-tail. "What's the matter with ye?"

"Nothing—we're goin' to the carnival." Raymond could not stand still.

France pulled the tickets from his pocket. "We got free tickets. A pretty carnival lady gave them to us. She came down in a balloon right in front of us." He handed them to Granny.

"Humph." She stared at the tickets.

"We gotta go, we gotta go, else they'll be wasted," France said.

"Well, then, lest you can git a *grownup* to go with ye, they'll just be wasted."

"*You* can go, Granny." France grabbed her arm and was shaking it. "Please, you gotta go with us."

"All five of us could go," I said. Met was jumping up and down.

"I don't see but three tickets." Granny seemed to be softening.

When Uncle John got home, we went through

the same litany. He went to his bedroom chifforobe and used a key to open the smallest drawer. He took out an envelope and removed a greenback dollar. "Now this'll be enough fer tickets and a bag o' peanuts each." All four of us commenced jumping up and down. Granny went to the kitchen and started getting supper, but I could tell she was as excited as we were. Soon a bouquet of mustard greens, sidemeat, and cornbread filled the house, and dishes clattered to the table.

The Ferris wheel arched high above the tents as we hurried to the fairgrounds. People stood watching it rotate. Many, like us, had never seen one before, and the line to pay a nickel and ride stretched fifty yards or more. Our tickets were good for most everything else, but not the big wheel.

Carousel music cast a mood with clowns and candy apples, gypsies with trinkets, and hot dogs on a stick. We stopped to buy our roasted peanuts. Next, the animal cages—elephants, lions, and giraffes, but Met and Raymond preferred the monkeys because of their antics. Met offered one of them a peanut, and he came to the edge of the cage where she stood. He reached through the wire gingerly, popped it into his mouth, then scratched his head. He commenced staring at her. "He thinks you're pretty," the trainer said.

"A monkey thinks she's pretty. That shows how pretty she is," Raymond teased.

She stuck out her tongue at him. With that, the monkey did a flip backwards, chattering wildly and sending Met and Raymond into fits of laughter.

France tapped Granny on the shoulder. "See that big ape over there? He looks just like Uncle Lowery, hairy chest and all."

"Fiddlesticks." Granny didn't think it was funny. She noticed the snake charmer's music and herded us ahead. "I expect that might be 'Jack o' Diamonds,'" she posed. We stood well back as the snake reared from his basket at the piped tune and poised as if to strike.

"'Tain't no real snake," France said. "I bet 'tain't real."

I nodded. "But you ain't about to find out."

A hawker stood in front of his tent with a megaphone. "Come right on up, gentlemen. Come and see the beautiful girls from the East. Twenty, yes, twenty in all." Hootchie-kootchie girls in veils and flimsy clothes undulated to oriental music. "Twenty, count them, twenty. And you'll see *more* of them inside." He let out with a nasty guffaw. France scrambled to the front and stood as close as a rope allowed.

"Get back, get back, sonny, and let paying customers through."

France gave him a smirk and mimicked, "Come

right up, come right up and see *ugly* girls from the *West*."

Granny huffed to France's side and took him by the ear.

"Ouch!" He came along with us to the fire-eater, then the bearded lady, and finally Punch and Judy. There Met kept wanting to see the show again and again, but Granny pulled her away after three performances.

Granny kept glancing at the Ferris wheel. We hadn't pestered her about riding it since we knew it cost more than we had.

"Wait right here." Granny turned, reaching into her bosom and pulling out a small bag tied to her clothing. She dumped the contents into her hand and out rolled three nickels and a dime. "We can all ride onct," she said.

We moved to the end of the line and waited excitedly. Granny, Met, and I took one seat and France and Raymond another. As the wheel filled with riders, we ascended to the top and stopped. Below us lay the town.

I drew in a deep breath. "There's Main Street, there's the courthouse, there's the depot, there's the school." It seemed we could see the whole world. When we began to descend, leaving stomachs behind, I held tightly to Granny's arm. Then upward we swept, and over the top again.

Granny was quiet, but her blue eyes sparkled like stars. France and Raymond rocked to and fro, "wheeing" and hollering. "Lookee there. Lookee there!" It was a long ride.

When we got off, Granny said it was time to go. John would be coming home, tired and hungry, expecting his supper. On the way home, France begged Granny to let him join the carnival show. He could be a fire-eater or a lion tamer or maybe a parachutist. Raymond said he would be a clown. Granny kept plodding along, not saying anything. Suddenly she stumbled to her knees.

"What's wrong, Granny?" I tried lifting her by the armpits, but she wouldn't budge. She tumbled sideways to a sitting position and sat there. Her eyes were glazed, staring at nothing. She opened her mouth like she wanted to speak, but the words would not come.

Met started crying. "Granny, Granny, git up."

"Go git your papa," I told France.

The trip to the carnival was Granny's last venture into the world outside. She would not walk again without help. As winter approached, her feet and legs became too swollen to wear shoes, her breathing too labored to lie in bed. John sat her in an arm chair in front of the fireplace, and she spent her time gazing at the flames.

Uncle John began packing his own lunches to take to work. France and I packed the others. France learned to keep the fire stoked and shop for groceries. I learned dried beans had to be soaked before cooking. Raymond and Met helped with chores. Harve's wife came weekdays and stayed while we were at school, and Aunt Mary came Saturdays to give Granny a bath and treat the sores that rose on her backside.

That winter passed miserably for all of us. My tenth birthday came and went, then Christmas. I tried to make wheat bread like Granny's, but got too much milk, then too much flour. I took the bread board in to Granny. "What's wrong with this?" I asked. A gnarled hand rose above the dough, dropped heavily, then fell into her lap. I wiped the sticky mixture from her fingers and went back to the kitchen.

Aunt Mary came on Christmas Day, bringing us goodies. She was beginning to pack her belongings. She'd be married in a week, and she and Burzilla were moving to the apple orchard farm on Richland Creek. Were it not for our plight, she'd be "happy as a lark," she said. "Now, I want all you'ns to come see us. You'll git all the apples you can eat."

The first week of the new year—1911—Aunt Sallie came with big fanfare and a wagonload of her belongings, including her prized bedding. Custommade of curled white horsehair, the mattress she had John and France place on sturdy springs was French-laid top and bottom with lamb's wool, tied down with worsted tufts, and trimmed with pink silk ribbon binding. With the bed providing comfort for her nights, she was prepared to spend her days caring for Granny.

John was free to marry the woman he'd been seeing for about a year. Evie was a slender woman, blonde, a widow with two sons about the ages of France and Raymond. She and John would live in her house. France and Raymond chose to stay with Granny, at least for a while. Aunt Sallie would need France's help.

A week after Sallie's arrival, Papa came home from Gastonia. He had tickets for Met and me to go back with him. Clemmie did not come but had a good-paying job at the cotton mill there, he bragged, and so did he. Papa looked better than I'd seen him in a long time. His red hair was barbershop cut, and he wore a brown pinstripe suit and brown wingtip shoes.

He tried to talk to Granny, but she appeared not to know who he was. He kissed her cheek and joked—"I look *that* different?" When he laughed and hugged her, she smiled.

"She ain't done that in days," Uncle John vowed. Evie was there, and John seemed happy. He held Evie's hand, and she blushed like a young girl.

She was better with Granny than anybody else, he claimed. Granny sipped soup when Evie was the one who held the spoon and coaxed her. Uncle John was so proud of that.

Papa told about Gastonia. "Boom town," he called it.

"Will I be in fifth grade in Gastonia?" I asked. Next I'd ask him about taking Nelse, my new kitty-cat.

"Well now, Clemmie thinks you're big enough to reach bobbins in the mill."

I made a face. "I want to finish school."

He laughed. "We'll see, we'll see."

ABOUT THE AUTHOR

From early childhood, Flora Ann Scearce listened to her mother's singing of folk ballads and heard her tales about growing up in North Carolina's Great Smoky Mountains amid hardships and a way of life that today no longer exists. Both mother and daughter felt strongly that these recollections should be preserved, and both set about to do that—Selena Sanders in journals and stories, and now her daughter—Flora Ann Scearce—in this novel. *Singer of an Empty Day* weaves events, songs, and games into a tale of mountain life in the early 1900s.

The author loves the mountains of North Carolina, although she, herself, has never lived there. She was born in Roanoke Rapids, North Carolina, where she met and married her husband, Herman Scearce. She has published short stories in *A Loving Voice II,* The Charles Press, Philadelphia, PA; *Mount Olive College Review,* Mount Olive College Press, Mount Olive, NC; and *Shoal,* the Literary Journal of Carteret Writers, Inc., Morehead City, NC; *The Dead Mule, An Eastern North Carolina Literary Journal; New River High Tide, A Collection of Poetry & Short Stories,* Council for the Arts, Jacksonville, NC, as well as other publications. She has won numerous awards for both prose and poetry.